CW01560339

A Reason to Grieve

M. Will (signature)

Mick Williams

DEDICATION

For my sister Lynn, who suffered through every page of my first draft.

For Baz Ashley, who cheers and encourages my every word.

For #1 Son and Callum.

For the people that put the Sparkle in my life.

And for Cathy.

Thank you all, and much love.

Chapter One

Funeral homes. They're all business and protocol, with gleaming surfaces and musty smells. And, after you weave through the regimented parking lot and the tidy entrance with its potted plants and smooth, lush carpet, there's a room with a dead body in it.

Tom Lewis approached the entrance to the room with the same feeling and expectation he always did. He expected grief and forced smiles. People dressed in stiff suits or floral blouses receiving hugs from other people they hadn't seen in years. Groups split off into mini tribes, piling cold finger food onto paper plates and comparing notes.

And flowers. Flowers everywhere.

An expensive token of commiseration that looked beautiful for the day, but soon became the topic of bickering and family feuds as relatives fought for possession. And then they died. Like the man in the casket.

An enlarged photograph rested against an easel outside the door, showing an aged man with puffy cheeks and jowls and cold eyes. The notice said his name was 'Big Frankie' Garcia. Multiple chins that hung over his shirt collar validated his moniker. He was an entrepreneur, whatever the hell that meant. Sixty-six years old. Four kids, six grandchildren. One grieving widow. Probable massive heart attack.

One of the presumed grandchildren sat on the edge of a fake stone fountain and made a gun shape with her fingers. She popped an imaginary round in Tom's face. He nodded and smiled. "Nice. Hello to you, too."

Eyes from every group turned as he rounded the corner and entered the main room, each pack attempting to work out which clique he belonged to. Dark-colored suits filled the place, resting on broad shoulders and long arms. The home could have been hosting a weightlifters convention. Maybe Frankie was in construction

1

because this was an impressive collection of muscled physique. Two man-mountains hovered, one either side of the casket, as a small spindly woman no wider than one of their thighs lifted her bony arms to receive hugs from a line of people that filtered by them. She wore a dark blue flowery dress that looked as if it would make a nice pair of 1960's curtains. Tom had that flicker of doubt that always gnawed away at this moment. He took a deep breath and strode forward, greeting and nodding and offering tight lipped smiles where required.

The line that led to the Widow Garcia wound from the casket and past a corkboard littered with family photos and an array of wind chimes and candles that Wal-Mart would be proud. Tom joined the line, still nodding and smiling. He could tell that people were trying to place him, work out who he was. The individual groups of mourners and well wishers floated around the room like well dressed jellyfish but, in the far corner, a girl stood alone. Dressed in a black suit, she looked to be about Tom's age, early thirties, very pretty. She scanned the room as if she was trying to find someone. He turned his attention back to the line as a tall man swooped toward her and they hugged, her standing on tiptoes to reach as he leaned forward to speak.

As Tom reached the front of the line, the widow raised her twig like arms and wrapped them around his neck. She was stronger than she seemed and dragged his head down until she planted a wet kiss on his cheek and then hugged him. Despite her strength, the hug lacked any commitment. There was no grief or feeling of loss in it. His frustration grew.

"And where do I know you from, young man?" she asked. Her voice didn't match her size. It was deep and strong and sounded like the product of a sixty a day habit chased with a bottle of whiskey.

Questions came with the territory and Tom had a set of answers already prepared. "Ma'am, I'm so sorry for your loss. I worked with your husband for a while, although I just try to stay out of the way and do my job."

She gave a knowing wink and glanced at the two giants either side of her. "I understand. Low profile, right? Get in and get out?" She laughed and gestured to the men. "Then you must know Russo and Scissors. We're one big happy family, no?"

Tom swallowed a basketball sized bundle of nerves as he glanced at them. Something about them seemed familiar but he couldn't place it. "Er, no, can't say that I do. Probably a different area. Separate department. Need to know and all that." He leaned forward and whispered, "And Scissors? That's his name?"

"Well, you know what they say. Never run with Scissors. It's dangerous."

She leaned back and let out a bellowing laugh that silenced the room. Everyone turned to look at them so Tom laughed, too, as a room full of eyes burned into him. The cute girl in the corner watched and smirked.

"Anyway," she said as she linked his arm, "you're coming to the graveside, right? Like I said, we're all one big family. Frankie would have liked to see you there, I'm sure."

Going to the cemetery wasn't part of Tom's plan, but there didn't seem to be enough grief in this room. Maybe everyone gathered around Frankie's last resting place would be the event to spark real grief. He needed the release.

"Ms Garcia? I wouldn't miss it for the world."

"Oh, listen to you," she smiled. "Bella. Call me Bella." She stroked his arm as the men either side glared at him. "You can ride with Russo and Scissors, they love good company. And I'm sure they'd like to get to know you."

"That would be nice," said Tom through gritted teeth. An image flashed through his mind, a report of a drive by shooting between rival mafia gangs a few weeks ago. A trickle of sweat ran from his armpit down his side. He'd gate crashed a mafia funeral. "It's warm in here, Ms. Garcia. I'll just step outside for some air."

He hugged her once more and slunk away toward the exit. The girl was still in the corner. Her eyes followed him as he passed her. Tiny dimples appeared on her cheeks as she smiled. He smiled back and hurried outside into the corridor.

It was as if she saw right through him.

****

Of all the funerals in today's paper, the Garcia's was the closest to the salon. Emma's last client left at 1.30. After cleaning her station, she had twenty minutes to change into the spare set of 'darks' she kept in her car and make her way to the funeral home.

Jen and Vicki, the girls working either side of her, were in their usual jovial mood. The banter between them and the clients made the job worthwhile as the three bounced remarks and jokes off one another while they styled. Emma didn't share their mood. A cloud hung over her chair.

A song on the radio during the drive in to work had resurrected old memories. They spread themselves like a drape over her shoulders and dragged her down as she worked through the day. The three of them carried out an impromptu group hug while she ate an early lunch. Both the girls were great, like family, and they understood her pain and cried, even though she was sure they couldn't feel it. The humiliation and rejection. Emma didn't cry. She needed release. If she let these feelings out here, they would destroy her. It would be like pulling a small cork from a dam and then trying to replace it. Impossible.

She resisted the urge to kick a snotty brat into the fountain on the way in and made her way into the viewing room to mingle with the mourners. The atmosphere was off. Even though the laughter seemed genuine, everyone seemed on edge, afraid to mourn properly. And afraid was the right word. The room was heavy with atmosphere as if fighting could start at any moment. She hugged and bluffed her way through a few conversations and then grabbed a piece of pizza and retreated to a corner to watch.

As the line to the widow moved along, a man breezed through the entrance and past her. He seemed out of place. He wore the appropriate clothing, a dark suit and gleaming shoes that screamed respect, but he didn't wear them like he meant it. After nodding and greeting a few people, he moved toward the casket and received an enthusiastic hug from the widow. Emma had to smile; he seemed cute, but the small woman looked as if she was about to snap him in half. Two guys by the casket watched him as if he was a threat and questioned each other in glances. They had no idea who he was.

After a few moments of conversation he turned and strode toward her. His face was ruddy and his eyes shifted around as if he expected to be ambushed before he left. As he grew closer, he caught her eye. She flashed him her standard non-committal smile, and he seemed to pause for a moment before he returned the gesture and rushed past her. The two men at the casket followed him seconds later.

Resigned to the fact that no tears would come today, Emma edged across the back wall and left the room. The brat still sat on the side of the fountain and glared at her as she walked by. The urge to dunk her was overwhelming. She kept walking and held the door for the two huge men and the red faced guy as they came back into the building.

****

Tom stamped his feet and rubbed heat into his hands. Plumes of breath clouded the November air before him and he shivered as the sweat cooled against his body. Four viewings per month for almost a year and, at last, he'd crashed one that could be dangerous. A mafia funeral. It was a stretch to think he'd seen pictures of them anywhere, but the way they carried themselves coupled with the lack of grief in the room screamed trouble. This was the real deal.

From across the parking lot his car beckoned safety, and he turned on his heels and took a step forward as the door behind him swung open. A heavy grip bit into his shoulder. Tom stopped and craned his neck. It was Russo. Or Scissors. Don't run with Scissors!

"We're a man down," growled the heavy. "We need another pall bearer. You look strong enough. Frankie, God rest his soul, was a whole lot of man. It'll take eight of us to lift him. You're up."

It wasn't a question or a request. Tom followed the men back into the funeral home and passed the cute looking girl by the doors. He attempted to beg for help with his eyes but she glanced at the floor and held the door open for them and then hurried out.

****

The mourners left in the viewing room had formed two lines from a side door to create a human corridor. The Tunnel of Death, thought Tom. Five black suits waited by the casket, all over six feet tall, almost as wide, all hidden behind dark sunglasses. Russo and Scissors donned the eye shades too. Tom's nervous eyes flitted from side to side as he reached the widow, and he turned his head to

5

avoid a full-mouthed kiss to the lips as she dragged his head down to her level again.

"Thank you for helping. Frankie would appreciate it. Load him up and then you can ride with the boys to the cemetery. I'll see you there."

She stroked his arm and, despite the heat in the room, he shivered again. He nodded with the slightest of movements and stood at the side of Frankie's final home. As if by magic, the side doors opened outward and the suits bent forward until they lined up with the brass handles of the casket. Tom didn't need to bend. He offered a silent prayer to the God of strength and grasped the cold metal. Please don't let him be the one to drop Big Frankie on the floor. Did they secure the lid closed just in case someone did? He took a deep breath.

Fingers wrapped around metal as one and they lifted the huge container off its table like an Olympic team. Something at the bottom of Tom's back popped and twanged. He grimaced and gritted his teeth again. Show no fear. They'd smell it like a pack of wolves and tear him to pieces.

The procession shuffled forward and Frankie got as close to daylight as he ever would again, until the shiny wooden box slid along rails and into the back of the hearse. A somber man locked him in place and closed the door with an air-tight thud. Not that Frankie would need air.

"You're with us," said a heavy, either Russo or Scissors. "This way."

Tom took two steps to every one of the giants', his back complaining at every footfall. Around the corner from the main entrance sat a tidy row of jet-black SUVs with tinted windows. They were identical but the two men made a beeline for the farthest vehicle. One opened the rear door and held it as the other climbed into the driver's seat. Tom glanced around once more to check for witnesses and, realizing he was alone, slid nervously onto the rear seat. The door slammed as the other man opened the passenger side door.

During the tense drive to the cemetery not much of the conversation reached the back seat but, after some light-hearted banter, Tom worked out which man was Russo and which was Scissors. Russo did most of the talking. Scissors drove.

"So, we haven't seen you before. What do you do?"

Tom thought fast, his mind whirring and skipping the list of regular answers he had for funeral questions. He wasn't built for heavy work.

"Cash," he said. "I make sure the cash is clean and goes to where it's supposed to."

Furrowed brows appeared in the rear-view mirror. "I thought Dave the Dollar took care of the cash," said Scissors.

It seemed so bizarre it had to be real, so Tom slipped into character and played along. "Yeah, well you know how it is. Dave got overrun with the volume, so they drafted me in to back him up."

"Yeah, business has been good," smiled Russo. "Shame about Dotty, though. Didn't see that coming."

"Dotty?"

"Dave's wife, Dotty. We lost her about a month ago."

Tom was slipping into the role now and, with his new found confidence, shared grief seemed miles away. Still, Dotty the Dollar?

"Ah, Dotty," he said. "Yeah, shame about her. Still, at least it was quick."

Both men strained to look over their broad shoulders at him. "Quick?" said Scissors. "That cancer ate away at her for months. What the fuck are you talking about, quick? A bullet would have been quick."

Tom's stomach flipped and his palms sweated. "Well, yeah. The cancer dragged on, but the end, her final breath. That was quick. You know, she breathed in and, er… didn't breathe back out again. It was quick. At the end."

They turned to face the road again and didn't speak until they pulled into the cemetery gates. Russo pointed across the landscaping at a mound of freshly dug soil and a large crowd. Scissors maneuvered the big vehicle around the narrow paths until they were yards from the burial site. Tom climbed out and followed the men to the hearse. His back complained again as they slid Frankie out of his taxi and onto a waiting gurney. Two of the bigger guys took over and wheeled him to his final resting place. Tom left them to it and took his place a few rows back, out of sight of the Widow Garcia. At the first opportunity, he could slip away and get back to his car.

The minister muttered a few words about grace and earning a place with the big guy while, in the background, a small crane trundled along the path toward them. It looked like one of those remote control things they used to defuse bombs. A wiry looking guy with a remote control meandered behind it. He guided the machine over the edge of the lawn and across to the waiting gurney. It all made sense. Even with eight men, there was no way they could manhandle Big Frankie and his casket into the ground with any finesse. The ropes didn't look as if they'd hold the weight. The men definitely didn't.

As the final words faded and the group bowed its collective head in prayer, Tom watched the small guy secure ropes around Big Frankie's new home and yank them tight. Motors whined, and the machine spouted support legs, then swung the oak box over the hole in the ground. The crane's feet sank into the soil as it absorbed the weight and, for a fleeting moment, it looked as if the whole thing was about to topple. Tom held his breath as the guy made a few adjustments and, after an impressive display of juggling, it seemed to balance. Big Frankie stopped and swayed in mid-air as his casket waved a last farewell. The minister dabbed his forehead with a handkerchief and continued.

"We therefore commit his body to the ground, earth to earth..."

At last, Widow Garcia let out a sob. Tom wished he could hug her, share that grief, and cry with her.

"... ashes to ashes, dust to dust, looking for that blessed..."

Something twanged, and it wasn't Tom's back. He looked over the bowed heads and saw that fronds of the blue nylon rope that supported Frankie's weight had stretched to snapping point. The narrower end of the casket closest to the widow, presumably Frankie's head, had dropped an inch and swayed again. The rope frayed and twisted.

"... hope when the Lord himself shall descend from Heaven..."

Big Frankie won his final fight, and the rope snapped. The slick oak casket slid through its remaining tethers with an unnatural grace, and the mob boss pitched forward into the gaping hole. Screams rose from the crowd as the box thumped against soil and the lid lifted enough to expose a pale, flabby arm. By the grace of all things holy, it slammed shut again as the casket wedged itself firmly upright.

Tom saw his chance. He backed away from the mourners and crept into the tree line that surrounded the site just as Widow Garcia's bellowing laugh echoed around the estate.

"Frankie. Who'd have figured," she yelled. "Why change now? The fat bastard dove headfirst into everything he ever did."

Chapter Two

So, we had the big conversation last night. I finally asked him how we were doing."

Emma listened as Vicki discussed her evening with her client, a seventy-nine year old mild mannered lady named Doris. Doris turned up every four weeks for a blue rinse. She was the salon's favorite client.

"And how did it go, honey?" drooled Doris through a set of loose-fitting dentures. "What did he say?"

"He said we were fine. Everything was fine."

Doris let out a deep sigh. "Oh dear, did he actually say the word fine?"

"Why? What's up with that?"

"Oh Vicki," said Doris, "I'm so sorry."

Vicki stepped away from the chair with scissors raised as Doris collapsed into a coughing fit. "Doris, are you okay? And sorry? Sorry for what?"

"I'm okay, dear. Don't you read Cosmopolitan? You should read Cosmopolitan. All modern women read Cosmopolitan, it's full of useful stuff. And you've seen my gray hair but, trust me, just because there's snow on the roof doesn't mean the fire's gone out down below. Anyway, fine is a word we use when we're either annoyed or we want to be non-committal."

"I'm not following," said Vicki with a shake of the head. "And I really don't want to picture your fires, Doris."

Emma stepped closer as Jen, the other stylist, sandwiched the old lady in on the other side.

"Vic, the word fine doesn't mean anything," said Emma. "If things are going well, they'd be good. If they were going really well, they'd be great, maybe even amazing. If things were incredible, you'd get what you're waiting for. But fine? Fine means nothing. Fine has no value or measurement. He's still not committing."

"How many years is it now?" asked Jen.

Vicki blinked. "Nine. We've been together for nine years. Adam's my high school sweetheart, the only man I've ever loved, and I give him everything. So why won't he set a date?"

"You kids," said Doris. "You give those boys everything too soon and they get to a point where it's all too easy for them. They get it handed to them on a plate. Bill and I had an understanding, and it kept him on his toes."

When Doris said 'understanding', her eyebrows lifted and raised her tight curls an inch.

"He's long gone now, as you know. Anyway, Bill had chores to do and, until they were done he'd have to cut his way through armor to get to me. Even after that, I wouldn't give it up easily. Almost fifty years of marriage, and he still passed away with a smile on his face."

"So how did that work?" asked Vicki. "If Bill didn't do his chores, what happened?"

"Well, he went to bed and faced the wall, didn't he?" said Doris with a smile.

"And if he did everything right?"

"Oh, honey, I rocked his world! That's why our marriage lasted fifty years."

Doris's laugh turned into another bout of coughing. The girls laughed, too, as Jen leaned closer. "At least you have someone." She glanced across at Emma. "Sorry Em, I'm not digging at you, but I can't seem to hold on to one for more than a few weeks. Everything starts great. First dates are always fun and I laugh at their jokes even if they're not funny. I always show a reasonable amount of cleavage without it looking like the candy store's open, but they still don't call. I've checked my cleavage and it's in decent shape. They should call."

Emma blushed and tried to ignore the comment.

"I mean," Jen continued, "I dated Jeff for three weeks and then he vanished, just like the rest of them. I've no idea what I'm doing wrong."

"Did you give it up easily?" asked Doris.

Jen spluttered as her client also leaned into the conversation. "Doris! No, I didn't as a matter of fact. We only had three dates. We'd got to the part where I talk about kids and what kind of house I want, and he went to the bathroom and never came back. I figured the seafood had got to him and he'd had to…"

"Stop right there, Jen," said Emma. "No need to elaborate."

"You talked about having kids on your third date?" said Vicki.

"Well, yeah. Why not? It's important to get that stuff out there. I'm not getting any younger."

"It is, and you're not," said Vicki with a wink, "but that's a conversation to be held when you've met someone special. That's when you want to take it to the next level."

"And what's the next level?" said Doris. "You girls talk in a foreign language. Do you mean world rocking?"

"Right after world rocking, Doris," said Emma. "Jen, you've got to stop going full-on by the third date. You're scaring them off. Men are simple souls. They want the basic things in life. Mention kids and houses too soon and its fight or flight. It's their only response because they're not built to handle that kind of stuff."

Doris craned her scrawny neck to focus on Emma. "And what about you, young lady? I don't see a ring on that finger, either. What's your story?"

Jen and Vicki shrank back to their own positions as Emma's face flushed red. "It's okay, girls," she said. "I'm off men, Doris. And I've had a ring on that finger. For five years."

"So what happened, dear?"

"Nothing worth talking about. It wouldn't change anything, and I've moved on now."

"It doesn't sound like it," said Doris.

"Well," said Emma, "that was two years ago. I've tried dating a few times…"

"… but her walls fly up," finished Jen.

Everyone turned and stared and Jen shrank into herself. "What? Look, I'm sorry, but if I go full-on too soon, then Em does the opposite. As soon as she gets a hint of a chance, she goes all hard-headed and puts up massive walls. There's no man alive that could climb them so they give up."

"And she's never faced it, either," said Vicki. "Never cried or showed anything. Not once."

"Okay, okay, you can stop putting me on the couch," said Emma. "I'm not that bad."

"Er, yes. Yes you are," said Vicki.

"Stop blocking that out," said Doris. "No good can come from boxing up all those bad feelings. Let them out, honey. Get yourself a good man and get your world rocked!"

"I wish it were that easy," laughed Emma. "Don't worry about me, Doris. It's my life. I'll work it out."

"So why do you keep going to funerals?" asked Jen.

Emma's head snapped around and her hard gaze locked on Jen's eyes. "What are you talking about?"

"You left your phone on the kitchen table the other day. The screen lit up, and it was on the obituary website for the newspaper. I didn't mean to pry, it was just sitting there. But I've seen you searching them a few times. Is that why you always have that black trouser suit in your car?"

Emma frowned and moved closer to her client. She continued cutting and dipped her head. "It's none of your business what I do. Let's leave it at that."

The room fell silent other than the sound of dryers and the snip of scissors. Doris leaned back. "Well honey, I'm seventy-nine years old so would you do me a favor? If my name ever pops up in your paper, would you cancel my appointment because I doubt I'll make it."

****

Rob Peterson peeled back the side of his shirt to reveal an angry bruise, a perfect circle of purple and gray. A few people in the bar turned to look, frowned and returned to their conversations.

"Yeah," he said, "so we did it three times last night, then she kept her legs in the air for half an hour like it said in the book. That way my little swimmers can go down bank instead of swimming upstream. She had to drop them after that, though, pins and needles set in. Her heel landed smack bang on my collarbone. I thought she'd cracked it. My collarbone, not the pregnancy. I was in agony for ages. I'm telling you, if it doesn't happen soon she'll trade me in for a better model with stronger soldiers."

Tom slid his bottle along the bar until its base hovered over the top of a well formed watermark in the varnish. "It looks as if you walked into a truck at the garage. Just keep at it, Rob, it'll happen. How long have you been trying now?"

An 'Irish' band from Ohio was coming to the end of a Van Morrison song, the guitarist wind-milling his arms in rock fashion across a small acoustic guitar.

"Almost two years," said Rob, raising his voice over the rising volume. He picked oil remnants from under his fingernails. "I've even been sneaking out from work. I've even left cars up in the air on a ramp while I go home and, you know, make a deposit. According to the internet I'm considered sterile if nothing happens after two years. I'm thirty," he shouted as the band finished the song and the bar fell silent. "I can't be sterile at thirty."

People turned to look again and a few sniggers sounded until conversation resumed.

Tom shook his head as the volume rose again. "Shit, sorry pal. That was bad timing. Didn't you go for fertility tests to see if your soldiers were up to military standard?"

"We both did." Rob rubbed his blushing face in his hands. "Apparently, everything's in good working order. Both of us. It better work soon, though, because Abby's getting frustrated."

The guy sitting on Tom's other side put his cellphone on hold. "How the hell can she be getting frustrated if you're giving it to her three times a night? That's high maintenance, Rob. Having said that, I did it three times this weekend as well, but it was with two different girls." Josh winked and resumed his call.

"Oh, here we go," said Tom. "Josh Davies. Gets burned once and becomes a serial womanizer."

"Hey, at least I'm getting some," said Josh as he threw a gentle punch.

"He's got a point," said Rob. "Anyway, what do you do with your nights? You never mention them. Do you get out and meet people? You know, if you talked to girls you might have more luck in the romance department."

Tom thought back to the Garcia funeral and the mad dash to escape mafia clutches. "I get out," he said with a shrug. "And I go to parties and stuff. In fact, I had quite a passionate hug and kiss just the other day, but it was more of a family affair."

14

"So you got no tongue then?" Rob laughed.

The image of the widow's mouth reaching up to him made Tom shudder. "No. No tongue. To be honest, she was on the old side for my taste. Dodgy family, too. I'll steer well clear from now on."

"So, what's going on? Girlfriend? Secret lover? Hey, you're not gay are you? You can tell me if you're gay, I'd be cool."

"No," said Tom as he drained his beer, "I'm not gay, and anyway, you're not my type so don't get your hopes up."

"You couldn't afford me," said Rob.

"It's just me and the cat. I'm all right, though, it's okay being single. I'm comfortable in my own company."

"Yeah, but if you don't use that thing soon it's either going to heal up or your virginity's going to grow back. It's probably got a 'best before' date stamped on it somewhere. You'll need pills soon just to make it work."

Josh disconnected his call and leaned back into the discussion. "You say you were gay, Tom? I knew it. I mean, it's okay and all, but I still knew it."

"Josh? Piss off," said Tom. "I'm not gay, I'm selective."

"Me too. I just selected Alison for a good time on Saturday, and Stephanie for Sunday. Life is good, my friend."

"Josh, you're either going to catch something itchy or you'll turn into a baboon. Whatever happened to your class? And how do you keep getting so many dates?"

"They come into the studio. It's a single guy's paradise, all of those models and single moms coming in for pictures with their kids. After I take the pictures I give them my card. Sometimes I write a little note on the back."

"That sounds creepy, to be honest."

"Whatever, it works. As for my class, it left with Sarah. You know what happened and it'll never happen again. Remember what Tom Arnold said; 'Women. You can't live with them and you can't kill them'. He was spot on with that statement."

"Yeah," said Tom. "The police don't like it much if you kill them, but they're not all the same, Josh. Just because she hurt you doesn't mean you shouldn't leave yourself open to the possibility of meeting the right one, you know?"

"Hurt me? Tom, she slept with two of my friends, left me and took my dog with her. Hurt me? She ripped out my heart, jumped up and down on it and then set it on fire."

"Jesus," said Rob. "What a drama queen. And he thought you were gay."

Tom signaled the barman for another beer as Rob continued. "Tell you what you need?"

"What, other than a lottery win and an interested supermodel?"

"Dream on. No, you need an angle."

"An angle?" frowned Tom. "I'm upright against the bar at ninety degrees to the floor. What other angle could I possibly need?"

"Funny. Girls like men to be different. We haven't got all the interesting parts they have. I mean, think about it. Have you looked in a mirror lately?"

"What are you saying?" said Tom. "I'm in decent shape. I try to look after myself." He chugged on the fresh beer. "Sort of."

"I don't mean that, you muppet. Imagine a naked woman. All sensual curves and smooth skin, long legs and lithe bodies and cute bums. Now think about a man's body..."

"I'm getting concerned here boys," interrupted Josh. "Did I walk into a different type of bar? First Tom comes out of the closet and now you want us to think about naked men?"

"For God's sake Josh, I'm not gay," said Tom as he took another mouthful of beer.

"I don't mean think about naked men literally," said Rob, "I mean figuratively. You see a naked woman and it's a beautiful thing. Think about a naked man and it's a pale, hairy torso on two legs with a tiny leg in the middle. Especially if it's cold."

Tom placed his bottle back on the bar. "Rob, is this conversation going anywhere or do we need to make you an appointment?"

"What I'm trying to say is that women have a beauty that men can never have. They've got that mystique about them. You know what they say, the second men understand women, it's all over. The human race might as well lie on its back and do the dying fly. So, men need an angle, something unique to offer."

"The night of your life," said Josh. "That's what I offer. Never failed me yet."

"I suspect your time is coming," said Rob. "So, come on. What makes Tom Lewis different from any other man?"

Tom sat back on his stool and considered the question. He stuck out his bottom lip. "Nothing. I'm just me."

"There must be something. How do you make a woman feel special?"

"They don't stick around long enough for me to find out. I just try to care. I try to make sure she's relaxed and having the best time I can give her."

"Okay," nodded Rob, "now we're making progress. So how do you relax them?"

"Well, nice music," said Tom. "Wine. Maybe a massage."

"Massage?" scoffed Josh. "That shit where you rub your hands all over them? Seems like a decent excuse for a grope to me. Does that crap really work? I reckon they want someone to show them who's boss. Take 'em and make 'em moan, that's what I say."

Tom shook his head. "It's not just about rubbing your hands all over them, Josh. It's about degrees of pressure, about kneading out tension and learning the curves of the body. Sleek, smooth movements that are sensual and relaxing. It's about giving."

"Well shit, Tom. Have you taken out a subscription to Bitch Weekly?"

"Josh, how do your knuckles not drag on the floor?"

"Because most of the time they're up here," he said clasping his hands to his chest, "unhooking bra straps."

"You're a Neanderthal."

Rob finished his beer and set it on the bar with a smack of his lips. "Okay guys, I'd better get home. I'm on a one beer limit. The boys are struggling as it is, I don't want them swimming under the influence. With my luck they'd get pulled over by the sperm police and have to spend a night in the cells."

"So what's next?" asked Tom.

"I'm going to a meeting tomorrow night, like a group session thing. The doctor reckons I could be suffering from anxiety, and he's worried I might get depressed. You know, low self-esteem and so on, because the boys aren't working? I'm nervous about it, to be honest. It sounds like one of those AA meetings, except I'll have to stand up and talk about not getting Abby pregnant."

"That could cause anxiety and depression," said Josh. "You should have another beer and relax."

"Isn't Abby going?"

"No, it's a men only thing."

"I've got no plans tomorrow," said Tom. "I could go with you, if you like? I'll just sit there like one of those group stalkers, but at least I'd be a familiar face in the room."

"That might be weird. I mean, I know none of the people there, so I could say anything to them and they'd never judge me. I know you."

"Rob, I've known you for years," said Tom. "I'd never judge. Tell you what, text or call me tomorrow if you want me there and I'll go with you. One condition, though. Name your firstborn after me."

"What if we have a girl?" said Rob.

"Well, high school will be a bitch, won't it?"

Chapter Three

S_ee you in the morning!"
Blinds clattered as Vicki closed the door behind her and walked to her car. Jen sterilized equipment as Emma turned the latch to lock up the salon. She jumped as a figure appeared through the blinds.

"Can I come in?" mouthed Doris through the glass.

The old lady looked tired. Emma wrenched open the door. "Hi Doris. Of course you can. What's up? Is there a problem with your hair? You just missed Vic, she left for the day."

Doris closed the door and took a seat in the waiting area. She placed an old leatherette purse on the chair next to her and clasped her hands between her knees. When she looked up, tears nestled at the bottom of her eyes.

"Doris? What is it?" Jen took a seat to one side of her as Emma moved the purse and took the other.

"I'm not sure how to say this," said Doris. Her voice wavered, almost lost beneath the quiet radio. "So I'll just come right out and say it. I've not long left the doctor's office since I've not been feeling too good lately. He said I have cancer."

Both girls gasped and placed supportive hands on Doris's shoulders.

"Oh my God," said Emma. "It's treatable, though, right? I mean, they caught it early enough and you'll be okay? And you know we're here for you. And your family, of course."

"I have no family. Bill and I had no children and I'm the last of my line. My younger brother left us ten years ago. Cancer got him too. I have to admit I've been a bit of a naughty girl, since I didn't go for my regular checkups. Lately, though, I've been getting tired early and I have this cough that won't go away. Then I coughed up blood, and it scared the life out of me so I made an appointment.

19

They did a load of tests and x-rays and said it started in my lungs and spread to my liver."

"I've noticed you coughing a lot," said Jen, "but they can still treat it, can't they? These days, chemotherapy can be really accurate and it doesn't completely drain you. You'll be okay, Doris."

Doris slumped into the seat. "They've given me three months. There's medication they can offer but I don't want that. I've had a good run and I don't want to go out rattling full of pills. I'm too old for that crap."

Jen dabbed at her eyes as Emma threw her arm around Doris. "We're here for you, Doris. Is there anything we can do?"

"The only thing that worries me is my funeral," she said. "That's what I wanted to talk to you about. Money's tight, and I don't have any of those stupid policies, so it can't be too extravagant. Would you help me plan everything?"

"Anything you need. You know we'll do whatever we can. Did you have something in mind?" Emma mentally kicked herself. She sounded like she was asking about a hair style.

"Well I don't fancy going up in flames," said Doris with a shake of her finger, "so no cremation." Her voice gained strength as if the support had already bolstered her. "Seems to be too much like Hell to go out with all that fire around you and, anyway, I don't like it when it's too hot. It brings me out in a rash. No, I'd like to be put in a nice box and buried next to Bill. We paid for a double plot years ago so they can just dig a hole and drop me in there."

"I'm sure we can take care of that, Doris," said Jen.

"And I need to be facing him. Poor Bill, he faced that wall enough times in the past. The least I can do is make it up to him now."

Emma found it hard not to smile. "Leave me with the information and I'll do a little research. Do you have friends we should invite?"

"Oh yes, hang on." A tiny hand gripped the purse and shook it open to retrieve a small notebook. "This has all of my contacts in it. I meet a lot of folks at the Veteran's Lodge. And then there's the bingo. I don't know how it works, what with getting all those folks together. And anyway, most of them are my age. There's no telling how many of them will still be around by the time it's my turn, they're dropping like flies."

"I love your spirit," said Emma as she squeezed Doris's gnarled hand. The skin seemed paper thin, stretched over bony knuckles. "We'll take care of everything. You just stay strong and leave it to us, okay?"

Doris's eyes filled again as she glanced back and forth between the girls. "I love you girls so much, but don't say anything to Vicki just yet, okay? Not yet. That girl's like a daughter to me. I don't think I could stand to see her cry. That's why I waited until she left. If you'd all left together, I'd have come back another time."

"Doris," said Jen, "would you like us to tell her?"

"Oh no, definitely not. I'll say something the next time she does my hair. Perhaps I'll take her to one side."

"You know you can come in here any time you like," said Emma. "Get your hair done every week if you like. We'll take care of that, too. It would be our pleasure. Plus, we'll get to see more of you."

"I think I'd like that. Thank you." Doris patted each girl on the knee, looped her purse over a scrawny wrist, placed her hands on her knees and pushed herself upright. "Well, I'll leave you girls to close up shop." She shuffled to the door. "Thank you again, it means the world to me."

"What are you doing for dinner?" asked Emma as she nudged Jen in the ribs. "We're going to the place across the road if you'd like to join us?"

"We are? Yes. Yes, we are," lied Jen. "And you're more than welcome to join us."

"Oh, I appreciate it, but you young ones should go and have a good time. There's a nice piece of fish in the fridge at home. You know what? I've never smoked and I've taken care of myself my entire life, but when your time's up, it's up. I might as well call and get a burger on the way home. And fries. With gallons of salt."

Doris almost doubled over with laughter until coughing seized her and her body racked with the effort. She pushed away helping hands. "It's okay, I've got it. I'm getting used to it now. Thanks again, girls. Have a good night and I'll see you soon."

The blinds didn't move as she opened the door. It closed behind her with a click.

****

The microwave dinged its happy song and Tom took his dinner from the glass dish and slid the plastic tray onto the table. Immediately, a fat cat leaped up and sniffed at it. He waved the cat away, poured a glass of milk and opened the newspaper.

Rob's group session began tomorrow at seven-thirty in the old library downtown. It was supposed to be an informal affair. Tom envisioned a rough circle of plastic chairs holding a small crowd of people who loathed making eye contact. There'd be one who goaded the others into talking about things they didn't want to, especially to a bunch of strangers. And there'd be a coffee pot, half filled with burned coffee that tasted like tar. Sounded like a date night.

He plunged a fork into the dish, scooped up a day's worth of sodium, and left the fork hovering before his mouth as he sighed. Some days were better than others. A darkness washed over him again and he dropped the fork with a plop back into the tray.

The sensation was like zipping up a sleeping bag, like being wrapped in something that smothered, only there was no warmth associated with this. Just the cloying feeling of something pressing down. Metal clanged as the tray hit the bottom of the trash can and Tom paced the apartment.

He picked up a picture from a display that nestled on a cabinet mounted to the far wall. Blue and red flashed in its glass as the neon sign from the store across the street sent its message through the window. Cindy would be behind the counter in a short skirt and high-heeled boots, her pink hair pulled into a pony tail. She'd be chewing gum and flashing a pearly white smile. Tom knew she liked him. She made no secret of it and had asked to cross the street with him a few times but he always politely declined. Her smile and dark eyes were bewitching, but there was no spark. He felt nothing of substance over the oppressive weight he carried inside.

A few times, temptation had nipped at him to saunter over there to buy a magazine or a bottle of milk. Maybe strike up a conversation to find out what time she finished. Then he'd invite her over to see what would happen; to see if the contact would awaken something in him, fire a spark that would ignite the fire missing in him. But then the weight pushed back and his conscience berated him for thinking of treating the girl with so little respect. She deserved much better.

He replaced the picture, one of a much younger version of him with two people he didn't really know. Not for the first time, thoughts of depression crossed his mind. It was annoying, the way people considered depression to be a mood. Tom wasn't sure if he'd be diagnosed clinically depressed, he'd never spoken to anyone or seen a professional, but he didn't need to. Restless nights. No appetite. Losing interest in the guitar he used to play. And the sensation of night closing in. The symptoms were obvious enough. The root of his issues were painfully obvious, too, and there was definitely no changing that. He'd lived with it since he was eight years old and the life-changing event that caused it was permanent. A doctor had suggested medication, but that was a dangerous and rocky road. Still, the funerals helped a little, the sharing of grief. One day, this feeling would meet its match and he'd be able to purge it from his body once and for all. Until then, there was always Rob's session.

The cat wrapped itself around his feet and he scooped it up and ruffled its fur.

"How're you doing Oswald? How's your day been? Bump into any sexy lady cats on your travels?"

The cat purred against his chest, the sound and vibration soothing. Oswald had entered Tom's life two years ago when the woman in the apartment next door had moved into a nicer, pet free complex. She'd been a glimmer of hope in an otherwise barren few years of dating. Like the few before her, she grew impatient and gave up waiting for him to open himself to her. After a few months of meals and conversation, she suggested friendship would be their best option and left the cat as a parting gift. She called the overweight ball of fur 'Cat' because she couldn't decide on an actual name.

When it first wandered into his apartment, Tom could sense the animal conspiring to take over and claim it as its own. As a fan of conspiracy theories, he picked a name from one of the biggest. Oswald just beat out Buzz and JFK.

They collapsed together on the sofa. Tom picked up the remote and powered up the TV. A random soap appeared. He skipped the channel and depressing news of bombings abroad flashed across the screen. He pressed the button again and a game show theme blared through the speakers. The screen went dark as he switched it off and tossed the remote aside. Outside, the sun was sinking. The small clock on the mantle glowed 6.10, and the street below grew noisier as the stores closed and people went home to their families.

Tom sighed. "Well, it's you and me against the world, Oswald." If the cat responded, it was too quiet to hear.

The newspaper beckoned from the table. Oswald leaped onto a pillow as Tom wandered back into the kitchen. The obituaries page was still open, marked with a circle of dark ink that ringed the announcement of a viewing at a funeral home.

Emelia Johnson, died aged 55, leaving behind a loving husband, two children and a few lines of relatives she probably hadn't seen for years. Viewing, service and cremation to be rattled off in quick succession by the look of things. The place was fifteen minutes across town. The service started in thirty-five.

"What to do, Oswald?" he shouted. "Stay here and be miserable, or get changed into some depressing clothes and be miserable somewhere else? If you nod, I'll stay here. Say nothing and I'll go out."

The cat glanced up at him but offered no advice.

"Well, that settles it then."

He jumped in the shower, washed and shaved, then changed into his dark suit and left the apartment.

Chapter Four

After leaving the salon, Emma sat for a few minutes in her car and tried to cry. As always, nothing came other than the suffocation and hand-wringing frustration. The local newspaper app on her phone mentioned a service and cremation close by. Her appetite had vanished and Doris's news had demoralized her to where even movement became an effort, let alone eating.

She grabbed her change of clothes, willed herself out of the car, and went back into the salon to change into her 'darks'.

The Blazing Oak Crematorium sat back off the road, surrounded by acres of gardens and forest. The entire area looked like the epitome of tranquility, other than the huge chimney that stood erect and proud at the back of a large white walled building. It pointed the way to the sky as if it contained an elevator for a quick trip to Heaven.

At the front sat a huge parking lot with optimistic rows of white lines begging to be filled. She swung the small vehicle into the middle of a row of empty spots by the entrance and walked up to the building.

Even in the dusk, the white walls gleamed and reflected any light. Ironic, she thought, that a place that specialized in creating smoke and a sense of finality was so bright and cheerful. The building should be caked in black soot, but the chimney and an impressive set of fans took care of that.

A glass-paneled door opened onto lush blue carpet that stretched away along a corridor that ran the length of the building. Multiple doors punctuated the wall down one side. Emma knew those rooms held bodies, lined up ready for cremation. She smiled and remembered a nicer conversation with Doris and other clients about the options available to the dead. Doris killed the chat by explaining how the human body was like a car. Mechanics, or doctors, kept it running for as long as possible. Regular oil changes and additives would maintain it but, over time, it would wear itself out and be ready for the scrap yard. The bodies were like cars. This was the scrap yard. The room opposite burned them up into a disposable size.

Each door held a small plaque. The one by the entrance said Eric Johnstone. This place wasn't like the viewing homes. There were no affectionate displays of loved ones, their lives documented with photographs and anecdotes. This building had a different ambience and was missing the odor that Doris had described as 'old people'. Those places smell like my living room, she'd said, so I speak from experience. And there was no twinkling fountain with a miserable brat climbing all over it either.

To the right, an ornate arch opened onto a large chapel. The blue carpet followed from the hall to form a walkway all the way to a raised platform at the far end. It was an ironically cold color in a room that had areas of extreme heat. White pillars supported a tall vaulted ceiling of glass panels that let in what little light was left of the day.

About two dozen people congregated at the front of the room, a rough dozen on either side of the walkway. A huge casket lay on a conveyor that led to a closed hatch. Glossy white glimmered like ice beneath a heavy red shawl that draped over it, adorned with wreathes and a framed picture. Emma smiled again and imagined it dinging as it passed over an imaginary scanner on its way to the furnace. When had she become so cynical?

She made her way forward and sat behind the last person on the left. A wash of expensive perfume drifted over her as the woman in front turned at the creak of the wooden pew. She flashed a forced smile. Emma smiled back and nodded her commiserations. Just like the last viewing, this room didn't feel sad. Despite the time of day, it was too bright. A part of her acknowledged that it was sad to see so few people gathered to say goodbye to someone. Another part was sad that there was not enough grief in the room and that this would be another exercise in frustration.

A man in heavy robes stepped out of a side door and made his way to a dais raised at one side of the casket. As he lifted his arms to speak, padded footsteps sounded behind her and she turned in time to see someone dressed in black take a seat in the opposite pew. The overhead lights danced on his shoes as he shuffled into place, but he turned his head before she could acknowledge him.

The man in front stepped up to a microphone and spoke and, although a sense of respect screamed that she should listen, Emma tuned out the voice and focused on the emotion in the room instead. As always, she tried to tap into the feeling of loss or the relief of unburdening. Either would do. The loss would provoke sadness. With enough sadness the tears would finally come. The elation of freedom, that the person in the casket was no longer suffering this life, would bring joy and laughter. Enough laughter would also bring tears.

Neither was happening.

A shuffling to her side broke her concentration, and she turned again. The man opposite was leaning forward as if he was trying to become one with the congregation. As if he felt her eyes on him, he stopped and turned to look at her. His own eyes widened, and he smiled an awkward smile.

Her heart raced. It was the cute guy from the previous viewing.

****

Tom hated to be late, but new construction outside the subdivision added ten minutes to his drive. The Chaplain had just started his sermon as he crept into the service and took a seat at the back of the small crowd. Emelia Johnson's casket was huge, larger than Big Frankie Garcia's and looked, from this angle, as if it wouldn't fit through the hatch and into the furnace. He trusted the professionalism of the employees, certain they would have checked to make sure it would roll through unhindered.

He leaned forward as a splinter from the wooden pew dug into his behind and glanced across at the people opposite. The nearest girl swung her head to look at him and, as they locked eyes, he smiled. It was the girl from the earlier viewing, the only other person in the room who'd seemed out of place. What were the odds of that? She returned the smile and flashed a pair of cute dimples that made his stomach tumble. Tom frowned and gave her an inquisitive look that said 'what are you doing here?' She shrugged and turned to face the Chaplain.

A speech followed about eternal life and reaping the seeds you sow, and Tom soon got distracted. He believed in something, but too many versions of the same words had left him hollow and cold. If there was a higher power, then why did it allow all the evil in the world? Why were they even sitting in this room if something held so much power? So many good people had gone before their time. Surely, something so powerful would have stopped their deaths. As if to answer his question, the Chaplain raised his voice a notch and almost shouted over the small congregation.

"And so, my brothers and sisters, The Lord has called Mr. Johnstone home."

The assembled heads turned upwards as one as the conveyor hummed into life. Tom frowned again. Did he say Mr. Johnstone? Emelia was not a male name.

The conveyor moved. An usher stepped forward, removed the flowers, picture and heavy shawl and gave the casket a small nudge. It rolled on well-oiled wheels onto the belt and trundled smoothly toward the hatch. The door rose to accept it.

Tom studied the casket. The glossed white wood with dulled silver hardware made it one of the nicer ones he'd seen. Probably a few thousand dollars, about to be reduced to ash. Mumbling broke out amongst the crowd.

"And so," continued the Chaplain, "as we send him on his way to eternal rest, let us bow our heads and offer our own silent prayers."

No heads bowed. Someone at the front pointed as the casket vanished into the furnace, the door closed, and orange glowed through the small aperture.

"Him? What do you mean, him? And didn't our casket have gold handles?" said a worried voice.

"I'm sure it did," came a reply.

The Chaplain looked from the source of one voice to the other as Tom glanced around the room. The cute girl turned to face him wide-eyed and mouthed the words 'oh no'. Tom still didn't grasp what was going on and, suddenly, she was sitting right next to him. As she nudged him across the pew, her hips touched his. The contact sent heat rushing through him before his face flushed, and then he winced as the splinter snagged his pants and pierced a cheek. He placed his hand over the rough spot. She moved even closer and sat on his hand.

"Ah…excuse me?" she whispered as her eyelashes fluttered and the hint of a blush appeared.

"Splinter," he whispered back.

She frowned as he slid his hand from beneath her and whispered in her ear, "There's a big splinter right beneath you. I've already been introduced. I was trying to save you the pain."

She lifted herself, rubbed her hand across the seat and nodded. "Thanks. Scoot down a little, would you?"

As he shuffled down the bench, she took a turn to lean in. "We should get out of here, I think it's about to go mental."

"Why's that?" asked Tom.

"I reckon they've just cremated the wrong person. Same initials, wrong body."

"I was late to the show," said Tom, "so please forgive me, but I'm not following you."

Her eyes held a mixture of concern and mischief that emphasized how cute her dimples were. Tom couldn't take his eyes off her.

"The paper said this service was for Emelia Johnson."

"The paper?"

"Yes. You know, newspaper? Where they print the news? It said in the obits that this was Emelia Johnson's service. But I saw some of the names in the hallway. There's an Eric Johnstone in the first room. I hope I'm wrong, but I think Eric just got toasted instead of Emelia."

"You check the paper for funerals?" asked Tom.

"For God's sake, they torch the wrong person and all you can do is ask if I read the paper?"

"Good point," said Tom. "Okay, do you want to get out of here? Damn, I sound like I'm in a bar and I just got lucky."

"Yeah, well you're in a crematorium. I've not met anyone that got lucky in one of those, so let's go."

Tom watched her slide out of the pew and followed her out of the room. As they reached the exit, an echo of angry voices bounced around the empty corridor behind them.

Outside, the sun had grown heavy and peeked out over the horizon, casting a warm glow over the gardens and landscaping.

"It looks like it could turn into a beautiful night," said Tom. "Since we're both here, do you fancy taking a walk?"

"I promised my mom I wouldn't go anywhere with strangers."

"Oh." Tom thrust out his hand. "Well, in that case, I'm Tom. Tom Lewis."

She shook it and spoke back in a deep voice. "I thought you were going to say Bond. James Bond." Those dimples flared again as she smiled. "Hello Tom Lewis, I'm Emma. Emma Cairnes. Pleased to meet you. Now, shall we take a walk in the gardens?"

"I'd like that," said Tom.

The melee behind them must have moved into the corridor as the shouting continued before a scream echoed through the grounds. Emma winced. "Sounds like they've seen the name tag on the first door. The other EJ. That's awful. Someone just got sent into the great hereafter without their family present."

Tom took a step toward the main path. A part of him wanted to run back and mingle with the grief that must be filling the place by now. Another part of him didn't want to disrespect the family. Also, he wanted to know more about this girl. "If that spills out here, I don't want to be anywhere near it. We should probably move."

Across the lot, an ivy covered trellis led into a well-tended garden with rows of tulips that lined clean gravel pathways. Shadows shot across a large central lawn that sat raised above the paths. It looked beautiful, a stark contrast to the cold building behind them. Tom pointed toward it.

"Come on," he said, "let's go in there."

He reached back to take her hand but she casually swung it behind her and set off toward the garden. "Come on then. Last one there supplies the picnic!" She ran away laughing as Tom strode after her.

Stepping through the trellis was like passing through a portal. Everything seemed to slow down. The mayhem behind was now out of earshot and an unobstructed view of the grounds lay before them. Emma swept the flat of her hand over the tops of the tulips while they followed the path, then stopped to smell it. She held her palm beneath Tom's nose. The scent was beautiful but he could still pick up the faint odor of musky and sensual perfume on her wrist.

They climbed a small bank and stood together on the lawn. At the opposite side of the garden was another entrance, this one tree lined, which led to a mini maze made with high clipped hedges. A solitary light in the center shone down from the top of a tall pole. She turned, her face glowing like a child's. "Shall we? I haven't been in a maze since I was a kid."

Tom glanced across the top of the hedges and tried to take a mental picture of the turns. "Yeah, that'd be fun."

She bounded away, her long dark hair flowing behind her. Somehow, she stayed upright in decent sized heels. Tom gave chase and caught her at the entrance to the maze where she turned to face him but continued to walk backwards.

"So, do you make a habit of attending the funerals of people you don't know?" he asked.

She laughed, turned again and walked away. "I could ask you the same question. Come on, keep up or you'll get lost."

She vanished around a corner. Tom sped up and turned it as she disappeared again. Each time he turned a corner she waited just long enough to catch his eye and then ran off onto the next. He didn't have to worry too much about losing her, her laughter bled over the top of the hedges as she moved toward the center. He broke into a jog and caught her as she reached a dead end. The single light shone down on them from above.

With his heartbeat racing, he slowed to a stop. "Wow, I'm more out of condition than I realized. Still, at least we made it to the center."

Emma leaned back against the hedge and smiled. "You need to get out and exercise more, Tom Lewis. That was hardly a marathon you ran."

The brilliant white of the sodium light reflected off her smile and danced in her eyes. Tom thrust his hands in his pockets, unsure of what to do with them. "And yet you seem to be quite fit, Emma Cairnes. What do you do, are you a gym instructor or something?"

She threw her head back and laughed again. "Not at all. I work in a hair salon, although I will let you into a secret. Since I'm on my feet all day, I do like to run and swim. It's nice to move about and get my blood pumping. What about you?"

"I need to try some of that," said Tom. "I work in a small advertising agency so I'm stuck behind a desk all day."

He watched her look him up and down. "Well in that case, you're not in bad shape. Maybe you need to do a little cardio and give your heart something to do."

Tom flushed at the compliment and resisted the urge to mention the other things his heart should do. He got the impression she was flirting with him and took a step closer and pulled his hands free from his pockets. She watched his approach and smiled.

Then it went dark.

"Oh, shit!" said Emma after she let out a tiny squeal. Tom looked around. It was pitch black. The building must have closed down for the night and someone had turned out the light.

"Sorry for my potty mouth," she said. "I'm working on it."

"Don't worry about it, you should work in advertising. Okay, I don't even know which direction we're facing. How about I give you a lift up the light pole and see if you can spot the entrance?"

"That's a great idea." Emma shucked off her shoes, holding onto his shoulder for balance as she did. Her perfume drifted over him again and something within him stirred.

"I'm glad I wore a trouser suit," she said. "I'd be paranoid you'd be looking up my skirt."

Tom smiled, although he knew she couldn't see it. "Hey, I'm just a man, but I'd try my best to be a gentleman."

"Yeah, whatever. You know you can't help it. Come on, give me a boost."

With the pole gripped in one hand, she balanced against him with the other while he scooped up a foot and hoisted her into the air. She squealed again, then laughed and stood on his shoulders. He gripped the back of her calf for support. It was solid, definitely a runner's, but it had a nice curve and it gave just enough to be as sensual as her perfume.

"Okay, you have your phone with you?" she said.

"Of course," said Tom.

"Mine's in my pocket and I daren't let go of this pole. Pass it up and I'll take a picture of the maze so we can work our way out of here. I can see the garden and the parking lot, so we should have no trouble."

A flash lit the night as the camera took a snapshot of the scenery, and then she stooped to climb down. She slid down the length of Tom's body as he gripped her to slow her fall. His hands traced the sides of her and, for a moment, they stood inches away from one another. He held his breath as time froze, until she took a step back and handed him his phone, then fumbled for something. A small light lit the space between them.

"My phone," she said. "When I saw yours glowing I had an idea. These will make it easier for us to see where we're going. Could I borrow yours again for a second?"

Tom frowned but passed his phone. She tapped at the screen and then passed it back. "Come on then, let's get out of here."

Ten minutes later they reached the arched trellis. Sure enough, other than a couple of security lights, the place sat in darkness. Their cars were the only two in the parking lot, hers by the entrance and his in no-man's-land, yards away.

"Well," she said, "this visit didn't turn out the way I thought it would."

"Really?" said Tom. "Dare I ask how you thought it would?"

She pondered for a moment, flashed those dimples again and simply said "No. I don't think so."

She almost trotted to her car and pressed a key fob. The car's lights flashed as the alarm beeped and she opened the driver's side door.

"Well, it's definitely been an eventful evening," she said. "Thank you for rescuing me from certain shenanigans in there."

Tom had to smile. Who said the word shenanigans these days? As she slid into the seat and reached for the door, he made a leap of faith.

"Emma. Can I call you?"

She pulled the door closed, fastened the seat belt and started the engine. He watched with anticipation as she wound down the window and put the car in gear. The engine revved as she pushed the accelerator.

"Yes, I'm sure you can."

"But I don't have your..."

Her laughter faded as he followed the car, until it merged with traffic at the exit and vanished.

Chapter Five

Doris stood and turned down the radio as the girls circled around their clients, cutting and molding styles.

"What a racket! Whatever happened to real music? Do you remember Frank Sinatra or Doris Day or Elvis? What the heck was that noise? And why does he keep shouting? Can't he sing?"

Emma laughed. "That's Fetty Wap, Doris."

"What on earth is a fetid wap?" said Doris as she took her seat. "Sounds like an illness."

"He's a rapper."

"A wrapper? Like a condom? Henry talks about those all the time at the club. I'm sure he wants me, he just won't come out and say it. I'm not asking him, though. It's the man's place to ask."

Vicki shook her head. "I'm not sure how we got from Elvis to condoms and I daren't ask. And how come you've not mentioned Henry? Who's Henry?"

"Yeah, come on Doris," said Emma, "you're always giving me a hard time and you've got a secret lover at the club? Spill the beans."

"Oh, it's nothing like that. We talk all the time and share war stories, but we're too old for much else. We might snap something."

"And you met at the club?"

"Yes, his son was wheeling him in one day when his colostomy bag fell off the side of his chair and Mavis Pickles rode over it. You should've seen the mess. Still, we got it clean. He had to leave that time but, when he came back, I made a point of saying hello. He's a lovely man. Still got some of his own teeth, too. That shows vitality."

"What more could you ask for in a man?" said Vicki. "So how many of you get together? At the club? Is it quite a gathering?"

Emma remembered Doris's contact book. She'd glanced through it last night between bouts of thinking about Tom and, if Doris wanted to invite everyone, they would need a big hall.

"Loads of us," said Doris, "but it's like a revolving door. Most weeks a new face appears, but it only replaces one that's missing."

The spark in her eyes dimmed a little as she gazed off into the distance. Emma caught Jen in the corner of her eye as she raised a hand to her face to dab a tear. As if she sensed the atmosphere, Vicki angled a mirror behind the knit of blue curls. "How's that then? I only did this a couple of days ago, though, so I'm not sure I've made much of a difference."

Doris nodded. She'd taken Emma up on the offer to come in whenever she liked and had reappeared the next day. The blue curls looked no different, but Vicki made the effort to take care of her without asking why.

"That's nice, thank you. I might try some of those corn holes next time," said Doris.

"The game?" asked Vicki.

"No, silly, the hair. When it's all plaited and in straight lines."

"Cornrows. Doris, why would you want cornrows? I'm not sure blue hair would carry it off, to be honest."

"Blue can carry anything off, dear, it's a soothing color."

Vicki placed her hands on the old lady's shoulders. "Doris, don't get me wrong, we love to see you, but did I mess up your hair the last time? I mean, you were here the other day and you're back again. Was it okay? Because you can tell me if it wasn't and I'll try to make it right."

Emma and Jen sensed the mood change. Their clients were oblivious, but the air bristled with tension.

"Would you mind making a coffee?" asked Doris as she gestured to the back room.

"Of course not. The usual?"

"Yes please, dear," said Doris and folded her hands in her lap.

Vicki turned and walked to the room. "Anyone else?"

The rest of the salon politely refused and Vicki disappeared through the door. Doris rose to follow her. Emma and Jen exchanged glances as the door clicked shut behind them.

A few minutes later Vicki reappeared. Emma watched her in the mirror as she meandered toward them, slumped into Doris's chair and cried. Her face was ruddy and mascara ran like little roadways from her eyes. The clients either side of her sat dumbstruck as Vicki sobbed.

"We're all done here, Mrs. Creamer," said Emma as Doris reappeared. Her client tilted her head in multiple directions, watched the results in the mirror, and nodded her approval. "Jen will take care of you at the front desk. Thanks again and I'll see you in a few weeks."

Mrs. Creamer wandered off bewildered, and Jen and her client followed her to the front of the salon.

Vicki dabbed her face with a towel, then spun to face Doris. "So, now what? There can't be anything wrong with you, you look perfectly fine to me. Perhaps they got it wrong. Go to a different doctor and get a second opinion."

"I'm having a good day, dear," said Doris. "Some days it's all I can do to breathe through the coughing. And I'll sleep this afternoon, too. I take lots of naps. No, I'm afraid they got it right. They showed me the x-rays. I've got good bones, though. I've seen them."

"It's just the rest of you," said Emma as she hugged Doris. "I looked through your contact book. That's a lot of names. If you want everyone there, then we'll have to find a good sized venue."

"Oh, don't worry about that," said Doris, "I had a brain storm."

"A brain wave?" said Vicki.

"One of those, too. Yes, we can use the club. Most of the people will already be there anyway so it'll be less of an effort for everyone."

"Well, they can hardly hold a service at the club, but that gives me an idea. Hang on a sec."

As the last client left the salon, Emma locked the door and flipped the sign to say 'Closed. Hair today and gone...'

The girls and Doris took seats in the waiting area.

"You know how you said you wanted a small funeral? Well, I want to give you what you deserve, and you deserve to go out in style, Doris. Let's arrange a fund raiser. Let's raise a load of money and get you the best funeral we can."

"That all sounds very morbid," said Vicki. "Doris, are you okay with all of this?"

"Fine by me," said Doris, "Anyway, I doubt I'll be paying that much attention by then. Still, if it makes you girls feel better, you should go for it. What did you have in mind?"

"I'm not sure," said Emma. "Let me think on it, but it would be nice to get all of your friends together. We should do something that would be a good night but also raise money so we can take care of everything for you. Is there anything you've always wanted to do?"

Doris stroked her chin for a moment. "One of those bungee things where they make you bounce on an elastic rope. I considered a parachute jump once but I've seen how men fold clothes. I wouldn't trust one with my parachute, he'd pleat it at the side instead of the front and I'd end up a splat on the ground."

"No bungee jump, Doris," said Vicki. She clutched a frayed tissue and looked like a panda as dark makeup ringed her eyes. "They're dangerous, you could…"

She trailed off as Doris smiled and patted her knee. "Don't worry about me, dear. Seventy-nine years I've been on this earth. Wars have started and finished in my time. I've seen people go from phoning home from a box at the side of the road to falling into a river because they couldn't take their eyes from one of those cell phones. And don't even get me started on that inter-web thing, mainly because I don't understand it. My point is, I've lived a good life. Sure, there've been bad times, but I've had moments where everything stopped and I knew I'd found true happiness, too. Bill and I could just glance across a room at one another. There were no words. We didn't need them. The silence said more than any words could. All I'm doing is going to meet my soul mate again."

Vicki broke down and sobbed again. Jen wiped wet streaks from her face while Emma wrapped an arm around Doris. "We love you, Doris. You're one of us."

"Well, let me give you girls some good advice," said Doris, "from an old tree to growing saplings. The moment you meet someone you can sit in silence with as comfortably as talking, hold on to them. And it's not just about the words and the sex, it's about finding someone who knows you and wants nothing more than to see you smile."

"Doris, that was beautiful," said Vicki.

"Too right," said Doris. "Fetid wap's got nothing on me."

****

The group session turned out to be a bust. The library itself was the highlight of the evening, all wood with row after row of books that gave off that smell that only exists in libraries and used book stores. The old building was comforting and familiar and reminded Tom of long days in his youth, sitting alone at a table reading a novel or researching homework. It was nicer than home. The library was full of strangers, but there were strangers at home, too. At least here there were books.

Ten men had sat in an almost perfect circle and shared stories of events in their lives that had left them filled with despair and sorrow. For a moment, Tom thought maybe this was it; funerals weren't the solution, and that the angst in this tight group could fuel his needs. Then the positive one, the ringleader, offered words of hope and encouraged the group to do the same and the whole thing descended into a big back slapping event.

Rob tried to express himself but failed and ended up discussing the best ways to get pregnant. No one else in the room seemed to be too interested although they did throw out the token 'keep at it' statement. After manslaughter and child abuse discussions, pregnancy seemed to be way down the list of priorities to an assembled group of depressed men. Rob and Tom apologized, finished the awful coffee and made their excuses, then drove back to Tom's place.

They made small talk as Tom stood in the kitchen and cleared the dishes from dinner.

Rob picked up the paper that lay on the table. "Newspapers are a dying breed now, what with the internet. It's no surprise." He waved it around like an extra limb. "Look at it, you've got a page of depression on the front. All the good sporty stuff is thrown to the back, and the middle's full of random shit and the hatched, matched and dispatched section."

Tom looked up from the sink. "What the hell are you talking about, hatched, matched and dispatched?"

Rob shook the paper open and presented the small, tidy columns punctuated by postage stamp sized pictures. "The three stages of life. Birth, marriage and death. Hatched, matched and dispatched. And they group them together in the middle pages where you have to go searching for them."

He glanced at the page and noticed circles marked in pen at random places. "Why have you circled these entries?" he asked.

"Did you know these people?" He looked up as if a bad thought had hit him. "Shit, Tom, I'm sorry if I've crossed a line, I had no idea."

Tom flushed and walked into the room. After a deep breath, he exhaled slowly. "You've crossed no lines." He played with his fingers and then ran them through his hair. "I, er, there's something I've never told anyone, actually."

"Is everything okay? Don't tell me you're suffering from something and planning your own funeral. Because that would be so far beyond messed up, it'd be on a different planet."

"No, it's nothing like that."

"Well that's a relief. I'm crap at funerals. They're no fun at all."

"I don't think they're supposed to be," said Tom. "Trust me. I've been to enough of them."

"Sorry man, but you've lost me."

"Well, you've already noticed that I never seem to date or show many feelings."

"I knew it, you really are gay," said Rob. "That's why we all wondered if you were into men."

"For God's sake, Rob, I'm not gay and I'll knock someone out if that conversation doesn't stop." Tom paused and took a moment to regroup. "Okay, I'm not sure how to explain this, so bear with me. You've known me, what, twenty years?"

Rob nodded. "Best friends since school, but you're starting to worry me now."

"Okay." Tom wrung his hands. "In a nutshell, I feel as if I'm emotionally stunted."

Rob skewed his head to one side like an attentive dog. "And you've lost me again," he said. "What the hell are you talking about?"

"Hang on," said Tom.

He retreated to the kitchen and returned with two beers, passed one to Rob and took a seat on the sofa.

"Are you having problems with piles, Tom?" said Rob. "Only I noticed earlier at the meeting. You look as if you're in pain. Unless it's a gay…"

"Stop! No more gay comments. Last night, I sat on a splinter, okay? It didn't seem too bad at the time, but it seems I was distracted. Anyway, let me get this out. When I was eight, I was with my folks for a night out. Dad was driving…"

"Yeah," interrupted Rob, "now you mention it, you don't talk about your folks much. I mean, their pictures are all over the…"

"Let me talk Rob, please."

"Sorry."

"Dad was driving. There was a horrible accident. He flew through the windscreen, no seat belt, and he was dead before he hit the ground. Mom didn't make it through the screen and had her neck broken. I flew through the hole that Dad made and the paramedics found me a few feet from the car, bumped and bruised, but otherwise okay."

Rob put down his beer. "Shit, I am so sorry. I had no idea."

"That's okay, you wouldn't. I've never talked about it," said Tom. "So anyway, I became an orphan at eight. Now here's the freaky part."

Rob leaned forward as if he was taking a confession.

"I've never grieved for my parents, I think because I don't remember them. Maybe that's why I'm not able to, but it's caused an emotional block in me. I go to viewings and funerals so I can wallow in that pain and sadness. If I can soak up enough of that grief, perhaps it'll pull it out of me, too."

There was a moment of silence.

"Tom?" said Rob.

"Yes?"

"That's fucked up."

"Tell me about it. I feel nothing. That's why I haven't been able to keep a girl for too long. They think it must be something about them. You've heard the old cliché, it's not you, it's me? That's really the case. It is me. I never get comfortable enough to explain it to them and, even if I did, they won't stick around for long after that, will they?"

Rob grabbed his beer, took a long drink, and let out a nervous laugh. "I'm speechless." He paused. "Can't you talk to someone, like a therapist or something? You should have said more tonight at that meeting. God knows, you might have saved me from myself."

"Tried therapy. Cost a fortune. It seems I've got all kinds of repressed shit inside me," said Tom as he made quote symbols with his fingers. "Like I didn't know that. No, I've got to find a way to get past it. I'll keep up with the funerals. One day it'll hit me and I'll be okay."

"You need to meet someone and get attached, form a bond or something."

"Well, it's funny you should mention that. I might have. Last night at a cremation."

Rob's laughter broke the mood. "You're shitting me. You met someone at a cremation? Thank God, romance is still alive and kicking."

Tom smiled, glad for the respite. "It was after the service, to be honest. They burned the wrong body, but I was late and missed it. This girl I've spotted before took me outside and we got lost in a maze."

"Tom, you're not even speaking English anymore. I recognize that language, though, it's called gibberish. You've devolved and now you're talking gibberish."

"Sorry," said Tom. "I'm not good at this stuff, Rob." He paused and composed himself. "Okay, I went to a cremation, they messed it up, and this girl I saw at another funeral sat by me and explained what was happening. We left before everyone went ballistic, and there was a maze outside, a real one, so we walked it until they turned out the light. I thought we'd be stuck in there all night, which wouldn't have been a bad thing, to be fair, but we found our way out. She used my phone to take a picture of the maze and we used the light off both our phones to get out. I asked her if I could call her. She said yes, then laughed and drove off before I got her number."

"You do need therapy, pal," said Rob. "So you've ringed all of these funerals so you can bump into her again? Do you think she's stunted as well?"

"No idea, she seemed normal enough to me but, no, I ringed those funerals yesterday as ones I could attend last night. I know her name, though, so I suppose I could Google her."

"You sound like a stalker. She seemed to like you, right?"

"Well, yeah, I think so. We had a good time, considering the wrong person went up in flames."

"Yeah, there's a statement you don't hear too often. And she said you could call her?"

"Yes. In a way."

"What do you mean, in a way? Did she say yes, you could call her and you had her permission, or yes, you could call her and you had the means to do so?"

"Shit, Rob, now you've lost me."

"She didn't give you her number?"

"No."

"Did she send you a text?"

"No. No text." Tom paused, frowned, and reached for his phone. "Although she took my phone and messed about with it before we parted ways."

He swiped the screen and looked at the icons. Nothing stood out. Then he pulled up his texts. Nothing new. Then his call history. Nothing received that he didn't recognize.

And then he found it. The last entry on the outgoing call log was a number, not a known contact. She'd called herself but, because of the funeral, she must have muted her phone so he heard no call. She'd given him her number and, in calling her own phone, had taken his too.

Tom felt himself blush and held out the phone. "It's here. And she has my number, too. I bet she's wondering why I haven't called."

"Don't worry about that," said Rob. "There's an unwritten rule. If you call to soon, you're desperate."

"To be fair, I am somewhat," said Tom. "What do you think? Should I call her?"

"Well, if you do, might you burst into flames or end up on the wrong side of the grass?"

"That's crazy talk."

"Well then... what have you got to lose?"

Tom's finger bounced along with his heartbeat as he dialed the number. Then he canceled it and sent a text instead.

Chapter Six

Wine was the answer. Emma wasn't sure what the question was, but she drove away from the salon and headed for the store. Talking with Doris and the girls had left her feeling morose. A months-old pizza lay buried under ice in the freezer at home while she tried to maintain a healthy diet and ate wheat bread and yogurt. Tonight was the perfect night for frozen plastic food. And a bottle of wine.

As she pulled into the store's parking lot her phone beeped from the cup holder and lit up the console. It fought against the lights bouncing and flashing from the bowling alley next to the store. Tom's name splashed across the screen.

She'd wondered how long it would take him to call or, in this case, text. For the whole day, the desire to tell the girls about a man with potential had driven her insane. A steady stream of clients had kept them all too preoccupied and, once Doris broke her news to Vicki, the time never seemed right.

As the car rolled to a stop, she switched off the engine and picked up her phone.

'For the first time ever, I had fun at a funeral,' said the text. 'Would you like to go out to a place with less dead people?'

A smile spread across her face. She hadn't had a meaningful date in months. Then she recalled the heat that had spread through her as he'd held her leg while she clung to the light pole. And the fact that she'd trusted him to do that. Then she remembered sliding down the front of him, close enough to kiss and for him to smell her perfume.

'That might be fun,' she replied. 'Did you have anything in mind?'

It would take him a moment to receive the text and respond, so Emma opened the car door and grabbed her purse just as her phone beeped again. He must have been holding his to have replied right away. She closed the door again and nestled into her seat.

'No. What do you enjoy?'

It would be so much easier to call and speak to him, but there must have been a reason he chose to text. Perhaps he was shy although he hadn't seemed to be when she mentioned him looking up her skirt. Or he was in company or surrounded by friends and he didn't want them to hear his conversation.

'Anything, I'm fairly easy...'

Her thumb slid and skidded across the send button and the phone transmitted the first half of her sentence. She panicked. 'I'm fairly easy' wasn't the message she'd be trying to send and her fingers scrambled to finish the sentence.

'Well, I wasn't planning on that kind of night, but... ☺' came the quick reply.

'OMG. I'm so sorry. I meant to say I'm fairly easy to please. I really don't mind.'

Emma imagined him laughing at her. If he was in a bar, surrounded by friends, they might see her message. If they got along and hit it off, she'd have to meet them. Then her phone rang. She jumped, and it fell from her hand, slid between her thighs and bounced into the foot well. She followed the glow of its light and retrieved it.

"Er, hello?" she stammered.

The voice on the other end of the call sounded perplexed and slightly amused. "Hello? Is this Emma?"

"Yes," she said. "Yes, it is. Sorry, Tom, I dropped my phone between my legs and had to go digging for it." Laughter chimed down the phone as she winced and blushed like a teenager.

"Well, I won't ask what you were doing," said Tom. "Anyway, I thought it would be easier to call. Safer too, by the sound of things."

"I'm certainly having communication issues, so I do appreciate you calling. How about I try not to be easy or fumble between my legs for the rest of our chat?"

"Let's be grateful this isn't one of those video calls. You'd never get me off the phone." He went silent as if he'd embarrassed himself. "So anyway, what do you enjoy? A meal? A movie?"

"To be honest," said Emma, "it's been so long since I went out, I really don't mind. Anywhere with food and alcohol. I need a glass of wine, though. What about you? What would you like to do?"

"We already have one thing in common. I haven't been out in months."

Emma glanced up and saw the bowling alley. "How about bowling? Do you bowl?"

"Not for a while. I'd give that a try."

"Okay, bowling it is. When would you like to go?"

There was silence again, and she imagined him fighting an inner battle with himself and his confidence. "How about tonight?" he said. "I know it's sudden, but I'm in a 'go for it' kind of mood and I'm asking before I lose the nerve. How soon could you be at a bowling alley?"

Emma glanced through the window. "You'd be surprised. Although I'm in heels, so I should probably change first."

"Emma," he said, "they loan you shoes, remember? They look like miniature clown shoes."

She felt like palm slapping her own forehead. "Duh. I knew that. Okay, believe it or not I'm sitting outside the alley on Southport. I can meet you in there if it's not too far for you?"

"Not at all, I know where that is. Give me twenty minutes or so and I'll be there. Is that okay with you?"

"I'll be right here. The first drink's on me."

"All right. See you soon."

"Okay, Tom Lewis. I look forward to it."

Emma disconnected the call and slid her phone into her purse.

"Sorry frozen pizza," she said to herself. "Maybe one day, but not today. Things are about to get a little warmer."

****

"I did it," said Tom.

Rob smiled and shook his head. "I can see that, on account of the fact I'm sitting right here. And I assume by the Cheshire cat grin and one half of a positive conversation that she said yes."

"We're going bowling. She's at an alley on Southport. Rob? I've never bowled in my life."

"But you just said you did," said Rob with a rising voice. "You shouldn't start a fresh relationship with a lie. That's bad form, Tom."

"I was so grateful she suggested something, I didn't want to nix it. And anyway, I've seen The Big Lebowski enough times. In my mind, I've bowled. And how hard can it be? You throw a ball at the pins and knock them down. And there's about a dozen of them. I can't see how you could miss."

"There are ten pins, idiot, hence the name ten-pin bowling. You'd better keep everything on the level and don't mess this up."

Tom sat and ran his fingers through his hair.

"And you're doing that nervous thing again where you play with your hair like a big girl. Relax and be prepared to have a good time. And don't mention the thing. You know, the thing that scares them off? Don't talk about it. Don't even think about it. Silence about the thing, okay?"

"Rob, it's not exactly a conscious thing, it's just in there."

"Well leave it in there. Push it down out of sight where it won't jump up and bite you on the ass again."

Tom stood again and walked to the bathroom. "I'll do my best. It's bowling, what's the worst that could happen?" He closed the door and picked up his toothbrush as Rob shouted through the door.

"Knowing you? Someone will keel over and you'll have to go to their funeral."

The door opened a crack and Tom mumbled with his toothbrush between his teeth. "That's not even funny."

"Come on, it was a little. So this girl, Emma? What's she like?"

Tom rinsed his mouth as he searched through a drawer. "Nice. Gorgeous eyes. Long brown hair. Or brunette."

"Same thing, Tom."

"Huh?"

"Brown and brunette. Brown is a color. Someone with brown hair is a brunette. It's the same color."

"Okay, smartass. She works in a salon so I can check later. And she likes to run and swim and she has a nice calf."

"What? Like a baby cow?"

Tom shook his head. "Rob, you can be such a muppet. The back of her leg, it was firm and curvy."

"Well, I hope for the sake of balance she's got two. What are you doing? You said you'd be there in twenty minutes."

"I know," said Tom flustered. "I'm sure I had a flyer for the bowling. Do me a favor. Find out where it is on Southport."

****

It turned out to be adjacent to a liquor store and had enough flashing neon in its windows to trigger a seizure. Tom locked the car door and took a moment to compose himself.

The phone calls had been easy. Eight hours a day hammering out deals and slogans at work with all kinds of people made it second nature to him. Talking with Emma at the funeral had seemed natural too, but the moment had created an adrenaline rush. The uncertainty, coupled with the warm familiarity of surroundings and the spontaneity, had made everything effortless.

They'd planned this. His stomach lurched, and he turned back and reached for the door handle, then stopped and mentally scolded himself. This wasn't a unique situation, other than it was in a bowling alley. He'd had dates before and, to be fair, the first ones turned out to be okay for the most part.

He took the first uncertain step toward the alley, then another. One at a time, he thought. Lights and noise bombarded his senses as he yanked open the heavy door. A maze of beeping arcade machines led the way to a round counter which housed the shoe section on one side and a bar on the other. Tom wandered through his second maze in two days and tried to peer through the distracting flashes to find Emma. He spotted her sitting to the side of the bar, perched on a tall stool. She looked pretty, in a white blouse and red skirt. The multicolored lights reflected off her blouse and her crossed legs, and he blushed as she caught his gaze and waved.

As he got closer to the bar, the noise behind it got louder. Balls rumbled down the lanes and pins crashed as they collapsed. He leaned toward her to speak and caught another whiff of her perfume.

"Hi," he shouted. "Thanks for coming at such short notice."

She placed a hand on his arm. "No, thanks for the invite. After the day I've had, it'll be nice to think of nothing and have fun. Sorry, I couldn't wait for you," she said, waving a glass in the air, "but I've opened a tab behind the bar. I said your first drink's on me so get what you'd like. What's your shoe size?"

The question caused Tom to back up and frown.

"For the clown shoes. Remember? Why don't you get a drink and I'll get our shoes. Our lane's reserved so they're waiting for us."

"Ah, sorry, it was an unusual question." He laughed and played with his hair, then realized and planted his hands in his pockets. "Elevens, please. I'll be right with you."

She wandered off as he caught the bartender's attention and ordered a beer. By the time he reached the other side of the bar she was already in the bowling shoes and held his in her hand. Tom wrinkled his nose. "How can you hold them like that? You don't know where they've been."

Emma laughed and tossed them to him. "Don't be such a big girl," she said playfully, "they spray them with a unique and deadly disinfectant and battery acid combination. Kills everything. Put them on and let's see if it kills your game." She licked out her tongue as he knelt to remove his shoes.

Their lane was at the far end of the complex up against the wall. Tom stood by while Emma keyed their names into the computer and then marched up to him. "Right," she said with a beaming smile, "let's see what you're made of."

She scooped up a decent sized ball, strode with purpose to the edge of the lane and lined up her shot. Tom watched as she bent, and traced the curve of her body when she knelt and released the ball. Her arm rose with a flourish as she watched the ball careen down the aisle and smash into the lead pin. All ten tumbled and fell backwards into darkness, and she leaped, punched the air, then moon-walked before him. "Follow that, bowler boy," she shouted and strode past him with a wink.

"I get the impression you're not very competitive then?" smiled Tom. "This is not your first time, is it?"

"Ha, you have no idea what you're letting yourself in for," she said, then turned away and reached for her drink.

The insinuation hang in the air as he reached for a ball of his own. Emma's returned through the conveyor system and clicked next to the others. Tom picked it up instead and moved to the lane while the pins jostled and dropped back into place. He followed her lead, lined up the swing of his arm against the marks in the center of the floor and rolled the ball forward. It didn't move as fast as hers, but it kept a good line and hit the lead pin. The pin fell backwards and began a domino effect until all but one remained. The last one wobbled and teetered, as if it was on tiptoes, and then fell alongside its comrades.

Emma clapped behind him as he turned, wide eyed with surprise. "Shit. I've not done that before."

"What?" she said. "Got a strike?"

"No, bowled."

She frowned. "Didn't you say you had, but not for a while?"

He held up his hands. "I have to confess, I told a bit of a lie. I was so grateful you suggested something, I went along with it so you'd come out."

She placed a hand on his arm and squeezed it. "Okay, my confession. If you'd suggested McDonald's I'd have still turned up. I've been waiting all day for you to call."

"Cool, I'll keep McDonalds in mind for next time," he said.

"Now listen to you," she laughed. "The boy gets a strike and grows confident. Let's see how you fare when the pressure's on."

Emma scooped up a ball and bowled again and, once again, ten pins scattered. An X appeared on the scoreboard under her name. Tom followed her and used the same technique. Again, ten pins collapsed. He stood back and watched in amazement as an X appeared alongside hers on the scoreboard.

He pointed to the display. "Look, it says Emma and Tom, and now there're two kisses under our names."

Emma glanced at the board, raised a hand to his cheek and pulled his head toward her. He shivered as her lips brushed his and she kissed him. Flushes ran down his arms and his breathing stopped as he returned the pressure.

"So that's how it is, huh?" she said as she pulled away. "Try to distract a girl with your manly passion. Right then, Tom Lewis. Challenge accepted."

She marched to the lane. All Tom could do was smile as she continued to accumulate strikes and spares. Pins scattered and collapsed after every ball she bowled while his game fell apart.

After the final frame they stood side by side and admired the scoreboard. She placed an arm around his shoulder and squeezed him. "So, just so you know, that's what's known in layman's terms as an ass kicking. How does it feel?"

"Painful," said Tom, "I won't sit down for a week, although look, our two kisses are still side by side."

She smiled again, looked at the board and kissed his cheek. "Thank you."

"For what? Letting you give me a kicking? Believe me, I didn't let you."

"No, not just that. I haven't smiled this much in a long time and, after today of all days, I needed to smile."

"Why don't you let me get us a drink and you can tell me about it. That's if you want to?"

"Yeah, I'd like that, but let's find somewhere quieter. Tell you what, I'll cover this if you take me somewhere half decent for something to eat. I'm starving."

"That sounds like a plan," said Tom.

****

They walked down the side of the three lane road and paused under a tram bridge to kiss again. Tom held her for a moment afterwards. Despite the good time they'd had, sadness seemed to roll off her in waves and he wondered what might have caused it. Perhaps he was about to find out. She squirmed free but took his hand and seemed to mentally shake herself. "Come on, I know a great place that's not too far away. Do you like donner kebabs?"

"I've never heard of them. What are they?"

"You're not vegetarian, are you?"

"No," said Tom, "I'm definitely a carnivore."

"Okay, it's easier to just show you."

She led him down a side street that plunged them into darkness. A distance ahead, a small sign flashed in the night.

"Is it safe down here?" he said.

Emma laughed. "In the nicest way, you can be such a wimp. Come on."

She pulled him along until the sign was legible. Ziti's Greek Food was a regular house, sandwiched in a row of similar buildings. Someone had remodeled the front to add a large window and a commercial door but, other than that, it was identical to the rest of the row. Dim lights hung at intervals but did little to brighten up the street.

"I know what you're thinking," she said, "but trust me. And don't freak out when you see the food either. Just try it. If you don't like it, I'll take it home with me and you can order a burger."

"As long as it won't kill me, I'll try anything once," he said as he held open the door for her. She brushed past him as a small bell rang above them, and he followed her inside.

It appeared bigger than it should. Eight red tables hugged the walls, four either side, supported on chrome legs. The clock on the back wall read just after 9.00, but there were still only three tables empty. A steel counter filled the far wall beyond them, topped with illuminated signs displaying the menu.

"It smells gorgeous," said Tom. "What is that? It's like a combination of fried food and spices."

There was a chunk of meat that looked like an elephant's leg spinning in the heat of a rotisserie behind the counter. "See that?" she pointed, "It's like spiced lamb. They shave slices off it and pile it into pita bread. Do you trust me to order for us?"

Tom nodded.

Emma summoned a waiter and ordered two donners with everything on them. Tom recognized nothing on the menu but resigned himself to try it. He paid, and they sat across from one another at a table to wait while the food was prepared.

He reached his hands over the table and she met him half way and clasped them in hers. "You said you'd had one of those days."

"Yes, although to be honest, it's been one of those weeks. There's a lovely lady who comes into the salon. We've known her for years and she's like a mother to us. Anyway, she told us she has cancer. It's heartbreaking. And Vicki, her stylist, is devastated."

"I hate the 'C' word. It's taken people I've known, too. Can she get treatment?"

"No, they've given her three months. To make matters worse, it also turns out she's alone. No family, although she has loads of friends. She has no money for a funeral either, so we're trying to arrange a fund raiser to send her off in style. She has such an amazing spirit, it's the least we can do. We love her."

"That's good of you. What sort of thing were you thinking?"

"No idea. She has access to one of those lodges, so the venue shouldn't be an issue, but what do you do with a room full of pensioners?"

"Not paint balling," said Tom, "or a disco. Old folks like to reminisce."

She pondered for a moment. "You could have an idea there."

"What, paint balling?"

"No," she laughed, "the disco and the reminiscing. I bet they'd love a kind of prom, but for old people."

A waiter sidled alongside them and slid two large plates onto the table. "Enjoy your food," he said with a heavy accent, and wandered off back to the kitchen.

Tom glanced down at the plate. "What the hell is that, and how many people is it supposed to feed?" The plate overflowed with a huge pita bread. Slices of meat spilled out of it, covered in a red salsa. He picked around in it to find cabbage, tomatoes, cucumber, and onion. "Seriously, that's three meals on one plate."

"Just dive in. I recommend eating some of it with your fingers before you try to pick up the whole thing, otherwise you'll find yourself wearing most of it."

He broke off a piece of meat and threw it into his mouth. His taste buds erupted. "Oh my God, that tastes amazing. Nothing like lamb, though."

"As far as I know, they never say what percentage of it is actually lamb, but when it tastes that good, who cares?" Emma dove in and wolfed down fingers full at a time.

"Wow, you were hungry!" said Tom.

"Mmmm, mmmmm," she nodded.

They sat in silence for a while as they tackled the food, and then Tom leaned back and wiped his fingers and chin with a napkin. "So, an old folks' disco prom? How would that work?"

Emma pushed away her empty plate. "I don't eat like that often, but when I do…"

"Then you go for it?" laughed Tom.

"Well, old folks love to dance, right? So, we should kit out the hall in a theme like, say, the 50's, and get a DJ to play classics they can dance to. Perhaps get one of those romantic arches they can kiss under and do a prom king and queen vote. There could be a raffle to raise money, and a small charge on the door for admittance. It would be a gathering of her friends, but a way to raise money, too."

"That sounds nice," said Tom. "And I know a photographer. I could ask him to take pictures and charge a small fee for them. And I can take care of tickets and flyers, too. My office has all kinds of printing equipment."

Emma tilted her head and smiled. "You'd do that for me?"

"Sure," said Tom. Something long lost and much deeper was developing within him. He gazed into Emma's eyes. They swirled like coffee and seemed to pull him closer. The sensation scared him a little. "I don't get out much," he said with a shrug. "It would give me something to do."

She seemed disappointed. The swirls flickered, and then she blinked. "Okay. I might take you up on it. Let me speak to the girls and maybe I'll get in touch."

She stacked the rest of his kebab onto her empty plate and reached for her purse. "Well," she said as she glanced at the clock, "it's after 9.30. I still have to get home, shower and get my things ready for work tomorrow."

"Oh, no problem, let me walk you back to your car," said Tom.

They stepped out into the cool night and walked along the deserted road, their arms swinging side by side, hands brushing but not connecting. Tom sensed a retreat and kicked himself. His statement and tone of voice had ruined a good moment, and he felt the need to reel it back in to try to salvage the evening. Everything he thought to say didn't sound right, so he remembered what Rob had said. Keep things on the level.

"I've had a lovely time tonight. Thanks again for dropping everything at such short notice. I'm sure most men don't ask you out twenty minutes before they expect to see you."

"No, that was a first."

Silence and awkwardness. Her mood had cooled as much as the night.

At the alley's parking lot Emma gestured to her car. Tom followed behind her. She unlocked the door and turned to face him.

"Thanks for a nice night," she said.

"Thank you. I've had a great time, despite the thrashing. I'd love to see again, if you'd like?"

She leaned forward and pecked him on the cheek, the softest of touches that was almost nothing but a gesture. "Let me speak to the girls and see what they say. Thanks again. Bye."

She climbed into her car and drove off into the night.

Chapter Seven

"You did what?"

"I drove off and left him there."

Jen shook her head. "You're crazy. He sounds like a really nice guy."

"He seems to be," said Emma, "but, in no time at all, he went from trying to please like a little puppy to stone-cold looking out for himself."

Vicki feigned amazement. "Oh, you mean it was like he put up a wall?"

"Well, I'm not saying…"

"The woman who uses construction companies to build her walls is put off by a nervous guy who might have done the same thing? Right now I can see a room full of teapots and kettles. They're all dancing around and calling each other black."

"Hilarious," said Emma. "I was hoping for a bit more support."

"Well, you should've bought a smaller size," said Jen. "What is wrong with you? I bet you stonewalled him, didn't you? Pardon the pun."

"Okay, I wish I'd kept my mouth shut. This is why I don't talk about my dates with you."

"What, this and the fact that you rarely have any?" said Vicki.

Emma sipped her wine and took a moment to calm herself. Recounting last night's events had been easy up this point. It took a pair of independent eyes to notice she'd done the same thing she always did, but this time on a first date. Even for her, it was an impressive feat of wall building. Normally, she got to at least the end of the third date. Not that the purpose of this wine bar visit had been to discuss her love life.

"Call him," said Jen. "Or even just text him and say hello and thanks again for a nice night. Anything, but offer an olive branch. I bet he's sitting at home sulking."

"Or he's already moved on and he's bowling someone else over," said Vicki. "Pardon the pun."

Emma tensed. For the first time in a long time, someone had come along who made her smile and, more importantly, had made her feel at ease and perhaps even a little special. Tom didn't push or probe or test her feelings. Jen was right. He was a nice guy. She reached for her phone but sat back again. Not yet. She wasn't ready.

"Okay, enough about me because I'm thinking I'm a lost cause."

"You're not a lost cause," said the girls in stereo.

"Whatever, we're not here for me. We're here to sort something out for Doris. And I may have an idea."

Jen and Vickie leaned forward, their hands clasped between their legs.

"Remember the lodge that Doris mentioned? Well, we can use that, I already checked. It's a good sized building and they'll let us have it for free provided we leave it as tidy as we found it. We'll need a cleanup crew. And Tom suggested that we should do a kind of prom night, but for old people."

"Tom suggested it, huh?" said Vicki.

"Yes, he said that old people like to dance and reminisce and he's right. We should find a theme, deck the lodge out like a high school, and get a DJ to play old people music."

Jen laughed. "And what do you consider to be old people music? My parents listen to AC/DC. That's old people music and I don't see Doris head banging to Hells Bells!"

"Good point," said Emma, "and now I'm fighting to keep that visual away. Tom said the 50's, but I'm inclined to try something more up to date."

"Tom said, huh?" said Jen.

"I see what you're doing." Emma emptied her wine glass and signaled for another. "So I listened to him. So what?"

"So," continued Jen, "it means he was listening to you, too. He was engaged and paid attention to what you said and showed an interest. Do you have any idea how rare that is? Most men struggle to get past the first sentence before they're mentally undressing you or trying to work out your cup size."

"To be fair," said Vicki, "your dates pay attention, too. As soon as they hear you mention houses and kids, they run."

Jen ignored the statement as Emma continued. "He also said that one of his friends is a photographer and we could charge a small fee for photos to add to the fund."

"I'd like to date a photographer." Jen's eyes glazed as she stared off into the distance. "I bet they've got really nimble fingers." She snapped to attention. "Shit. Did I say that out loud?"

"Not a word of it," said Emma. "And while we're talking about Tom, it turns out he works for an ad agency and has access to printing equipment. He pretty much offered to print the flyers and posters."

"You got all of this on a first date?" said Jen.

"Well, yes," Emma replied, "before I messed it up."

"And you weren't showing any excess cleavage or making offers of sexual favors?"

"Jen, you're scaring me. Please stop."

"No, I have to go out on the town with you. Together, we could conquer the world."

"Or plunge us into another Ice Age," said Vicki. "Girls, please shelve your hormones and let's get this thing sorted."

"Yes," snapped Emma, "focus! We need a theme. Remember on Back to the Future when Marty McFly traveled back in time to his parents' prom night? Let's do something like that. They had Under the Sea as their theme."

"We'll need something more up to date, though, like The Little Mermaid," said Jen.

"Or Finding Nemo," said Emma.

"Not Finding Nemo," said Jen, "the girl with the braces freaks me out. I can't watch it."

"Are you being serious? What girl? Are braces that bad?"

"Did you have braces," said Jen. "Ever? I endured high school with braces. Believe me, Emma, the struggle is real."

"I believe you," said Emma, "I'm struggling right now. Come on, then. A theme for seventy to eighty-year-olds."

At that moment, Are You Lonesome Tonight twinkled out of the bar's sound system, just loud enough for Emma to hear. She pointed up into the air at an imaginary speaker.

"The music God's have spoken. Elvis."

Both girls frowned.

"Remember? Doris asked what had happened to 'good' music like Elvis or Frank Sinatra. We should get an Elvis impersonator and theme it around one of his films."

"He made films?" said Jen.

"Go back to your photographer," said Vicki. "We've got this."

"No, imagine it. Those hips…" Jen dazed away again, dreamy eyed. "Proper child bearing hips, but on a man…"

"I'm fighting off the scariest image of Elvis running down the street being chased by Jen," said Emma. "There are some things you just can't unsee."

****

"You did what?"

"I know," said Tom. "It was going so well, but I felt this pulling sensation that scared the crap out of me. I'd only just met her, well, to actually talk to anyway, and it was like she was reeling me in. It scared me and I panicked."

"And you didn't mention the thing?" asked Rob.

"No."

"What thing?" said Josh as he sipped his beer.

"Nothing," said Rob with a dismissive wave. "Different conversation. So, on a first date you managed to put the brakes on a potentially good thing without even discussing deep stuff? That's impressive, even for you."

"Tell me about it." Tom put his head in his hands. "I'm doomed."

Other than a couple by the entrance and a few people lined up by the TV, the bar was quiet. At weekends the place bounced, and the sound of chatter and clinking glasses drowned out any noise from the television. During the week, only the regulars made the pilgrimage for a couple of 'wind down after work' beers.

Josh leaned forward and clapped his back. "Don't talk rubbish. You've got us in your corner and we'll get you through this. When are you seeing her again?"

Tom sat back, unable to hide his surprise. "Thanks Josh. I'm not sure. We left it where she's going to speak to her friends about the fund raiser and get back to me."

Josh and Rob glanced at one another, and then glanced as one at Tom. "Okay," said Josh. "Bit of a squirrel moment there, pal. What fund raiser?"

"Oh yeah, about that. Josh, I may have volunteered you for some work."

Josh rubbed his hands together. "Cool. I can never be too busy. Work is good."

"This is the free kind, though."

"The free kind? I'm not following you. That sounds like something I might be allergic to."

"Emma has this client that comes into her salon, an old woman. She's found out she has cancer."

"Oh. That's not cool. How old is she? And why would she want pictures?"

"Old. About a hundred and something, I can't remember. It doesn't really matter. The thing is, she can't afford to pay for a decent funeral, so the girls at the salon are doing a fund raiser to help. I might have inadvertently on purpose volunteered your excellent photographic services."

"Thanks. Well, as long as I'm not already booked, it couldn't hurt. It sounds like a good cause and I could hand out business cards. Has she got any good looking mates?"

"I'm sure she does, but they'll all be eighty-something and wrinkly," said Tom.

"Emma, you clown. Does Emma have any mates?"

"Oh. I'm sure she does, but I haven't seen them. Some of the old folks might have nurses with them, though. In uniform."

"Okay," said Josh, pointing with his beer bottle. "Now we're talking. Count me in."

Rob laughed. "A man easily swayed. I've never got the whole uniform thing. I don't see what the fascination is."

"Press-studs," said Josh. "A lot of uniforms are designed for speed, so there are no buttons, just press-studs. And what goes on quickly must also come off quickly. It's a law of physics."

"And you have firsthand experience of this?" asked Tom.

"Not really, I researched it on the internet."

"You researched press-studs on the internet?"

"Hey, I was alone. There was nothing on TV and I was bored."

"Moving quickly on," said Tom, "what am I going to do with Emma? She's the first girl I've met in a long time that might be worth pursuing."

Josh looked at Rob and thumbed in Tom's direction. "Pursuing, he says. I'm an internet weirdo who researched press-studs and yet he pursues girls and it's okay."

"I'm not sure what you should do," said Rob. "It's the age-old dilemma, isn't it? If you wait for her to call you, she'll think you're not bothered. The longer you wait, the more she'll lose interest. Women seem to like the man taking the lead."

"Yeah, that's not good. I could take the lead."

"Alternatively, you could call her. Then she might think you're weak and desperate. Most women don't like weak and desperate men."

"Well shit, Rob, that's a nice choice. Thanks."

"You like her, right?" said Josh

"Yes. She's really nice."

"So, you'd be gutted if you never saw her again?"

"Well, yes, I guess I would."

"But you can't just call unannounced? You know, weak and desperate, right?"

"Right."

"Tom, women like men to make an effort for them. If she's worthwhile, then show her. Make an effort for her. If you think she's special, show her she's special."

Tom sat back in his chair, wide eyed. "Well I'll be damned, Josh just turned into Dr. Phil."

"Seriously," said Josh. "This fund raiser. It sounds as if it means a lot to her, so count me in. I'll do the photographs. Rob, I'm sure there's something you could do. Maybe enlist the mechanics from the garage to dress up and help serve food or wheel the old folks into the place. Or even offer a taxi service so they can have a few drinks. Let's get a plan together, and then you can call her and have something to offer other than desperation."

Tom took a drink from his beer. "Josh, I don't know what to say. Where the hell did that come from?"

Josh shrugged. "I dunno," he grinned. "Perhaps there's hope for this young ho after all."

Tom pulled out his phone. "Be right back, guys."

He wandered to the far side of the bar away from the TV, sat in the corner, and dialed Emma's number. The call connected and the ring tone burred in his ear. Once. Three times. It continued to call, and he braced himself for voicemail. Should he leave a message? He needed to talk to her, to let her know he was invested and that he wanted to help her and see her again. Eight rings, still no answer. Just as he lowered the phone a faint voice chirped from the speaker.

"Hello?"

He quickly brought it back to his ear. "Hello? Emma?"

"Hi, Tom."

"Hi. I er... how are you?"

"I'm okay, thanks. Still at work, but we're done for the day."

Was that an invitation? Tom's head whirred and played out every possible meaning for the eleven words. She was okay, she was still at work, but she was done for the day. Was she done and going home, or was she saying she was done and he should swing by and pick her up?

"Me, too," he offered. His head still spun. Show her she's special, Josh had said. "Er, look, I had a great time the other night. I've done nothing but think about you."

It may have been the connection, but Tom was sure he heard a sharp intake of breath at the other end of the line. Voices were chatting in the background.

"And I'd love to see you again," he continued. "I'm in a bar with some friends of mine and we'd like to offer our services for your fund raiser. We'd like to help, if that's okay?"

Silence. She must be weighing up options.

"Okay." She paused. "Thank you, that would be very good of you. I'm here with the girls from the salon trying to work it out, too. We're going to need an Elvis impersonator."

Tom grinned. Talk about being on the same wavelength. "Well, you can relax because I happen to know one."

"Anyone else would have thought that was a weird statement," she laughed. "Fancy a drink tomorrow?"

"I'd love it," said Tom. A huge weight rolled off his shoulders.

"Okay, call me when you get done at work."

"I'll do that."

"And Tom?"

"Yes?"

"I was thinking about you, too. Bye."

Tom slid his phone into his pocket and sauntered back to the bar like an old Wild West gunslinger.

"Well, someone looks like he won the lottery," said Rob.

"I got a second date." Tom's smile lit up the room.

"Hang on," said Josh. "Let me get a pen. Okay, 'Dear Diary, today was a special…'"

"Ha ha, very funny. Do you guys remember Colin? I can't remember his surname, but he used to hang around with us. Did karaoke all the time and we kind of gave him a hard time? And rightly so, he was about as unusual as a man could get."

"Yeah," said Rob, "I remember him. Didn't he have a…"

"Yes," said Tom. "Him. We need to get in touch with him."

"Hang on." Josh opened his phone. "He's on Facebook. He does all kinds of shows these days. Nothing fancy, just private parties and weddings."

Josh flipped through a few pages. "Here he is. Colin Archibald. Why do we need him?"

"Because he's an Elvis impersonator."

Rob looked at Josh. "Of course he is. That clears that right up. Tom? Why do we need an Elvis impersonator?"

"The girls want one for the fund raiser. I remember Colin used to do a mean Elvis on the karaoke and he branched out and did a full act with it."

"What?" said Rob. "Even with the…?"

"Yes. Find his number and we'll book a date with Elvis."

Chapter Eight

Seriously, Steve. You want to lead with this?"

Tom gestured at laptop that sat on the desk before him. The screen's image was of a large boat with its bow sticking proudly out of stormy waters. Tiny passengers held onto the guard rails and covered the side of the ship. Beneath the image was the slogan 'Keep it up, even in a raging sea. Use Viagra'.

"Yeah," said Steve. Tom's laughter didn't seem to offend him. "The sea represents a turbulent relationship and the ship…"

"Yes, I get what the ship represents," said Tom. "It's sticking up enough to get its own porn movie. And I get the people spewing everywhere too, but this could be a huge account and we might not get the chance to put in a bid like this again. We want to be evoking sensuality and intimacy, not people holding on for dear life."

"I've had a few romantic encounters like that," said Steve with a devilish grin. "I call it 'Rodeo sex'. Mention their sister's name and then try to hang on. Twenty-five seconds is my personal best." He laughed and held onto his paunch as it shook like jelly.

"Thanks for the visual. There's a possibility I just re-ate some of my breakfast."

"So, the ship's not going to work then?"

"No. Give me a small boat, perhaps a row boat, floating gracefully on a lake. The water's calm and serene, and there's an older couple sitting in it, facing each other, sipping wine. Imagine swans milling around them. Paint me a sunset in the background that's casting an orange glow onto them and make it subtle, but still obvious, that they want one another. At any moment, they're going to row that boat ashore and enjoy one another. The old guy just needs a bit of help with his paddle."

"His paddle?"

"For God's sake Steve, his…"

"Ah, I get it now," said Steve. "Okay, leave it with me. Back to the drawing board."

The office door closed behind the graphic artist and Tom took a seat behind the desk and slammed the laptop closed as his phone beeped. Instead of a text from Emma, he found a message from Josh.

'Colin Archibald's cell # 312 555 1598. You might want to stick to texting!'

The thought of speaking to Colin after all this time held the same appeal as sucking on a pair of sweaty gym socks. Tom opened his text app and typed.

'Hi Colin, it's Tom. Do you still do the Elvis show? I may have a gig for you.'

As the message sent, he spotted Emma's name in his text folder. She'd be styling hair right now, and he relaxed back into his chair and remembered the time he spent with her in the maze. The curve of her leg, the smell of her perfume, and the kiss she'd given him at the bowling alley. As his imagination kicked into gear, his phone pinged.

"Shit," he whispered to himself, "if that's Colin, that was quick." He picked up the phone and opened the screen.

'Tom who?' was all it said.

Seriously? He began to doubt the impression he left on people. And it wasn't that long ago.

'Sorry. Tom Lewis. We used to go to the same karaoke at O'Sheas.'

A few seconds passed.

'Sorry. Still don't remember but yes, still do Elvis.'

Bastard. But whatever, he's still game.

'Great. Might have a gig for you if you're interested?'

Instant reply. 'Okay. Let me know details and we'll talk fee.'

Tom hadn't considered a fee but, for now, it didn't matter. He had an Elvis impersonator he'd be able to talk about later.

'Will do. Be in touch soon.'

He slid the phone back onto the desk and then pulled it back. Tonight was his second date with Emma, a date he hadn't expected, and he thought back to their first proper meeting to gain inspiration. Emma had supplied the venue last time, so he had to at least appear to make an effort. He went for the element of surprise and dialed her number. It rang a few times before she answered.

"Hello?"

"Hi Emma. Tom."

"Hi Tom, what's up? Surely you've not finished work already? It's not even lunchtime yet."

"No, I'm still hard at it. Listen, do you remember when we were racing to the maze at the crematorium and you said last one to the garden supplies the picnic?"

"Of course," she laughed. It instantly brightened his mood and swept away the stress of the Viagra campaign. "Are you going to step up?"

Tom could hear the laughter in her voice and it stirred something deep within him. "Yes, I am. How long will you be with your current client?"

The phone was quiet for a while. He could almost hear the times being worked out. "Well," she said, "I'm waiting for a color to set, so about an hour."

He glanced at his watch. "That's two o'clock. Tell you what, how about I meet you at 2.15 at the clock tower in Regency Park. Do you know it?"

"Yes, I do. Should I bring something?"

"Just bring you," said Tom, "and I'll take care of the rest."

After a quick goodbye, he pocketed the phone and walked out into the office. "Guys, I'm taking an extended lunch. Client thing. If you need me, my phone's on."

Pairs of inquiring eyes watched as he waltzed through the room and went to his car, then drove to the grocery store.

****

At 2.00pm, Tom stood beneath the clock tower and scanned the entrances while a breeze ruffled his hair, not warm, but comfortable. Brilliant sunlight cut through the trees to throw spears of light across the grass and sprinkle diamonds around the lake.

The park had its usual occupants. A mother strolled by with a buggy and offered a weak smile. He waved at the baby and returned the smile. Dog walkers bent to scoop up smelly parcels in grocery store bags as kids ran around and tried to avoid them. The cackling sound of fighting geese echoed through the half empty park until, after a lot of wing flapping and splashing water, they gave up the fight and waddled off into the undergrowth. The scene was finally as he hoped. Peaceful and romantic.

At 2.10, she appeared. Tom watched her walk toward him, wearing a burnt orange blouse that seemed to catch the sun, and an ankle length white skirt that billowed in the breeze. It turned almost see-through when the light caught it a certain way to show a silhouette of her legs. She held her head high as she walked. It made her look confident and assured. And very attractive.

He waved his arm in the air and she caught his eye, smiled and walked toward him.

"Hello again," she said, and leaned to give him a peck on the cheek. She pointed to the basket at his side. "What on earth is that?"

"Lunch," said Tom. "Come on, follow me."

He picked up the handle of the brown wicker basket, took her hand, and led her deeper into the park. "Remember at the maze, when you said the loser provides the picnic? This is the picnic."

"Nice," she said. "I work a block away, and this is only the second or third time I've been here. It's actually quite pleasant."

As they walked, he swung her arm playfully between them. "I have to confess, this is the first time I've been here. I had to use Google to find it, but I did a little research, too. There's picnic area around the corner that looks beautiful. How long do we have?"

"A couple of hours. How about you?"

"I run our department," said Tom, "so I've got as long as I like, within reason. Consider me on an extended lunch, and thereby you can also consider yourself my client."

She let out a short laugh as he smiled. "Tom Lewis, are you trying to sell me something?"

Tom winked as they rounded the corner. The path opened onto a lawn surrounded by a low fence. Trees with large overhanging boughs dotted the area to offer shade. In the middle of the grass was a small fountain that twinkled in the sunlight.

"Pick a tree," he said, and gestured toward the space. "Any tree."

"You sound like a magician," she said as she looked around. "Okay, that one next to the fountain. It looks peaceful. Let's sit there."

They ducked under the branches and Tom laid down the basket and took out a large fleeced blanket. "Please step aside ma'am," he said and spread the blanket across the grass.

She softly punched his arm. "I'm way too young to be a ma'am," she said. "You'd better come up with something else."

"Okay, I'll work on that, er, young lady?"

They sat under the tree as Tom took a fruit tray from the basket and laid it between them. Then he produced a sandwich tray and a carton of apple juice.

"How many people are coming on this date?" she asked. "And I hate to say this, but I don't like apple juice."

"Just us, but I wasn't sure what you'd like and the store was all out of kebabs," he smiled. "And the apple juice is a diversion."

Emma frowned as he turned and fumbled with something, and then a loud pop sounded. He turned back with a bottle of sparkling white wine.

"Tom Lewis! Don't say you brought alcohol into the park. You bad boy. I hope you brought glasses to go with it."

She giggled as he plucked two plastic cups from the basket and poured the wine.

"So how is your fund raiser coming along?" asked Tom as he removed shrink wrap from the sandwiches.

"It's going okay. The hall's booked and I have feelers out with some caterers. The entertainment's not sorted yet, and we'll still need to decorate the hall in a kind of Elvis movie style."

"About Elvis, I may have you covered. Turns out I know a guy who does that. To be honest, I haven't seen him for quite a while, but I remember him being pretty good. Not corny like a lot of them. He's unique, though."

"That sounds ominous. Unique in what way?"

Tom laughed. "Let me see what he wants to charge first and then, if I suggest you try him, I'll let you know."

"Okay, I'll let it slide for now. But I really appreciate the offer for help. Thank you."

"You are more than welcome," said Tom. He took a bite from a ham and mayo sandwich. "So, since we're not trapped in a maze or gazing at a dead body, tell me about you. I won't lie, you've been on my mind a lot but, in truth, I don't know a lot about you."

Emma blushed and played with her hair for a while, before she reached forward and grabbed a sandwich. "Well, there's not that much to tell. I co-own a salon with another girl, Jen. She's a trip. If you've got any single mates and they fancy a challenge, let them meet Jen. Imagine a man-magnet, except the poles are reversed. As soon as she gets a sniff of security, she plans their future and they scurry off back to where they came from. It's a shame, because she's really attractive and, underneath the desperation, she'd make someone an amazing partner."

Tom laughed again. "I think I just learned more about Jen than about you, but fair enough, I'll play along. I also have a single friend named Josh. He's a photographer, and he's a decent looking guy. Not in a gay way, mind you. Just lately, I've been having issues with that."

"Oh, I can tell from the way you held my leg that you're far from gay."

It was Tom's turn to blush. "Yes, well it is perfectly formed. I can appreciate that."

"Well thank you." Emma smiled and stretched out her legs. "There's another just like it."

He gazed down at the shape that formed beneath the thin skirt. "Yes, there is, so I'd better distract myself before I get into trouble. Josh got hurt a while ago and now he thinks he's some kind of gigolo but, beneath it all, he's a good guy. He just needs to meet the right girl who'll treat him well and rebuild his trust. As for me, I'm an account manager for a decent sized ad agency. At the moment we're busy competing for some big names."

Emma sipped the wine and carefully placed the cup in a divot in the blanket. "Would I know any of them?"

"Well, I'm concentrating on Viagra right now."

"I'm sure you are," she laughed. "That has to be hard."

"What? Well, the…" Tom stammered.

"Competing for a name like that," she said with a coy look. "It must be hard. You know? A challenge?"

"Yes. Yes, of course. I have a decent team, but they're being too obvious. I want intimate and romantic and they're drawing a bull in a china shop."

She leaned a little closer. "So you want intimate and romantic. Is that a reflection of you, like a subconscious thing? Other than bowling, we've not exactly met at intimate and romantic locations, have we?"

"No, we haven't," said Tom. The brown in her eyes was so dark her pupils almost vanished even though he knew they'd be wide in the shade of the tree. They drew him in and made him want to tell her everything. It was too soon, but he didn't want to throw up another wall. "Tell me about your client. The old lady. How's she doing?"

"Doris? So far, so good, although I'm sure she's putting on a brave face when she's with us. We had her give Vicki her cell phone number so we could check in each day. It's weird seeing old people with cell phones, it doesn't look right. They handle them as if they're about to explode, like they're holding a hand grenade."

"Oh, I'm sure teenagers think the same thing about us. Do you mind me asking what type of cancer she has?"

"Every kind. It seems as if she's riddled with it. I hate cancer, even the word. It sounds evil. I wish they'd find a cure for it."

"Oh, I'm sure they have," said Tom. "We had this discussion at the bar. When you consider all the things we've accomplished, and you consider the billions they throw at cancer research, there's no way they haven't found something. They couldn't release it, though. Think of the money health care makes from cancer treatment. And how many people would actually exist on earth if there was no cancer. Where would we put them all? And what would they all do? And how could we afford to house and keep them all?"

"God, that's depressing," said Emma.

"It is, isn't it? What a way to kill the mood. Sorry. Let's talk about something cheerier. Hey, I've got an idea. Josh and Jen sound like the perfect antidotes to one another. Josh needs someone to rein him in, and it sounds as if she needs someone that can keep their distance, at least for a while. If I can get him to send me a picture, do you think Jen would do the same? Then, we could send each of them the others picture and see if we can get them together."

"That sounds like a great idea. Honestly, she's a lovely girl, she just needs someone who won't panic and run at the first sight of a jeweler!"

Tom dug out his phone and sent a message to Josh. Emma texted Jen. Jen's reply arrived first.

"Ha, she sent it," said Emma as she turned the screen to Tom.

"Wow, she's pretty. Josh likes long blondes so I'm sure he'll say yes. How old is she?"

"Twenty-six. How old's Josh?"

"Twenty-eight, although mentally he can be thirteen sometimes. Hang on, here he is."

The screen of Tom's phone lit up and he opened the text and then turned the screen to Emma.

"That's a mop of curly hair," she laughed. "Jen would have a field day with that. He's pretty cute. Nice eyes, too. Okay, send that to me. I'll send Jen's picture to you and we can forward them on. I've never been a matchmaker before, this could be fun."

A few key presses later and they laid their phones on the blanket as Tom poured another cup of wine.

"So, tell me what you've got planned so far for the fund raiser, and I'll check in with the guys and see what we can do to help."

For the next hour they talked and laughed. Tom listened to Emma's expectations for the event and made mental notes of anything he could help with. One by one, they considered Elvis movies and narrowed the choice down to three. The time passed by so quickly that Emma jumped when she glanced at her phone.

"Oh God, I'd better get going," she said. "And I can't believe we drank all the wine."

"It's only two glasses each. I doubt you'll get into too much trouble for that. Come on, I'll walk you back to the entrance."

Tom packed away the empty bottle and the cups, re-wrapped the sandwiches and carried the basket in one hand while his other held Emma's. When they reached the entrance, he took out the sandwiches and handed them to her. "Here you go, take them back to the salon and treat everyone to a quick bite to eat."

"Thank you," she said. "That's good of you. And thank you for the impromptu lunch. I had a really nice time."

"Me too, and I'd love to see you again. Would you mind if I called you after I check in with the guys?"

"Absolutely. Let me know what's going on and we can compare notes."

She reached up on her tiptoes to kiss him, and he dropped the basket to the ground with a rattle, reached behind her waist and pulled her closer. His kiss grew firmer as her mouth opened to allow their tongues to meet and he held onto her until she pulled away. Her face was flushed red, and she seemed slightly breathless.

After one more kiss, she rested her head on his shoulder and whispered in his ear. "I really don't want to, but I have to go. Talk soon, okay?"

"Count on it," smiled Tom.

"Good. Talk to you soon, then. Bye."

She waved and gave him a cute smile before she walked off toward the salon. He watched her with a grin plastered to his face until she vanished around the corner.

Chapter Nine

"Tom? Something's happened, and I'm not sure what to do. Can you come over?"

Tom glanced at the Mickey Mouse alarm clock on his bedside cabinet. Through blurry eyes it read 7.10, while his brain struggled to work out whose voice had woken him. Today was Saturday and there were no alarms set.

"He's in the bathroom with the door locked and I can hear him crying in there." Sobbing sounds bled into the earpiece. "Please, Tom. He won't listen to anyone else but you. Please help me."

In an instant, he pieced it together. It was Abby, Rob's wife. She sounded distraught.

"Abs? What's up? Are you okay?"

"Yes," she said. Her voice was thick and wavered. "No. Shit, I don't know. I'm okay, but I'm not sure what he's doing. Please, can you come over?"

Tom rolled his legs out of bed and planted his feet on the carpeted floor. "I'm on my way, Abs, it's going to be okay. I'll be right there."

Twenty minutes later Tom pulled to a stop outside a quaint, one story patio home. Two rocking chairs sat on its wraparound porch, along with an array of potted plants that would make a nursery jealous. Yellow shutters framed the clean windows and bracketed hanging baskets of colorful flowers that cascaded down the siding to the wooden floorboards. Abby stood in the open doorway, wrapped in a housecoat, red-faced and desperate looking.

Tom raced up the steps, and she gathered him in her arms. "Thank you so much for coming. Please, come inside."

Tom stopped by the sofa and held her at arm's length. "Abs, what's going on?"

Abby was a strong woman. Just short of six feet tall, she was toned with the body of an athlete, but she folded and caved as sobs racked it and she clung to Tom.

"I'm late," she said. "My period? It's late, so I did a pregnancy test. Tom, we were so excited. I don't know if Rob's told you, but we've been trying to have a child for so long. This isn't the first time I've been late, but it's been a while. So, he sat on the edge of the bath while I peed on one of those stick things."

"That must have been a tender moment to share," said Tom as he tried to break the tension that sucked all the air from the room. It didn't work.

"He watched the whole thing like a hawk. He's so proud Tom, please don't tell him I mentioned any of this."

"Of course not, Abs. Come on, what's going on?"

"Well," she continued. "We sat and waited for the damned thing to give us its reading. Honestly, we're so ready to be parents I can't even begin to explain. Anyway, I held the stick in front of us, and it came up negative. Again."

Tom felt his stomach do flips as he held the wife of his best friend. "Okay. It's okay, Abs, I'll talk to him."

"Would you? Please, Tom, I'm scared. I know he blames himself. He's been going to these stupid meetings to clear his head, but I don't think they're working."

Tom held his tongue and hugged Abby close once more. "Hang on here. Let me talk to him. Okay?"

"Yes," she sniffed.

"Put some coffee on. I'll be right back."

She nodded, sniffed again, and pulled her housecoat around her and shuffled off toward the kitchen. Tom steeled himself and moved further into the house to the bathroom. He knocked on the door.

"Rob?"

After a pause, Rob spoke. "I thought I heard your voice. Did Abby call you?"

"Yes. Come on pal, open the door. Let's talk."

"Nothing to say, Tom. Go home. We'll work it out."

"Rob, you've locked yourself in a bathroom while your beautiful wife is out here crying. She's in pieces and she's worried sick about you. Now I'm not exactly trained in negotiation tactics but, from where I stand, you're being a dick. Open the door and let's sort this out."

"As subtle as ever, Tom. Go home, pal. Leave us alone."

"Sorry, Rob. No can do. There's an amazing woman out here who looks as if her world got stripped away from her. I can't walk away and leave things like that. Come out and talk."

Nothing happened for a while, and then the door clicked as the latch turned from the other side. It swung open and Rob appeared. "You bastard. Why'd you have to make me feel so guilty?"

A crack echoed through the house as Tom's hand connected with Rob's cheek. Rob fell back, raised a hand to his already reddening face, then recovered from the slap and scowled.

"And that's what you get for being a bitch, you moron," said Tom. "You've got a woman that worships the ground you walk on. She's in the kitchen, breaking her heart. Grow a pair and treat her as you should. You think you're the only one going through this? Don't you think she feels the same? And what's this bullshit about you going to all of these meetings? You went to one that I know of, and I went with you. The biggest contribution you made was pouring a cup of fucking coffee. And it was shit coffee."

Rob recoiled and then forced himself to face Tom. "You curse and swear a lot when you're pissed."

"No shit, Sherlock," said Tom. "It's not a quality I'm proud of. Now you might be a hair bigger than me, but you're suffering from fluid loss and lack of sleep. If you don't go out there and show that woman how much you love her, so help me God I'll kick your ass into next week."

Tom sat on the side of the bath as Rob lumbered past him and headed to the kitchen. He heard faint sobs and gasps and snippets of 'sorry babe' as he took deep breaths and tried to think of a way to ease the pain of his friends.

"There's fresh coffee here, Tom," shouted Abby.

It was almost 8.00 on a Saturday morning. The three of them sat around an old teak kitchen table. Rob and Abby were across from each other, their hands clasped over the table as they mumbled words of apology and love. Tom sat at the head of the table and gave them space.

"Sorry you had to come out," said Rob. "I bet you were sleeping and woke up to this."

"No, I was awake anyway. And if we can't look after our friends then all hope is lost, right?"

"Tom Lewis, you're a first class liar," said Abby. "Your voice was so groggy you could have spent the night drinking Nyquil."

Tom laughed, and a cloud lifted from inside the room. Smiles appeared, and the mood brightened. At least for a while.

"Fair enough Abs, you've got me. Still, we have to look after our friends. I didn't realize you guys were suffering so much? Rob, what's going on man? Talk to me."

Rob mussed his hair and rubbed both hands across his face. His eyes watered and Tom felt a little jealous until a flash of guilt ripped through him. Now was not the time to be thinking of his own problems.

"I feel like a failure," said Rob. "Every time we walk down the street there's kids everywhere. Couples pushing buggies, ads on TV about diapers and what cream you should use for this rash or medicine for that illness. There's teething crap and couples on chat shows that shouldn't have kids even if their lives depended on it. And then there's us. Two normal people who love each other. Not bothering anyone."

Tears left his eyes and traced a line down his cheeks. "All we want is to complete our family. There are idiots all over the place having kids that have no business being anywhere near one but, try as we might, we can't seem to do it. We're perfect. Why can't we make a baby?"

Abby stood and held her husband as he cried. Tom joined them and they hugged as a group.

"Did you ever think you're putting too much pressure on yourselves?" said Tom. "That you're trying so hard you're setting yourselves up for failure? I'm no expert, but I'm sure I've read that the more you relax, the more chance you'll have."

"I think that applies to erections," said Abby, "but I appreciate your insight, Tom."

Rob laughed and wiped his face. "Thanks for coming over, man. I needed someone to give me a kick." He stood and took his wife in his arms. "Abby, I love you more than life itself, babe. I'm sorry. We'll make amazing parents and I promise to carry my share of the burden and not be the idiot that hides in the bathroom when the going gets tough. I love you and I want to make another life with you."

Abby cupped his face in her hands and kissed him as Tom stood and moved toward the door.

"Well, my work here is done, as they say. I should leave you two alone. I'd also say get a room but you've got a house full of them, so just choose one and try again. Practice makes perfect and all that."

After one more group hug, Tom walked through the kitchen. When he turned to wish them well, they'd already vanished.

****

Tom's drive home took him past Josh's studio, a converted two room apartment above a Laundromat that had its own entrance door set into the wall beside a huge plate-glass window.

Tom bounded up the stairs and then slowed to a quiet walk as he heard voices inside. He paused to look at the images that hung on the side wall. Josh was an excellent photographer who used imaginative backdrops and lighting to create stunning pictures. Tom smiled as he realized that all the pictures were of attractive single moms with their children.

Josh always said that Saturdays were his busiest day by far. People who worked all week booked up his time weeks in advance, so he crammed in as many appointments as possible during the weekend.

Strobes of light bounced off the wall as Tom eased open the door at the top of the stairs. Josh definitely had a client. The first room looked like the backstage changing room of a theater. Racks of props and costumes filled the floor-space. The back wall looked like Hawaii thanks to a massive and very realistic beach scene that hung from a hook in the ceiling.

He walked through the racking to the far door and peeped into the room. Josh was kneeling in front of a stage, angling his camera one way and then the other as the flash continued to dance against the walls. A middle aged couple reclined on a patch of fake grass while a large lake hung from a stand and sparkled behind them. Throw in a row boat, thought Tom, and you have an image for the Viagra campaign.

Josh stood and clipped the camera to the top of a tripod. "One more batch of static shots and we'll wrap it up, folks."

The couple posed, and the camera whirred and clicked and more lightning flashes lit up the room. Tom remained behind the door until they stood and picked up their jackets.

"Thanks again, Josh," said the woman. "It's our twenty-fifth wedding anniversary this weekend and we wanted something to remember it by."

"It was my pleasure, Mrs. Brewer. Let me go through these and get them onto a disk for you. I'll call you as soon as they're ready. And congratulations, I hope you have many more happy years to come."

"Who said they were happy?" said Mr. Brewer. His wife shot him a playful glance and slapped his rear. "Kidding! I wouldn't change a thing. Thanks again, Josh."

Tom walked into the studio as the couple reached the door. He spoke as their footsteps echoed down the stairs. "It's weird watching you be normal."

"Hey, I can be normal," said Josh, "and professional. Just because I'm a man for all women doesn't mean I can't cage the savage beast and live a regular life."

Tom frowned and looked at his friend. An unruly mop of dark hair topped a kind face that also held a mischief primary school teachers would dread. "The beast? Give me a break. The only beast I've seen come out of you was after eight pints of heavy beer, and it was projectile, not savage."

"Yeah," said Josh, "fair enough. So anyway, to what do I owe this pleasure?" He collapsed the camera tripod and unhooked the background scenery.

"I was just driving past," said Tom. He neglected to mention Rob. "You got the picture of Emma's friend then. What do you think?"

"You're out of the loop, pal. I've already got her number and we've been texting."

Tom frowned again. "Really? And how is that working out for you?"

Josh put down the large print of the lake and sat on the edge of the stage. "She's different."

"Oh? How so? Like, she could be a future Miss World different or, oh my God, this girl should be committed to an asylum different?"

"Well, most of the girls I text have already met me, so they have no expectations. Jen's different. She's just... well... normal. We've been talking about normal stuff. She got a new car, you know?"

"Er, no," said Tom. "Surprisingly, I didn't."

"Yeah, one of those German things that runs forever. Anyway, she's left no hints about meeting, she just seems content to chat so I'll see how it goes. I haven't come across anyone like this before. I'm intrigued."

"She seemed to like your picture."

"That's a good thing. Did you see hers?"

"Yes," said Tom, "She is very pretty."

"Pretty? She's frigging gorgeous. I'm going to take this slow, because I know it reflects on you, you know, how I behave? So I'm going to make an effort to see this through and see where it ends. Hey, I even canceled my date tonight with Allison."

Tom stood and clapped him on the shoulder. "I'm proud of you, son." He glanced at the backdrop. "Do you have a load of these?"

"What, these scenes? Yeah, they're all back there in the other room. Why?"

"Anything you could tie in to an Elvis movie?"

Josh's eyes flitted while he thought. "Well, I have a decent Blue Hawaii thing hanging already, but didn't Elvis do Viva Las Vegas?"

"Yes," said Tom, "he did. And funnily enough that movie is on the shortlist. Why do you ask?"

Josh stood and walked toward the front room. "Follow me. I may have just the thing."

Chapter Ten

So, he really likes her then?"

"Yes," said Tom. He paced around the kitchen with his phone jammed between his shoulder and his ear as he scooped a mound of gravy- covered mess into a bowl. "And he says he's taking things slowly. That's a big step for Josh. By now, he'd normally be smoking a cigar and moving on."

"Ew! He smokes?"

"No, that was a metaphor for, you know, after the event."

There was silence for a moment until the penny dropped. "Ah, I get you now. So he doesn't hang around afterwards?"

"No. To be honest, he rarely finishes the cigar." Tom turned and almost fell over the cat. "Shit, Ozzy. Come on, over here. Get out from under my feet."

As Emma laughed down the line, he placed a dish in a corner. "I'm sorry? Who's making you curse?"

"Sorry about that, it's Oswald, my cat. He's wrapped around my foot because it's time to eat. They're creatures of habit."

"I'm never been too sure about cats. They seem cold and aloof. It's not like they greet you at the door with wagging tails, is it?"

"I wouldn't say that. They're like kids. It's all about how you raise them."

"So you raised an affectionate cat?"

"Hell, no," said Tom. "I adopted him. He was raised before I got him. Oswald doesn't give a crap about anything as long as I feed him. I had a cat growing up, though, who'd reach up and pat your leg for attention."

"Sounds like you had a nice childhood," said Emma.

Tom was unsure of how to answer, so he shifted the conversation. "It was okay. Did you guys discuss your charity night? Thanks to Josh, I may have found something that might clinch which movie theme you use."

"Oh? What's that?"

"Do Viva Las Vegas. He did a photo shoot a while ago for a young couple. They couldn't afford a big wedding, so they got married in an office and told everyone they'd eloped to Vegas. The plan was going great until people asked to see the pictures. So they hired Josh to find some Vegas backdrops and take a few they could use."

"Sneaky."

"Yes, but they went to the right guy. When Josh does something, he does it right and goes above and beyond the call of duty. He's got a pile of stuff we can use to decorate the hall, and then we can get Elvis to play a kind of residency. Rob volunteered the guys from his garage, too, they're a decent bunch. I figured we could have a card table and a roulette wheel and turn part of the hall into a casino. The mechanics are a beefy bunch of guys, so they'd make great croupiers. And they've volunteered to help taxi everyone around, too."

It took a while for Emma to answer. "Wow. You've given this a lot of thought, haven't you?"

"Yes, I have," laughed Tom. "I'm fortunate to be surrounded by good people."

"Well, speaking of being surrounded by good people, how do you feel about seeing if Josh and Jen would like to join us on a date?"

Tom thought for a moment. "Have you spoken to Jen?"

"No, not yet. I thought I'd run it by you first."

"Josh mentioned that he's trying to take his time and not rush into things."

"He'll be lucky if Jen lets him do that for too long. Do you think it's a bad idea?"

"I'm not sure," said Tom. "Let me speak to him and see what he thinks. He's behaving himself at the moment, and I'm worried it might be like poking a bear with a stick."

"No, don't poke him with a stick."

"Tell you what, let me make a couple of calls. I'll check in with Josh and I'll give Elvis a call if you're okay with that?"

"That sounds great. I don't imagine many people come out with a sentence like that too often. And I do appreciate your help. Doris will be so happy with all of this. Thank you, Tom."

"Don't thank me until we get everything in place... with both things."

After saying their goodbyes, Tom steeled himself to make the first call.

The last time he'd spoken to Colin Archibald had been at a karaoke bar downtown. Colin was stone cold sober while Tom had been at the wrong end of a marathon drinking session courtesy of another failed attempt at a relationship. He couldn't remember anything he'd said that night, but the fact that Colin had returned his text must have meant that it was nothing too dramatic. And Colin had a thick skin. He had to have.

Tom dialed the number, and the call connected.

"Hello?"

"Colin? It's Tom. Tom Lewis."

"Oh, hello Tom. I remember you this time. What can I do for you?"

So far, so good.

"Remember me mentioning the Elvis thing?"

He had to stop to think. What was Emma to him? More than a friend, certainly, but how much more?

"A kind of girlfriend is throwing a fundraiser to help a cancer sufferer. They'd love to have you do your Elvis show, if you'd be interested?"

"Sure," said Colin without a pause. "Count me in. And I'll do it for free. I haven't played in a while, I need the practith. And I hate canther."

And there it was. It all came rushing back. He remembered making fun of Colin's lisp, just like everyone else had.

"Great," said Tom. "I really appreciate it. Look, the last time we met I was stupid drunk and..."

"Tom."

"Yes?"

"Water under the bridge."

It was obvious that Colin had got used to choosing his words. Each one seemed measured and deliberate. He continued. "People can be cruel when they're drunk. It'th okay. I'm uthed to it. And anyway, you know what happenth when Elvith things."

Tom nodded somberly and smiled. Why couldn't everyone have Colin's humility? "That part I remember well, despite the drink.

Thank you, Colin. Let me get back to my lady friend and find out dates and times and I'll be in touch."

"No problem. Talk thoon."

Colin disconnected the call before Tom could say goodbye.

One down, one to go. Tom pulled up Josh's number and called him.

"Josh?"

"Tom."

"We're going with your Vegas stuff, so thanks for that. If you can dig it all out, we can look at what you have and then check out the hall. As long as the girls are okay with it, of course."

"I'll get it together," said Josh. "I'm just texting back and forth with Jen. She's got a great sense of humor."

Tom shook his head. Who was this man and what had he done with Josh? "About that. I know you're taking things slow, but do you fancy a double date?"

"I don't like men, Tom. Remember? We've had that discussion."

"Not with me, you muppet. How about you and Jen go out somewhere with me and Emma?"

There was silence as Josh must have pondered the question. "Hmmm… has Emma mentioned anything to Jen yet?"

"No, I said I'd check with you first. It sounds as if Jen would be up for it anyway, to be honest."

More silence. Then, "Okay. We're texting right now, so let me see what she says. Did you have anywhere in mind?"

"Not yet," said Tom. "Tell you what, since this would be your first date with Jen, why don't you two pick it out and surprise us?"

Josh laughed. "I always go to bars or restaurants, but I should ask Jen what she'd like to do. Or maybe I could suggest something different. How about bowling?"

Tom scowled. "Not bowling. Been there. Done that. I'm not very good at it either."

"Okay. Laser tag?"

"No."

"Zip lining?"

"Now you're being silly."

"Well help me then. I'm no good at this romantic stuff."

"Okay," said Tom. "I read about a new hibachi grill they opened downtown. Why don't you suggest that?"

"Hibachi? Don't they make videos?"

"For crying out loud, Google it when we hang up. It's fresh cooked food and they cook it right in front of you. The chefs use big knives and make a show of the actual cooking process."

"Huh. That might be fun. All right, leave it with me. Let me check it out and chat with Jen and I'll call you later."

"Sounds like a plan. I'll get Rob to meet us at the studio later and we can go through the Vegas stuff."

Tom redialed Emma's number. The tone burred until her cheery voice interrupted. "Hi, you've reached Emma's phone. I'm either cutting someone, or someone's dyeing. Either way, a serial stylist's work is never done. There'll be a really annoying tone in a moment. Speak after that and I'll get back to you when I've disposed of the evidence."

He smiled and spoke to nothing. "Hi, it's Tom. Although you'll see that from my missed call so I'll just get on with it. Anyway, I spoke to Josh, and he seems okay with a double date. I said he could choose the venue if that's all right with you? Okay, well I'm useless at talking to these things so I'll chat with you soon."

He put the phone on the counter and flipped open the newspaper. The circled viewings in the obituaries glared back at him like evil eyes. After a moment, he realized that, at least for the time being, he was okay thumbing past them to the events section nearer the back. An ad for the hibachi place was somewhere near the last page. Then his phone made a meowing sound. His ringtone.

"Hi, it's just me," said Emma. "Sorry I missed your call. I was finishing up with a client. I'm free for a while now."

"Oh, it's no problem. It's a good thing you're busy, it keeps..."

The phone muffled. Tom could hear voices in the background and Emma saying "no", and then more voices.

"Sorry about that," she said, "I'm back. Are you doing anything right now?"

Tom's stomach flipped. He looked around the room as if it would supply an answer. "Er, no. No, I'm hanging out at home."

"Well, this might seem odd, and I promise I'm not being pushy. Rather than chatting on the phone, would you like to come over to the salon for a coffee? There is an ulterior motive, of course."

"Of course," said Tom. "And what would that be?"

"I told the girls about you and they want to meet you. Which, in girl-speak, translates to they want to give you the once over and make sure you're suitable before I spend any more time with you. They can be very protective. No pressure, obviously!"

"No, none at all," said Tom. Oswald bumped against his ankle. Tom looked down for support as the cat wandered off nonchalantly into the next room. "Thanks, bud," he mumbled. "Okay, I'm game. Why don't you text me the address and I'll head your way."

****

The salon nestled in the middle of a row of small buildings that sat on the outskirts of downtown. It was a great location, close enough to the center to attract lots of passing customers, but far enough away to keep the rent affordable. Tom cast his mind back to 'Heavy Frankie' Garcia as he took in the front of the place. It had taken the Chicago gangster theme and painted it like a cartoon. A sign spanned the main window that said "We'll Cut You" in vivid, eye popping color, as cigar smoke drifted from the edges of the 'W' and the 'u'. It should have looked cheesy, but it worked.

Blurred shapes moved inside, but too faint to work out who was who. He checked his hair in the mirror, as if the hurried ten minutes in the bathroom before he left hadn't been enough, and then raced across the road. The door chimed as he edged it open. Emma waved and breezed past the counter.

"Hi, I'm glad you came."

"Thanks for the invite." He stood like a statue with his hands thrust into his pockets. "It'll be cool to see where you work."

Her smile lit up the room and her eyes sparkled with excitement while she twisted her hands in a whirl of nerves. He returned the smile and relaxed. It seemed to be the sign she needed that everything was good, and she leaned forward and kissed him on the cheek.

"Come on, let me introduce you to everyone."

Tom followed as she swerved around the side of the counter. A blast of warm air hit him when he walked into the main area and the strong smell of ammonia blasted his senses. A radio played a rap song from a shelf high in the far corner. It looked down over a row of mirrors and chairs, backed with another row of machines that looked like a collection of mind control devices. A woman sat under one of them with a towel wrapped around her shoulders.

He recognized Jen from the photo he'd sent to Josh. Long blonde hair flowed down her back as she waved a hair dryer over the head of her client. Another girl got to her feet as he approached. She was about his height, a couple of inches under six feet, and dressed to kill. Framed in a brown bob and with minimal makeup, her face was naturally pretty.

"Tom, meet Vicki. Vic, this is Tom," said Emma.

Tom held out his hand and Vicki took it with a firm grip and shook it. "It's a pleasure to meet you, Tom. I'd like to say we've heard all about you, but trying to get information from Emma is like trying to plait fog. Still, she's our girl and we're a tight group, so don't you dare hurt her." She gestured to the woman sitting under the machine. "Otherwise, we'll stick you under a dryer like Debbie and turn it up to full heat until you come out with an Afro."

Tom stared, open mouthed.

"I'm just kidding," said Vicki with a smile, and then her eyes closed to slits. "Unless you hurt her, and then I'm being serious."

Emma laughed. "Pay no attention to Vicki, she's our resident bouncer. And she's only about eighty percent serious. I'm sure you recognize Jen over there, since I saw your jaw hit the ground."

"Oh, it's not that," stammered Tom. "The Afro threat concerned me. I'm no expert, but I don't think it would be a good look for me."

Emma brushed up against him and ran her fingers through his hair. The sensation sent shivers through his body and the hairs on his arms rose. "I'm sure we can work with this," she smiled, "although I like the way you already have it. So play nice, it would be a shame to have to 'fro you."

Tom smiled again and looked around the salon as Emma wandered off toward a door built into the back wall. The place was clean, but the fixtures had that look that said they'd been there a while and they weren't going anywhere. The girls had built up a successful business. He glanced at the three of them. Jen, with her waves of blonde hair that shimmered across her back as she swayed in time to the dryer motion. Vicki, with her tight, controlled bob, as she tidied magazines on a small side table. And Emma, her long brunette hair trailing behind her cute form as she turned to him from the doorway and motioned for him to follow her.

He snapped out of his reverie and quick stepped to the doorway. Emma lifted her finger to her lips, pulled him inside the room, and pushed the door closed behind him.

"I hope you don't think I'm being too forward," she started as she flattened him against the wall and pushed her body onto his.

"No," squeaked Tom.

"But I've not felt like this for a long time. I know we're still getting to know each other, but right now I don't really care."

Something stirred in Tom as he tried to form words.

"And I know that we met in the strangest of places," she continued, "but I feel like I've met a kindred spirit."

Tom was transfixed. Her body moved every part of him and he still struggled for words.

"Oh God, I've gone too far haven't I?" she said. "You're too quiet. It's too soon. Damn, I should have known I'd..."

Tom kissed her, a deep, full kiss that took her words and her breath away. He clasped the sides of her head and held her there as he pressed his mouth to hers and shared himself. The breath from her nose washed over him, heavy and warm as their tongues met. And then she broke away.

"Can I suggest something?" she said.

Tom controlled his breathing. "Of course. What is it?"

"Let's see each other. Not dead people."

He grabbed her again as she lifted her knee and pressed the inside of her thigh against his hip. Warmth enveloped him and his blood rushed and pulsed in his ears. She reached around the back of his head and pulled his kiss even closer and he began to explore her mouth.

A cry stopped them both in their tracks, followed by a pounding on the door. Vicki's voice sounded panicked from the other side.

"Emma. It's Doris. They just found her on the floor at home."

Chapter Eleven

After a manic drive and a few hairy moments at red lights, the group reached the hospital and raced up the stairwell to the Intensive Care Unit.

The nurse's station at Mercy Hospital looked as if it was hosting a medical conference. It was in the middle of a shift change. One team in, one team out. The trading of information and update of conditions. Emma had nothing but respect for the people in blue. Overworked and underpaid couldn't apply anywhere more than here. Without nurses, the place would grind to a halt.

She rushed with the girls to the front of the desk while Tom stayed behind them. The nurse front and center looked up, her face lined and her eyes blurred with exhaustion. Regardless, she was attentive and listened.

"Hi. We're here to see Doris," said Emma.

The nurse glanced at a whiteboard behind her and shook her head. "I'm sorry. We have no Doris here. Are you sure you have the correct hospital, or do you have any more information you could give me about the patient? A surname, maybe?"

Emma turned to Vicki. "He said Mercy Hospital, right?"

"Definitely," said Vicki. As she craned her head forward to study the board, a panel of lights lit up like an airport runway and scary sounding machinery beeped in the distance. The desk was an instant flurry of action. Clipboards hit the countertop and the group of blue turned as one and rushed away down the corridor.

"Oh God, not Doris," said Vicki. She took off after them and disappeared around a curve.

Emma turned. Tom was keeping a respectful distance. He was behind Jen, leaning against the back wall. "Come on," she said to them both. "We'd better go after her."

She ran down the middle of the corridor, wary of people coming out of the side doors. As she rounded the curve, the team in blue had already vanished into a room somewhere ahead. Vicki stood a few doors down with her arm leaned against the doorframe. Her body shook.

"Vic, what is it?" said Emma as she grew closer.

Vicki turned and smiled through her tears, then pointed through the glass window. Emma drew alongside her as Jen wrapped an arm around her from the other side. Through the window they saw Doris propped up on a mountain of pillows. IV lines ran from her arms and she looked as if she'd aged twenty years. Her skin sagged and her tight blue curls now hung like limp noodles from a pale scalp.

Tom pointed at a paper clipped to a frame to one side of the door. "I thought you said her name was Doris?"

"It is," said Vicki. "Doris Wellnick."

Tom gestured again at the notice and they stepped back to read it. At the top of a list of hastily written and barely legible medical notes, someone had printed the name Angel D. Wellnick in capital letters.

Jen raised a hand to her mouth. "Doris's name is Angel? Why doesn't that surprise me?"

Emma glanced up and down the corridor again. Nothing else moved, with the team of nurses shut away in another room somewhere dealing with an emergency. "Come on, I'm not waiting here all day. I'm going in."

She pushed open the door and walked into a wall of antiseptic and old age that almost stung her eyes. Doris's eyes fluttered open as the hinge clicked. Everyone filed into the room. Tom entered last and closed the door behind them.

Vicki pushed her way to the side of the bed and took a frail hand in hers. "Doris, what are you doing to us? You had us worried. Are you okay?"

Doris spoke over the constant and steady beep that came from the machine beside her.

"I'm okay, dear."

Each word seemed to punch through a wall of exhaustion. She nodded at the IV lines that trailed like puppet strings from each arm. Purple circles mottled her forearms where the failed attempts had marked her.

"I don't know what all the fuss is about. They've poked and prodded me like a pin cushion to get these stupid things in, and they keep saying I need fluid. I'm perfectly capable of drinking water, I'm not useless. I've been doing it for years."

"They have your best interests at heart," said Vicki. "Do as you're told and they'll have you out of here in no time."

"I hope so. Have you seen the gown they put me in?" Her voice dropped to a whisper. "It has no ass in it. What if a hunky older doctor comes in and it's the first thing he sees? I know it sags. I've got mirrors."

Vicki stifled a laugh. "Doris, I'm sure they've seen much worse. So, tell us what happened? How did you get here?"

Doris shuffled upright and spoke a little louder. "Well, I'd got up to make a cup of tea. I've been drinking a lot of that green tea, it's supposed to be good for you. So far, all it's done is make my pee a weird color. Anyway, I was in the kitchen when the phone rang. I stood to answer it and it was Henry, checking in on me. And I remember chatting for a while but then I got so dizzy. I held onto the counter but I must have tumbled. Next thing, I'm lying here while they put these tubes in me. Apparently, I'm dehydrated, and it's part of the cancer working its evil on me."

Vicki's eyes welled up, and she turned as Emma stepped forward. "Is there anything you need? Can we call anyone for you?"

"Yes, would you call Henry and thank him for me? His number's in the little book of mine you have. And I need my hair doing. I can't see it, but it feels awful. It doesn't feel very blue."

"I've already thanked Henry," said Vicki. "He called me at the salon. I'm glad you gave him my number."

"And your hair's fine," lied Emma. She changed the subject. "So Doris, what's with your name being Angel? That's a beautiful name, why would you change it?"

"Pfft, you have no idea," she said. "Can you imagine going through high school with a name like Angel? Can you imagine the jokes? Every time the dinner bell rang, it was like 'oh, listen everyone, someone just got her wings'. And then I grow up and escape high school and they make a vampire show and guess what his name is? Angel. And not only does he have my name, but he's a man." She turned to Vicki. "Good looking fella, though. He had dimples, and even his muscles had muscles."

The girls smiled and crowded around the bed, leaving Tom exposed by the door. It was obvious that the company had rejuvenated Doris. The sparkle had returned to her eyes, and she seemed to draw strength from those around her. "And who might you be, young man?" she said.

Emma walked around the bed and took Doris's other hand. Tom froze like a deer in headlights and, for the first time, she doubted bringing him here. It was like introducing a boyfriend to the family. Was he even ready to get to know these people, these extensions of her? And what had happened at the salon? The girls' insistence to invite him over had almost led to her jumping him. Not that he'd seemed to mind. For whatever reason, she relaxed around him. She'd dropped her guard faster than she'd expected, but what if he was too good to be true? Still, they were here now. It was too late to back out.

"Doris, I'd like you to meet Tom. He's, ah, a good friend of mine." She glanced across the room and locked eyes with him. "Tom, this is Doris. It's her fund raiser you've been helping me with."

"Come closer then," said Doris. "Don't be shy. Just because they named a vampire after me doesn't mean I bite, too. Let's see what you've got to offer my girl."

Tom blushed, tried to relax his bunched shoulders, and edged forward as if he was the last kid picked for a sports team. He held out a trembling hand. "It's a pleasure to meet you, Doris. I've heard a lot about you."

"Well, you can forget the boring stuff and remember anything interesting or illegal. So, you're after our Emma, are you? Well you don't look half bad so let me give you some advice, the words of a wise lady."

Tom leaned in closer and nodded. "Of course, a man can never get too much advice."

"Never a truer word said. Listen carefully, young man. Emma's a lovely girl, and she makes a nice cup of coffee. I try to stay up to date with what you young ones are doing, so my advice for you? If you like this single lady, then you better put a ring on it."

"That's excellent advice, Doris," said Tom with a smile. "I'll be sure to keep it in mind."

The girls gathered around the bed and spent half an hour getting Doris up to date with salon talk and then made their excuses.

"We'll be back again tomorrow," said Vicki. "Do you have your phone with you? Keep us posted, okay?"

Doris pointed to the tiny bedside cabinet. "One of the nurses put it in there somewhere. And don't worry, I'll let you know what's going on. Thank you for coming to visit an old crone. I do appreciate it."

"You're our adopted mom, Doris. We love you."

The old lady's eyes misted over and she squeezed each of their hands as they left the room.

Vicki left her contact details at the desk and got an official update on Doris's condition. As long as she responded to the medication, they expected to release her after twenty four hours.

As they made their way to the parking lot, Jen's phone beeped. She held it up with a smile. "Josh. He seems really nice."

She read the message and glanced at her watch. "I love hibachi food. What a lovely man to think of it. It's almost six. Are you hungry? Do you guys fancy it?"

"Fancy what?" said Vicki.

"Oh, sorry, Vic. You already have a man. Now it's our turn. We're going out on a date."

"I like hibachi, too," said Vicki with a pout.

"Sorry again, you'll cramp my style."

Vicki laughed. "Jen, your style went out with the Human League. That's okay, I know when I'm not wanted. My car's over here, so you all have a nice time and have a shrimp for me."

"They can eat shrimp for you," said Emma. "I can't stand the things. Tom, would you mind checking in with Josh? See if he's free, that is as long as you fancy it, too?"

"I'd love to," said Tom. "Give me a minute."

The girls hugged as he wandered off and dialed his phone.

"See you Monday, Vic. Have a nice rest of the weekend, and text me if Doris calls. Come on Jen. Let's find out if we have a date with destiny."

Tom turned back to them. "He's just finishing up at the studio. Said we can call by and check out the Vegas stuff." He stopped and shuffled uncomfortably. "That is, you know, if you think it's still relevant. Sorry about Doris, by the way. She seems lovely."

"It's more relevant than ever," said Emma. "Lead the way, Tom. We'll follow you."

****

They clambered up the stairs to Josh's studio. Tom stopped at the top and shushed them with a finger to the lips. "Let's wait in the first room until we're sure he's done."

Tom pushed open the door to find Josh sitting crossed legged on the floor, sifting through a mountain of props. As soon as Josh set eyes on Jen, he clambered to his feet and brushed paper dust off his shirt. His smile seemed effortless and genuine.

"Hi, it's great to finally meet you."

Jen grasped his outstretched hand in both of hers and shook it. "Great to meet you, too. And look at your hair, I could spend forever shaping that."

Tom glanced at Emma, then at Josh. "Have you two been texting for months, or just the last couple of days?"

Emma swung an arm and slapped the back of his head with her palm. "Tom Lewis. These kids have been itching to meet each other. Be respectful."

Tom smoothed down his mussed up hair and apologized, then wandered over to the scattered papers, while Jen and Josh wandered off into the studio in a babble of excitement.

"Look at all of this." He knelt and rested his forearms on his knees, then rummaged through the stack. "Wall banners. Posters. Garlands. We need to see how big the hall is, but this stuff will definitely work."

Emma stood behind him and placed her hands on his shoulders. He jumped at the initial touch, then relaxed and enjoyed the contact. "This could turn out to be a good time. I'm not used to the men in my life being this giving, you know? Ha, who am I kidding? I'm not used to men in my life. You may have to bear with me but, for now, I'll take it. Especially if you'll feed me hibachi."

Tom laughed. An urge rushed through him to turn and hold her in his arms and carry on where they left off at the salon. The way she'd taken the lead had taken his breath away. Jen laughed from the other room to break the moment, so he stood and took her hand instead. "Of course I'll feed you hibachi. Dare we check in the other room? The Josh of old would have Jen splayed out on the floor in all kinds of poses. But this new guy? I don't know what to expect."

They peeked around the corner to find Josh demonstrating how the lighting umbrellas changed the tone of a shot.

"You kids ready?" asked Tom.

Josh and Jen looked at each other and nodded in unison. "Yep," she said. "I'm starving. Let's go."

All four of them piled into Tom's car. It was like a family holiday drive, with the adults in the front and the excitable children bouncing around on the rear seat. Tom glanced in the rear-view mirror from time to time to see two beaming smiles. Something had changed in Josh during this last week, starting with his comments in the bar. It seemed as if Jen had come along just at the right time. He smiled and glanced across at Emma and caught her looking back at him. She returned the smile as if she'd read his mind.

Something had changed in him, too, although Josh seemed to find it much easier to deal with. The nagging feeling was still there, but it bubbled beneath the surface instead of overwhelming his entire being. The need to wallow in grief hadn't manifested itself since he'd ran into the maze with her. It was only days ago, but it felt as if something had already filled a space inside him. Still, she seemed to hold something back. They'd met under the most unusual circumstances, but maybe she was more like him than he realized.

He made a mental note to ask her about her funeral visits when they next had time alone.

****

The Sizzling Wok sat back from the road under one of the overhead tram tracks. Faded vinyl siding and wood panels clad the outside of the building. For such a new place it looked dingy, but there were plenty of cars dotted around the parking lot. Tom pulled up close to the entrance and followed the rest inside.

A tiny Oriental woman greeted them at the door in a babble of broken English. Her name badge said she was named 'Candy'.

Candy seated them along a bench that stretched out in front of a gleaming steel grill top. A taller man stood behind it, hefting a shining spatula in each hand. The grill reflected his rippling forearms and made him look like an extra from a Bruce Lee movie.

The faded appearance from outside did not carry through to the interior. Everything in the room dazzled as if it had been buffed to a high gloss. From the varnished table tops to the gleaming tile behind the far counter, everything shined.

Candy slid menus across the table as Jen leaned forward. "Have you been here before, Tom?"

He slid his finger down the menu. "No. First time. It's had great reviews, though. The writer mentioned bulgogi. I've never heard of it, so I think I'll try that."

"And you're getting shrimp, right Jen?" said Emma.

Jen smiled. "Ongoing joke," she said to Tom. "She hates them. I love them."

Emma screwed up her face. "It's like chewing worms with gristle."

"Okay," said Jen with a grimace, "I used to love them."

Candy took their drinks order and returned with glasses of beer. Condensation ran down their sides and pooled on the table.

"That's cold beer," said Tom. He took a sip and smacked his lips as the cold liquid lit up his taste buds.

"Always serve cold beer," said Candy. "Always. Other place serve flat, warm beer. That bad for business." She flipped open her notepad. "Ready for order?"

The group gave their orders and Bruce Lee leaped into action. His name badge said he was Tony.

"We may be new, but we come from cooking background," he said in almost perfect English. The steel top sizzled as he emptied a cup of rice onto it, then scooped up an egg with a flat spatula and tossed it into the air. It seemed to hover as he played a mini drum solo with the spatulas that pinged against the surface, before he caught the egg again, cracked the shell with the slightest of taps and dumped its contents next to the rice. Smoke plumed up to an overhead fan as he did the same thing again before mashing the mess into a mound of scrambled egg that he mixed with the rice.

Shrimp danced and popped alongside beef and chicken as they hit the grill top, but Tony kept them moving. He looked up at Josh. "You cash?"

Josh frowned. "Er, no. Credit card."

"No," said Tony. "You cash."

With a flick of the wrist he flipped a shrimp in Josh's direction. Josh jerked back as the food sailed through the air and bounced harmlessly off his chin.

"Cash," said Tony, and mimicked catching the shrimp in his mouth.

"Catch! You mean catch? Okay," said Josh, "now I understand. Try again."

As Tony flicked another shrimp, the entire room shook and vibrated as a tram trundled overhead. Most of the other patrons seemed to take it in their stride and continued to eat. Tom glanced at Emma wide-eyed as cooking utensils clattered and clanged against one another and the salt shaker vibrated its way an inch closer to the edge of the table. The shrimp landed with a damp splat on the floor and skidded under a chair.

Tony laughed and pointed to the ceiling with his spatula.

"See? This is why Sizzling Wok so clean. Vibration from tram make dust fall everywhere. Bad for business. Mister, please pick up shrimp."

The tram faded into the distance and the room settled as the four nestled back into their seats. Tom and Emma held hands while Josh and Jen babbled like school kids. Tom looked along the row of them and smirked.

"What?" said Emma.

Tom took a moment to understand the question. "Oh, it's nothing. Well, actually it's everything." He lowered his voice and leaned closer to her. "Josh got hurt a while ago. To be honest, he's an all-or-nothing kind of guy. You know, keep the girls at arm's length and just have a good time, or plow headlong into marriage and have a dozen kids. I haven't seen him smile like this, like really smile, in ages." He paused. "Would you do me a favor? Tell Jen to be nice to him."

"Don't worry, I don't think I'll need to. From what I can gather, she thinks he's great. And you don't know Jen. That thing with the dozen kids? That's a strong possibility. In fact, she's probably already named them all."

"As long as she doesn't hurt him, I'm cool with whatever names she comes up with."

Tony prepared their meals in no time. The top gave off enough heat to tan everyone present and was large enough to cook everything at the same time. He lined up four plates and somehow separated the mass of food into individual servings, each heaped like a mini mountain. He smiled and ladled another spoon of rice on to each. "Always good portions," he said. "Small portions no good. Bad for..."

"Business?" chorused the group.

Tony smiled. "Yes. Bad for business."

Chapter Twelve

The lake shimmered like a field full of tulips as the sun cast a warm glow across its surface. A small boat sat marooned in its center. Inside it sat an elderly couple that gazed into one another's eyes. In the background, a pier ran out of the water and up to a small cabin that had a tiny wisp of inviting smoke trailing from its chimney.

Steve wrung his hands as Tom looked over the image once more. "Well? Is that more like what you had in mind?"

Tom looked up. "Steve, that's perfect. Even the slogan placement is perfect."

The bottom left of the screen had a discreet logo of the company. Floating beneath the boat and the male figure was a slogan that glowed out of the orange ripples.

Viagra—coming soon…

"You don't think the slogan's too, you know, suggestive?"

"We're advertising erection medication, Steve, not Jelly Beans. I hope the only people that'll get it are the people that are…well, you know, going to get it."

"You should meet my young cousins," said Steve. "They make my toes curl."

Tom snapped the laptop lid closed. "The youth of today. It worries me, too, but I'm not a parent so I take no responsibility. Okay, it's too late in the day to do anything with this now. Run it off to processing and have them produce a few proofs and we'll see what the board says tomorrow."

Steve grinned, snatched up the laptop and opened the door.

"And Steve?"

"Yes, boss?"

"Nice work. Thanks for taking note."

"Does this mean I get a raise? Pardon the pun."

"Have a nice night, Steve."

Steve grinned once more and closed the door.

Tom reached across the desk and picked up his phone. The blue text notification light had flashed like a beacon in the corner of the screen during Steve's presentation. He opened it.

'Hi. Busy, but thought I'd let you know the hospital let Doris go home x'

He read the message again. Emma had put a solitary 'x' at the end of her message. A kiss.

A text routine had started since the hospital visit where whoever woke first would send the other a message to say they hoped the day went well. Then, in the evenings, they'd get a recap on the days' events. Tom figured it would have been easier to call, but Emma mentioned that she had clients in the salon at all hours, plus she and the girls drove to the hospital after work to see Doris. There'd been no mention of another date yet.

His thumbs flitted across the phone's screen. 'Great news, thanks for the info. She seems nice. Any idea on date for fund raiser? Xx'

The first 'x' came without a thought but, after a pause, he added another. Was it was a step too soon? Tom got the impression that Emma needed to know he was okay, and that he liked her. On one hand she was strong, like the way she'd taken the lead at the hospital to plow forward to find Doris. In other ways she seemed fragile or vulnerable. Something in her past had shaped her into the woman she was now. Tom felt the need to reassure her, to show her he had no intention of hurting her.

His screen lit up. 'Thanks. We love Doris. Or Angel! ☺ Spoke to hall. Poss a week on Sunday if we can pull everything together x'

'No problem,' he typed. 'Want me to print posters? And I'll check with Elvis xx'

Her reply was instant.

'LOL… check with Elvis. Give me a while and I'll confirm for posters x'

Still just the one kiss. Baby steps, thought Tom. A little at a time. No overwhelming and no pressure.

'Will do. Enjoy your evening xx'

He dialed Rob's work number.

"Vincenzo's. This is Vinnie."

Vincent Hope owned the garage that Rob worked at. It sat downtown in what the locals called The Italian Block. Vinnie's blood pumped New Jersey, but he moved to Chicago with his parents. He kept his accent and opened Vincent's on the corner of a busy road. Once the neighborhood accepted him, he gained more and more local custom, moved into a larger business unit and changed the name to fit in with the Italian surroundings. Vincenzo's was a huge success, even though the only Italian thing in the place was a Ferrari poster on the office wall.

"Hi, Vin," said Tom. "Is Rob available?"

"Sure thing, Tom. Gimme a sec."

The phone clattered to the counter and a booming voice echoed around the building. "Yo, Rob! You got a phone call. It's your boy, Tom."

Tom smiled. Vinnie shouted like a mobster. The phone clattered again.

"Tom. What's up?"

"Nothing much. Just checking in. I haven't spoken to you since, well, since Abby called."

"Yeah. We're good. In fact, I'm just wrapping up here, got to reconnect a couple of hoses and I'm done. Abby's at her sisters for a girl's night, so do you fancy a beer?"

"Would love to. I'll call Josh. Usual place?"

"Yep. Meet you there. Save me some beer."

****

When Tom walked in, Rob and Josh were at the end of the bar and already half way through their first beers. He dragged a stool closer and signaled the bartender.

"Josh was telling me about Jen. She sounds nice," said Rob.

Tom nodded. "She is. They seem like a decent group of girls, to be honest. Listen, the fund raiser might be a week from Sunday. Does that work for you two?"

"Fine by me," said Josh. "I don't work Sunday's anyway, plus I have an ulterior motive for turning up. Count me in."

"And I've got no plans other than baby making, so count me in, too. And I'll check with the other guys at the garage. They're always up for supporting a good cause."

99

"And how's that coming," asked Tom. "Pardon the pun."

"The baby making? I saw someone about it the other day. Abby suggested I might be depressed, so I got a number off a friend of hers. It went pretty well, much better than I expected. I'm better about a few things, but it's ongoing. We'll keep trying and see what happens. Hey, at least the practice is good. What about you, lover boy? How many dates have you had now?"

Tom smiled. "Three. That's tied for first place. If we make it to this fund raiser, it'll be a record."

"She's good for you," said Josh. "I don't remember seeing you smile like that before."

"Smile like what? When did you see him smile?" asked Rob.

"We went out for an impromptu meal the other day," said Josh.

"Where was my invite?"

"It was more of a single person thing and, anyway, you were probably home getting some exercise."

"But you're okay?" asked Tom. "We're here if you ever need someone to talk to. Even Josh. Something's happened to him. Maybe aliens landed and whisked the old one away. This new version's got feelings and sensitivity."

"Hey, I'm sitting right here," said Josh.

"Seriously, don't underestimate depression, Rob. It's dangerous. People might assume you're just being miserable, but it can affect a lot of different things."

"And when did you become such an expert?" asked Josh.

"We had someone at the agency, one of the sales guys. It's like there were two versions of him. Sometimes he waltzed into the office, laughing and cracking jokes, other days he'd walk to his desk and say nothing. We knew he was under pressure at work, but we didn't realize his wife had left with the kids."

"What happened?"

"I worked with his manager and tried to help. People don't realize that it's a genuine disorder. You don't come into work pissed and then suddenly get better, it's a permanent, mental thing. Talking with him seemed to be the best solution, but we messed up."

"I wouldn't say you were qualified to talk to anyone about something as serious as that," said Rob. "And that's coming from someone who's talked to you."

"In the end we didn't talk," said Tom. "We gave him time off instead, to get help. What we didn't realize was that work was the only thing keeping him together. You've seen the parking garage on 5th Street? He jumped from the top of that."

Tom sipped his beer while the others gazed at the floor. Then Rob's head snapped up.

"I need another beer. Anyone else need a beer?"

****

A small boat rested on the shore as the setting sun cast an orange glow over the background. A middle-aged couple sat together, their backs to the boat. They held hands and smiled for the camera. The woman was instantly recognizable.

"So that's Bill?" asked Emma.

Doris craned her head to glance at the photograph, even though it had probably hung in the same place for years. "Yes, that's my love," she said. "We were in a bay somewhere near Myrtle Beach. We used to drive there as often as we could and hire a little boat, relax, and laugh all day."

"That sounds like paradise," said Vicki, "but you have to keep your head still while I finish your hair."

Since Doris wasn't able to get to the salon for her appointment, the salon had gone to her. "I'm sorry, dear. It already feels much bluer than it did at the hospital. I appreciate you calling around."

Emma sat on the sofa. Doris sat across from her in a wingback chair, with pillows either side of her to keep her upright. Her bruised arms rested in her lap as Vicki moved behind her tightening up a mop of blue curls. "We don't mind at all," she said. "Have you had any thoughts on what you'd like to do at your fund raiser? Some male friends of ours are helping, too, but we'd welcome any ideas you might have. So far, we're thinking of decking out the hall like…"

"Don't tell me," interrupted Doris. "Keep it a surprise. Unless they involve me waking up on the kitchen floor, I normally like surprises. You girls do whatever you think would be fun. I'm not too concerned about raising funds, more about being around everyone again. If I'm going out, I'd like to go out after saying goodbye to everyone."

Vicki raised a hand and wiped away a stray tear as Jen came in from the kitchen with a cup of steaming tea. "Doris, this stuff smells like something I've thrown down the toilet. Does it taste any better than it smells?"

"You get used to it, dear. At first it reminded me of sucking an old sock, but I'm okay with it now. I'm certainly not drinking it because it's doing me any good. It's a bit late for that."

"How about doing your fund raiser a week from Sunday?" said Emma. "Would that be enough time for everyone? And we were thinking of charging a small fee to get into the hall, and then we'd have events set up inside, too. I doubt we'll raise a fortune, but everything helps. And if everyone could bring a guest, that would double revenue right away."

"Oh, I'm sure everyone will already be either there or at the rest home down the road, so time shouldn't be a problem. And most of them have a regular visitor, so as long as we let everyone know then it should be quite straight forward."

"Okay. I have someone print up posters. We can dot them around the hall and at the rest home and give everyone plenty of notice."

"And I'll call Henry, too." Doris's eyes shone. "I'd like to ask him if he'll be my chaparral."

Emma stared blankly.

"The man on my arm. Isn't he supposed to turn up in a big car with a rose stuck between his teeth? He's still got his teeth. He could do that." She frowned. "I'd better warn him about the thorns, though, I'm not sure how much he knows about flowers."

"Don't you mean chaperone?" asked Jen. "And you're supposed to be on his arm, but don't worry about that. We'll make sure you get well taken care of."

Doris laughed and her eyes sparkled with mischief. "It's been a while since I was well taken care of. I'm not sure these old bones would cope, to be honest, but still... be nice to go out with a bang, wouldn't it? Speaking of which, how are you getting on with that young man from the hospital?"

Emma blushed. "We've both been busy with work, but I'm sure we'll see each other again soon. And he's coming to your fund raiser, so you'll get to meet..."

Her sentence was cut short as her pocket vibrated and then rang. She smiled and dug out her phone. "I'll bet that's him right now."

The screen said 'Dad'.

"Give me a sec," she said as she wondered into the kitchen, "I have to take this."

After a messy divorce, Dad had taken a military job, moved to Columbus, Ohio, and stayed there after retirement.

"Em?"

His voice sounded heavy and hoarse.

"Hi, Dad, is everything okay?"

"No, love. I know it's a long drive, but could you come home? Sammy died."

Chapter Thirteen

Emma's car crunched and popped its way along the gravel driveway and into a turning circle outside a large Victorian looking home. Glass paneled double doors swung open as she braked to a stop and Dad appeared in the doorway. He held onto the frame with one hand and seemed to struggle to stand up straight as he forced a smile. His shoulders sagged like a man dealing with defeat. Emma's stomach churned as she took in his crumbling posture.

Dan Cairnes pushed against the wood to propel himself upright as Emma noticed the other thing that had changed. As soon as the car turned into the driveway and the large stones announced her arrival, she would have expected the door to fly open. A Springer spaniel would come bounding across to meet her, his ears flapping as he galloped as if he was trying to get airborne with excitement. A welcoming bark would bounce around between the trees that surrounded the property, and she'd have to use all the mirrors to maneuver the vehicle to a stop without clipping him.

Emma had not had a pet since she moved to Chicago. It was hard enough keeping hold of a man, and almost as much maintenance. The silence that greeted her when she got home was as much a part of her surroundings as the sofa. Now it was her Dad's turn to get used to it.

She climbed out of the car and rushed up the steps to the door. Before she'd braced herself, he collapsed into her arms and buried his head into her shoulder. Emma felt him tense as she squeezed him and pulled him close. The divorce and its reasons had crushed him, and the strong military man she grew up with had never recovered. The final piece of his old life, Sammy the Springer spaniel, was gone and the silence around the property was as loud as cannon fire.

"Thank you for coming, love," he said. "I know it's a drive, and I wouldn't normally bother you, but…"

"Don't worry, Dad, it's okay." Emma peeled away from him and held his hands. His eyes were ringed in red. "Dad, I'm so sorry. You loved him so much. "Come on," she said. "Step inside, and I'll make us a drink and you can tell me everything."

The interior of the house gleamed. Landscape paintings hung on the pale walls next to shadow boxes of medals and old rifles. Light from the chandelier that hung from the ceiling sparkled off a tile floor that looked clean enough to eat from. A dark oak stairwell wound around up to the next level and vanished into shadow at the top. Emma glanced into the darkness.

"I know what you're thinking," said Dad. "And no, I still don't go up there."

Since the divorce, Dad hadn't set foot in the bedroom he'd shared with his wife. Mom's dresses still hung in the closet, the way they had when Emma had first called him with the news. She remembered the way his voice had caught, and the silence that followed it. And she'd heard something unique.

Her Dad had cried.

Now he slept on a single bed in a converted office at the rear of the house that also held Sammy's fur lined basket. The office cum bedroom backed onto a large living room and a well equipped kitchen, along with a small guest bathroom. The set up rendered the upper level of the house useless.

After a few minutes, the pungent smell of strong coffee wafted through the kitchen as the two sat at the kitchen table.

"The vet found a lump in his side a few weeks ago," said Dad. "Cancer. I didn't call because they said it was treatable and I thought everything would be okay. After a while, he became very weak and would fall onto his side instead of lying down. It was like his legs would give up on him. Then I noticed that he didn't seem to walk in a straight line either, but weaved from side to side, so I took him back. The cancer had spread much quicker than they thought it would and the treatment wasn't working. I asked if he was suffering. They said he was, but they gave me some medication for him."

His eyes welled up and Emma leaned across and took his hand. "I'm sorry Dad. Cancer. I frigging hate that word."

"Me too, love. I brought him home and, for a while, he was okay. Then he'd wake in the night, twitching and whimpering. I couldn't bear to watch him suffer, Em, it broke my heart. After a few days I took him back and had him put to sleep. Other than my beautiful daughter, he was the most loving soul I've ever known." He paused, shook his head and uttered a cynical laugh. "And way more trustworthy than most humans."

Emma wanted to tell him that everything would be okay. He was still only in his mid-fifties. Despite his recent appearance, he was in good shape. She wanted to say that women would find his gray flecked dark hair and strong jaw line attractive, and would enjoy his wonderful sense of humor. And she wanted to say it would be possible to move on, to find a new love, and to rescue another loving dog from the shelter once the wounds had healed. Then she looked into herself and knew she couldn't, in all fairness, utter those words until she believed them about herself first.

"And what about you?" he asked. "What's my gorgeous daughter up to these days? Business still good at the salon?"

"It's going great," said Emma. "We're working well as a team and we've built up a solid list of regulars."

She was about to mention Doris when her busy mind gave her a jolt. Tom was still waiting for instruction on how to arrange the fund raiser and they had a little over a week to pull everything together.

"And I might have met someone," she continued.

Dad smiled. "There's hope for at least one of us." His eyes grew brighter although the effort caused the lines in his face to deepen. They rippled away from the corners of his eyes like sand dunes. "I'm glad they didn't ruin both of us. Well, come on, tell me more."

Emma cringed at the comment, but told him about the picnic and the bowling date. She neglected to mention the funerals. Dad suffered enough, he didn't need that depression. "And if you can excuse me for a moment," she said, "I have to call him about an event we're scheduling for the salon. A charity night."

"Okay," he nodded, "but Em? Would you mind staying a couple of nights? Just a couple? It would be nice to have someone else around the place, it seems so quiet at the moment. And you know there's always a room here for you if you ever…"

"I know. Of course I can stay." She leaned across the table again, squeezed his hand and swerved the mention of moving back into her old room. "Let me make that call and then I'll see what's in the fridge. I'm starving."

****

"We've got to work with the girls from the salon and put the thing together this week," said Tom. He paced around his living room, stepping over the cat as it weaved between his feet. "Emma said Jen spoke to the folks at the hall so we can get in and decide how to dress it. We just need to get the things over there and check with Colin to see how he'd like to set up the stage."

"Come over then," said Josh. "I'm at the studio now. Where did you say she went?"

"Emma's visiting her Dad in Ohio. He's suffered a bereavement. She didn't say who."

"She's almost as bad as you for funerals. Perhaps you should both open a funeral home and move in together."

"Funny," said Tom. "Before I get there, I'll swing by the office to pick up some flyers I designed for the event. I wouldn't mind a second opinion if you'd give them the once over. And I'll get in touch with Colin and see if he can meet us there."

Tom fed Oswald and drove to the office to pick up the papers. Twenty minutes later he parked opposite the studio and ran up the stairs. Boxes of posters, banners, props and decorations sat piled at the entrance.

Josh burst through the door with another box. "Last one. Come on. Load up your car with what you can carry. The bigger stuff will fit in mine. Then you can text me the address and I'll meet you there."

"Josh, this is amazing. Thank you so much," said Tom.

"You don't have to thank me. Doris sounds like a lovely lady and I'm sure Jen will appreciate this, too. It feels good to be a part of it, to be honest."

"I don't know where you buried the old Josh," said Tom, "but I quite like this new one so leave him there." He clapped Josh on the shoulder, picked up a box and walked down the stairs. "Let's load up and go see what we're up against."

The Lodge was conveniently close to the Blazing Oak Crematorium. Tom thought back to his meeting here with Emma as Josh sidled up beside him in the parking lot. "I've driven past here plenty of times," he said. "I had no idea this was here."

Josh grinned. "Talk about efficiency. You'd waste no time and just roll them from the Lodge to the crem when they croaked."

The building sat back behind a tree line that hid it from the busy road out front. A parking lot surrounded it, much like the Crematorium, although there were no tall chimneys here. Or mazes.

Tom backed open the entrance door and swung around with a box to look into the room. The hall was huge. A small bar that ran down part of the side wall looked as if it had been tacked on as an afterthought. A tall stage took up the entire front side, bookended by sweeping red curtains. Facing it stood row after row of rectangular plastic tables arranged like a troop formation waiting at attention for orders.

"Holy crap," said Josh. "How are we going to fill this? It's huge."

Tom dropped his box and dug around inside it, then pulled out a sheaf of papers and spread them over the nearest table. "Okay, see what you think of the flyers first."

Emma had taken a picture of Doris sitting in the salon, loaded down with a head full of curlers. Her wide smile beamed and her eyes blazed with mischief. Tom had transferred it onto his laptop and merged it with a photo of a Las Vegas Elvis, and a gambling image borrowed from an Ocean's 11 film clip. Roulette chips tumbled down the side of the picture to an announcement, with the date, venue and admission. Food and drink would be available, of course.

"Excellent," nodded Josh. "That's actually pretty good, Tom. Couldn't have done much better myself."

"Great. I'll pin these up and then drive over to the rest home and drop a few there, too. Let's get the rest of the boxes in and behind the stage. Then I'll show you a rough plan I've sketched of how we can set up the room."

Midway through ferrying in boxes, Colin rolled into the parking lot in a jet black BMW with tinted windows and gleaming chrome wheels. Josh whistled. "Life is good in the Elvis impersonation world. Look at that for a ride."

Colin climbed out of the car and waved and, once again, Tom marveled at his humility. For the entire time he'd known him, Colin had suffered nothing but grief and humiliation for his speech impediment.

"Tom. Josh. All okay?" he asked, still picking out each word.

"Hi, Colin. We're good, thanks," said Tom. "Come inside. Let me show you the hall."

As soon as they entered, Colin strode forward as if he owned the place. Something seemed to click in him, and he went from being a mild mannered man with a lisp to a confident performer. He climbed the small staircase to the stage and surveyed the room. "Perfect. It'll thound exthellent in here. Thith room is the perfect shape for thound."

Josh turned to Tom. "And you're positive he can do Elvis?" he whispered. "I'm not being mean, but the front rows might get drowned in phlegm before he's finished the first couple of numbers. And if he sings She Thinks I Still Care, I'm running for a life jacket and water wings."

Tom glared at Josh. "That sounds like the Josh of old. Rein it in, then wait and see what happens."

Colin wandered the stage as he seemed to mentally plan his show. Two steps forward, then three back, followed by a twist of the hips and that famous Elvis pelvic thrust. An imaginary microphone was brought to his lips as a few words sneaked out, before he took a line of measured steps, turned, and spun and choreographed a full routine.

Tom stared in awe, then nudged Josh. "He seems so professional. It's all coming back to me now. Don't quote me, but this might actually work."

Chapter Fourteen

Despite Emma's absence, the work week flew by.

Steve's Viagra presentation was a resounding success, and the board agreed to take it to the company itself. Rob called to say he and Abby received a call from a company to enroll in a clinical trial to test a new drug to increase fertility. He sounded ecstatic and Tom wished them both luck and suggested that they get practicing right away. Josh called to say he and Jen were going to the Sizzling Wok and he was welcome to join them. He thanked them, but said he didn't want to be the third wheel and that he was waiting for Emma's phone call.

The first day, when she drove to Ohio, Emma didn't call until late in the day. She sounded exhausted and only called to tell him about the hall and to get in touch with Josh to contact Jen for more information. The next day she didn't call at all. He picked up his phone many times, lit up the screen, saw nothing, and thought to text or call. Then he put the phone down and left it. This was her time with her Dad.

Daughters had a special bond to their fathers. It was the natural way of things. But there seemed to be something more here. Toward the end of the week she called again and talked about her Dad and how he was doing. When she spoke of him, it was as if she wanted to say something but couldn't find the words, or didn't want to. It was more in what she didn't say that hinted at something different and unique between them. At one point, she also hinted at questions about Tom's family but he steered her away and onto different topics. Now was not the time for that conversation. She promised to be home in time to check out the hall ahead of the fund raiser.

He paced the apartment again. For someone used to being alone, it felt weird and empty to him. He missed chatting with Emma. She spent no time here, but her presence filled the place when they were talking. Tom glanced at his phone again, sure that she'd call soon.

The event started in three hours and she still hadn't made contact. He put the phone on the table and, as he stepped into the kitchen to make a drink, it buzzed and chirped. His stomach leaped a nauseous dance as he snatched it up.

"Hello?"

"Tom? It'th Colin. The hall ith perfect, the thound is perfect, and it lookth amazing. You did a great job."

His heart sank while he translated Colin's lisp. "Thanks, Colin. And I know I've already mentioned it, but we appreciate you doing this. I hope you get a load of bookings from it."

"No problem," he said. "Thee you later. Bring your danthing shoeth."

Tom disconnected the call, then fumbled his phone as it rang again.

"Did you forget something?" he said.

"I'm sorry? Tom? Is everything okay?"

This time, his stomach leaped and churned while his heart somersaulted. "Emma. I thought you were Colin. Sorry."

"Er, an easy mistake to make, I guess."

He could hear the smile in her voice. "Are you back in town?"

"I am," she said. "Sorry I've been so distant this past week. I'll explain everything one day. Dad needed someone and the choice these days is either me or me, so it was a no brainer. I'm back now, though, and I can't wait to check out the hall. Can I meet you there in an hour or so? I need to shower, do my hair and put my face on."

"Of course," he said. "I can always pick you up?"

Tom still hadn't seen Emma's home. It seemed like the next step, the bridge to the next level of trust and closeness.

"That's okay." She spoke in a breezy, carefree fashion, not in a guarded and insecure way. Maybe next time, he thought. "I'll just meet you there. To be honest, I'm a little tired. A lot of driving and all that. And anyway, you might want to stay with the boys and I'd hate to cramp your style."

He laughed. "Wait until you see my best Elvis moves. Most of them involve me not putting a hip out of joint. How about I wait by the door for you?"

"Okay. Oh, and what about Doris? How is she getting there? Did you sort something special out for her?"

Tom smiled. "Have you seen Pretty Woman?"

"Yes, although it was years ago."

"Don't worry about Doris. We'll be there in plenty of time, so you'll get to see her arrival."

****

There were already at least a dozen cars dotted about when Emma pulled into the parking lot. Tom stood at the doorway as promised. He looked handsome in gray dress slacks and a white button down shirt. His hair shone against his head, slicked back in a sixties style, and his ear to ear smile screamed that he was pleased to see her.

The car locked with a click and a beep and she strode as confidently as she could toward him. She rarely wore heels and felt as if she was wading through jelly. A small breeze tugged at the willowy fabric of her lace skirt, so she thrust her hands down to her side and smiled back.

"Long time no see, Tom Lewis."

He leaned forward and kissed her cheek. Emma didn't recognize his cologne, but the muskiness of it lingered in her nose and snapped awake her senses.

"Welcome back, Emma Cairnes."

"The sixties suits you," she said, "and you smell lovely."

He brushed a hand against her arm. "Thank you. You look amazing. It's weird, but I've missed you."

"Of course you did," she said, stepping past him. "It's not weird, I'm very missable. Come on. Show me what you did in here."

She pushed open the door and stepped inside as he followed. "Is Doris here yet?"

"No," said Tom, "but she shouldn't be too long. They had a problem with Henry's bag, but it's sorted now."

"Henry's bag? Dare I ask?"

Tom laughed. "His colostomy bag. Someone ran over it at the Lodge one time and that's how he got talking to Doris. He's paranoid about it, so they're trying to hide it so he's not as conscious and so it doesn't get trampled again."

"Mavis Pickles," nodded Emma. "Mavis ran over it. So, Henry's coming too?"

"Oh yes, she was very insistent that he take her. And I'm sure Henry thinks he's getting lucky tonight, he keeps asking Rob for a little blue pill. Rob's going to slip him peppermint tic-tacs to keep him quiet."

"You boys are so bad. He might pop them and try something and then be gutted if nothing happens to his... you know, his... I can't believe we're discussing this. Come on, show me inside."

The music grew louder as they walked through the foyer and approached the main room. Light pulsed beneath the doors before Tom threw them open. Emma gasped.

"Oh my God." She raised a hand to her mouth. "Tom, it's incredible."

The beige walls danced with color as lights bounced and flashed from the stage. Beads and streamers hung from the bar, and two young men dressed in sharp suits flitted behind it making last minute changes as early arrivals waited for drinks.

A stars and stripes table cloth covered every table. Glitter and confetti sparkled across them and a mysterious small box sat in the center of each one. In the far corner, a few tables were pulled together to create a mini casino. A large man was testing a roulette wheel and an even bigger mean-looking man stood behind him with folded arms.

"That's Vinnie," said Tom as he followed Emma's gaze. "Rob's boss. He's from New Jersey so he's got the accent. He'll be our croupier tonight. The guy behind him is one of the mechanics. He's there for effect, although I don't see the residents of a care home giving us too much trouble. And the boxes on the tables? They're filled with poker chips so everyone can play a few games of cards or roulette. We've even got a few prizes we pulled together too."

Emma shook her head, walked further into the room and did a pirouette to take it all in. "It's amazing. Oh, and what's with the stage?"

Tom grinned. Colin had pulled out all the stops with his show. A backdrop hung behind the stage, a midnight blue velvet cloth that shimmered in the changing light. Spotlights beamed circles onto the floor and a huge mirror ball sent snowflakes of light drifting around the room. Center stage, a solitary old style microphone waited patiently on its stand.

The crowning glory was a huge banner that stretched the length of the stage and hung from its front edge. It had a picture of a young

Doris on one side, and another recent one on the other. They sandwiched a simple phrase that said 'Doris…with love'.

Emma grabbed the back of Tom's head and kissed him. "I don't know how you've done this, but it's so far above and beyond what I expected, I don't know where to start."

"Start here," said Tom. He cupped her elbow and led her to the bar. "Doris should be here soon. The room is already filling up, so everyone should be ready and waiting before she arrives. Grab a drink first. I made sure they had fizzy wine."

She gestured to the bartender. "Thank you. Seems you've considered everything. Did you get Doris a cab?"

"No. The guys at the garage where Rob works have volunteered their time as chauffeurs. They're on a tee-total mission to make sure everyone gets here and leaves again in one piece. They've got something special planned for Doris, though."

As the bartender placed a glass of wine on the bar, Emma lifted an arm and waved. Josh and Jen were sitting in the corner with Rob and Abby. Vicki sat across from them with Adam.

"I guess that's the naughty corner," she smiled.

Tom craned his neck and scanned the group. "Who's the other guy?"

"That's Adam, Vicki's lifelong partner. They've been together so long she's thinks marriage will go out of fashion by the time they get there."

The corner table backed onto a space the size of a small room, but the entire area hid behind fabric draped from hanging rails like huge shower curtains. Emma turned to ask the obvious question but Tom beat her to it.

"That's a surprise for later," he said, "for when the booze has been flowing and our pretend Elvis is doing his thing. It should be fun. Trust me. We'll be in there later."

Emma glanced around. The room was almost full now, other than a table in front of the stage reserved for Doris and Henry. She relaxed and put her faith in this man beside her. Then someone waved from across the room. Tom strode over to him, talked for a moment, and then returned.

"Are you ready?" he said. "Doris is almost here."

He took her hand and led her outside as a strong voice behind her marshaled the waiting guests.

"I'm really excited about this," said Emma. "Thank you, yet again. I couldn't have done this without you. And I'm so sorry for vanishing on you at the last moment."

Tom turned, pulled her close and kissed her. "I couldn't have done this for anyone else but you. Come on. Let's go outside before they get here."

As they stepped out of the entrance, a stretch limousine coasted around the corner. Its sunroof was open and a man's upper body stood upright out of it with both arms aloft. He was singing along to a Beach Boys song thumping from the cars' sound system while his hair flapped in the wind like a rooster's comb.

Emma collapsed into fits of giggles. "That has to be Henry. I've been dying to meet him. From what Doris has said, he's quite a character."

"I thought he was wheelchair bound?" said Tom.

As if to answer him, the car slowed to a stop, and the door swung open. A guy built like a lumberjack knelt inside and lowered Henry back into the seat. Then the opposite door opened, and another guy walked around the back of the limo and pulled a wheelchair from the trunk. The sound of teenage laughter drifted out of the vehicle.

"God, can you hear Doris laughing?" said Emma. "That has to be worth the price of admission alone."

"Did you see me?" shouted a strong male voice.

One of Rob's mechanic friends lifted Henry into his wheelchair with ease as the old man turned back to the car and searched for his companion.

"Did you see that, Doris? Just like Kate Winslet in the Titanic. I leaned forward over the bow of the ship with the wind in my hair while Brian Wilson serenaded me with Good Vibrations. I've always wanted to do that. Not the vibrations, the bow leaning thing. Would have been better without this damned bag of piss taped to me, but still, you work with what you've got."

Emma skipped down the steps, shook Henry's hand and then leaned into the dark car. "Doris, you're here. Come on and give me your hand. Let me help you inside. Tonight is all about you."

She looked into the back section of the limo. Doris slid back against the leather seats so hard she dented them and blended into the far corner.

"Is everything okay?"

For the first time, Emma saw fear in the woman's eyes. She'd lost a husband. The same husband had returned from war while she waited. Terminal illness had tested her. And now she appeared to be quaking in the back of a stretch limo while her date for the night was singing Beach Boys songs in an awful key.

"Doris," said Emma. "What's wrong?"

She climbed into the back of the car and pulled the door almost closed. Henry's wailing and the noise from the Lodge faded as she looked up. Small tears trickled across wrinkled skin as Doris tried in vain to stem the flow and wipe them away.

"Oh Emma, I don't know what to say. No one has ever done anything like this for me before. It's all a bit overwhelming, to be honest. These hunky men turned up and manhandled me into this car. That was nice. We picked up Henry, although he might have had a whiskey or two beforehand. He hasn't had a date in a while and, underneath the bravado, I think he's nervous. Then they took us on this tour of the city while we sipped champagne." Doris nodded to an empty bottle lying on the seat opposite her. "I'm worried Henry's bag will be full before we can share a tender moment."

Emma put a hand to her mouth to hide a cheeky giggle and then composed herself. "Doris, if you're looking for a tender moment with Henry, then we'll do all we can to make sure you have that opportunity. I can't believe I'm saying that, but against everything I hold holy, I promise. I mean it. Tonight is yours. Are you ready to enjoy it?"

Doris smiled and held out a hand. "Yes, dear. But just check my hair would you? Is it blue enough? Are my curls nice and tight?"

Emma leaned back and sank into the leather upholstery. She looked at the woman in front of her.

"Doris? I pray that one day I'll be just like you." Tears hovered behind her eyes and Emma thought that, at last, this was the moment of release. But they held on for dear life and refused to fall.

"If I could be half as proud as you. As selfless. I hope I can be myself, the way you are, and live life as if every day counts. I'd love to have your fire and your way of boiling everything down to basics. And I want to do away with the complicated stuff that makes life so difficult."

"Well," said Doris, "when you've only got weeks left dear, that shit doesn't seem so important anymore."

Emma held out her hand and smiled. "Come on then. Let's party like there's no tomorrow."

Chapter Fifteen

s the doors opened, the room erupted into a chorus of claps and cheers. Tom glanced to his left to see Doris. She stood behind Henry with a trembling hand held to her mouth, but she remained bolt upright and proud. It was hard to believe a vile disease ate away inside her. Camera flashes lit up like lightning in her eyes as she scanned the room. She laughed and pointed and tottered for a moment as emotion seemed to wash over her, and then gripped the handle of Henry's wheelchair for support.

On her other side, Emma held an arm to steady her. Tom discreetly looked Emma up and down. She wore a white shimmering skirt and a black and white blouse, with no jewelry other than small earrings which sparkled beneath her hair. When she smiled, small explosions went off in his stomach. Maybe this was what proper love felt like.

Dates had come and gone before. No one had really reached inside him and connected, and he wondered whether that was down to them not being the 'right person', or down to him not letting them in. Ultimately, they all gave up and disappeared after a while. Emma seemed different.

And she was still here.

There was an article he read in a magazine about a glass bridge that stretched out into the Grand Canyon. The writer had stood at the precipice and gazed through the clear floor to the canyon's basin almost eight-hundred feet below. He'd wavered before taking a step of faith and edging out, inch by nervous inch, to the far rail.

Tom looked across at Emma and slipped an arm behind Doris's back to touch her. The brush of his finger did no more than ripple the fabric of her blouse but she noticed, caught his eye, and smiled again.

It was time to take a chance.

He decided to tell her everything the next time they were alone and then try to hold on. He was ready to step out onto the glass and reach for the rail.

Doris gripped the other handle and pushed Henry's wheelchair forward before someone stepped up and placed a huge hand over hers.

"Sorry, ma'am, but you're not allowed to do that. Let me take over for you while you say hello to everyone."

For a moment, Doris looked as if she was about to put up a fight and then thought better of it. "Thank you, young man." She craned her neck to look up into unfamiliar eyes. "And who might you be? And look at the size of your arms. I've seen thinner waists. I bet you work out."

The guy blushed and smirked. "It's my pleasure, Doris. I'm Shane. I work with Rob at the garage."

"Well, Shane," she said, "I have no idea who Rob is but I thank him and you for all of this. And would you mind if I squeeze one of your arms? Just one, I don't want to get carried away, only I'm sort of promised to someone else tonight and he might get jealous."

"Totally understand," laughed Shane as he flexed a bicep. "Just the one then, otherwise I might feel disappointed later."

She laughed, squeezed the muscle and patted it. "Lovely," she said, her eyes dreamy. "Just lovely. Now, I think I need a drink."

Shane wheeled Henry to his seat as the girls from the salon gathered around Doris and escorted her to the table. Tom looked around the room. Everything seemed in order. The people young enough to still be mobile were at the bar keeping the two bartenders busy, and the tip jar was filling up with crumpled bills. The tables down one side of the room held small nibbles of food, and plates were already being carried away. A small crowd had gathered around the 'casino', where Vinnie was doing a great job of encouraging the spectators to get to their tables and gather their chips.

Emma had given Doris a hug, along with a glass of wine, then moved into the corner to sit with everyone else. Tom followed and sat next to her.

"Hi, gang. I've met most of you before," he said as he pointed across the table, "and I assume you must be Adam?"

He held out his hand and received a firm handshake.

"I am," said Adam. "I've heard all about you, Tom. Fair warning; you'd best be nice to Emma."

Tom's eyes widened as Adam held his gaze.

"Otherwise," he finished, "Jen will track you down and take care of you."

Everyone laughed, and the ice was broken.

Time flew by as each couple relaxed, drank, and exchanged stories. Tom checked the time on his phone to find that Colin's Elvis show was ten minutes away. He leaned across to Emma. "Since this is such an important night," he asked, "don't you think someone should say something?"

"Like what? I'm a hairdresser, not a public speaker." She addressed the group. "Does anyone here want to stand and say a few words, like a toast or something?"

No one stepped up and Tom grew frustrated. "Okay. I'll do it. Elvis starts in a few minutes. Someone needs to thank these people for coming and let them all know what's going on. And we need to acknowledge Doris."

Emma rubbed his arm. "Thanks for volunteering, Tom. You'll do a great job."

Tom huffed, then stood and clinked against the side of his glass with a fork. "Everyone. Everyone? Could I get a moment of quiet, please?"

A hush settled over the room. Someone turned down the music, someone else coughed and apologized, and then there was silence. Expectant faces stared back at him. The average age of the crowd must have hovered around a hundred-and-ten. He took a deep breath.

"Ladies, gentlemen and mechanics," he started. Vinnie threw a poker chip at him, which he caught and passed to Emma. "Thank you all so much for coming. Before I start, I'd like to thank Vinnie and the boys for scrubbing up and doing a great job so far."

Vinnie tipped a wink, and the mechanics took a small bow as applause echoed around the room.

"Also, my friends at the table here who all chipped in create this amazing set-up."

More applause.

"Obviously, the girls from the salon."

Shouts mingled with the clapping, and Tom let the noise settle before he continued.

"I'll be honest, I know perhaps five percent of the people here tonight, but I'd like to thank one-hundred percent of you for showing up and caring."

Tom paused for more applause but the crowd sat and waited. The pressure of a few hundred eyes pricked sweat in his collar, and a bead traced a cool trail as it trickled down his back.

"I, erm, I had the pleasure of meeting Doris, but in less than normal circumstances," he said, "but despite the situation, her spirit and humor won me over in no time."

He glanced across at Doris and found her staring at him with a small smile painted across her face.

"The girls at the salon consider her to be their mom," he continued, his confidence returning, "and it's a testament to her character that you're all here. Again, thank you all for coming. I'm sure it means a lot to Doris, so I'll just say that everyone, every single one of you, needs to say a few words to her tonight."

The whole room gazed and looked at him and he felt a wave of emotion hit him. It didn't threaten tears, but his stomach leaped as the importance and meaning of the evening hit home.

"Time goes by too quickly, folks," he said. "None of us are guaranteed tomorrow. No one knows what the future holds or what's around the next corner. It could be a nice surprise or it could be a curse. Whatever is waiting, we should approach it with a smile and a positive attitude. Just like Doris. She's an example to us all and I'm proud to say I know her."

He smiled and raised his glass. "Please join me in a toast. Here's to Doris. Let's make this a night to remember."

The room erupted into a thunder of applause. Jen sobbed as Josh wrapped his arm around her, Vicki rested her head on Adam's shoulder, while Doris still smiled and joined the toast.

Tom sat with a thud, heaved a huge sigh of relief, and drained his drink in one huge gulp. Emma leaned over, kissed his cheek and whispered in his ear. "You smooth bastard."

Moments later, a taped voice broke through the chatter. "Ladieth and gentlemen. You've theen the movieth. You've heard the thongth. Now it'th time to thee the clotheth thing to the real thing. Welcome to the thtage… the one, the only… Elvith Prethley!!!"

The room's lights dimmed and the stage burst into life. Lights shifted and danced, music blared from the speakers and the unmistakable start of Blue Suede Shoes swam around the room. Heads turned and feet tapped as Colin swaggered onto the stage. Tom's mouth dropped open. Colin was completely transformed and looked every bit the part. He swung the microphone around and hit his first cue precisely.

"Well it's one for the money," he sang, "Two for the show. Three to get ready, now go cat go, but don't you... step on my blue suede shoes."

There was no hint of a lisp. With eyes closed, Elvis was in the room. Every word, note and inflection was perfect. Tom turned to Josh, who sat wide-eyed and slack-jawed while he stared at the stage. Tom shrugged and smiled. Josh just looked and shook his head while the room jostled and people milled onto the dance floor.

"That's frigging ridiculous," shouted Josh over the music. "What happened?"

"Well, I thought to tell you but figured it'd be more fun to watch," said Tom. "When he sings, the lisp disappears. Colin becomes Elvis and overcomes it. I've never seen him dressed up, though, it's amazing. He's really good."

The show went on. Love Me Tender, Jailhouse Rock and Don't Be Cruel were fired off in quick succession. When Colin announced Are You Lonesome Tonight, Tom turned to Emma. "May I have this dance, beautiful lady?"

"Of course," she said. "Wouldn't miss it for the world."

As the melody bled through the sound system, Tom whirled and spun Emma around the dance floor, never allowing her body to leave his by more than a few inches. At one point, he noticed their surroundings. Josh serenaded Jen, Adam was cuddling Vicki, and Doris had draped herself over Henry's wheelchair while she held his hand and rocked with him. There was no sign of Rob and Abby.

"You realize," said Emma, "that this is actually a sad song. It's not at all positive."

"Really?" said Tom. "I've not heard a lot of Elvis. Always thought he had cool hair, though."

Emma laughed and held him closer. "If you like, we could do that to you. There are gallons of gel at the salon. We could Elvis you up."

Tom buried his nose into her neck and kissed it. "I've got a list of things I'd rather do."

Emma pulled him even closer and moved with him until the song finished and Colin announced a small break.

"I'm burning up," she said as they parted, "and not in a hunk a hunk of burning love kind of way, either. Would you mind getting me a glass of water?"

"Of course not," said Tom. He went to the bar and returned to find everyone sitting around the table, deep in conversation. It was good to see that the two groups of friends had mingled well.

"I've got this theory," said Josh. "Have you ever noticed that old people always have water features? There must come a time when they look in the mirror and realize their skin no longer fits them. I think they keep loads of water around in the hope they'll re-hydrate and fill out again."

Tom leaned over and whispered into Emma's ear. "The water fountain they always have in the funeral homes." They collapsed into each other in fits of laughter as everyone looked on.

Then Josh leaned over. "Do you think it's time? Before Colin starts his second set?"

"Yes," said Tom. "As soon as he starts, I reckon you should pull down the curtain and start snapping."

Josh nodded and, as Colin took to the stage again, he stood and unclipped the curtains that hid the space in the corner behind them. The people on the surrounding tables turned to watch and their smiles spread across the room like a wave as Josh revealed his mini studio.

He pointed to Doris and curled his finger to beckon her. Shane stepped forward and wheeled Henry over to the corner while Doris followed. Josh picked up an old Polaroid camera as Shane positioned Henry under a trellised arch lined with roses. A sign spanned its top that simply read 'Doris'. They stood on a patch of faux grass with hedges on either side. The whole set was lit by a 1960's style streetlight plugged into an outlet behind the hedge. A tip jar sat on a small table at the front with 'Doris Donations' scribbled on the front of it. Tom threw in a few notes to get things started.

Doris posed as Josh shouted over the music. "Okay, come on guys. Work the camera. Come on, give me sexy. Henry, love the camera. Work it, baby."

They hugged and burst into laughter. Josh captured the scene and waved the resulting piece of card in the air until the image appeared. The girls gathered around him and watched the picture develop and then cooed together.

"That's beautiful," said Vicki. She took the picture and handed it to Doris.

Doris tilted her head as she gazed at it. "Look, Henry," she said, "Forever frozen in time."

He stared at it for a moment and then clutched it in his lap as if it was a jewel.

"Thank you, dear," said Doris. "And thank you, Josh, that's really special." She pointed across the table. "Is that your Adam?" she asked Vicki.

Adam was talking to someone and was oblivious to the attention. "Yes, it is," she said. "Why?"

"Would you mind if I had a quick word with him?"

Vicki frowned.

"Don't worry," said Doris, "I promise I won't hurt him."

"Oh, I know, but please don't…"

"Vicki? I've known you for a long time now. I won't be able to know you for too much longer, so let me do this one thing, okay? And I promise I'll be nice."

Vicki bowed her head as Doris walked past her and prodded Adam between the shoulder blades. He spun and listened as she spoke in his ear and then nodded and wandered off into the room with her.

Tom slid his arm around Emma's waist. "What's that all about?"

"I have my suspicions," said Emma. "I suspect Adam is about to the get the adopted mom talk."

The surrounding space grew tighter as people jostled into Josh's small studio to get a Polaroid memory of the evening. Colin waltzed down the stairs at the side of the stage to the sound of A Little Less Conversation and gyrated with a younger couple as Josh captured the moment.

"Come on," said Emma. "Elvis has a point. A little less conversation. This girl wants to dance."

124

The night moved along without a hitch. Smiling faces filled the dance floor as Colin put on the show of a lifetime. All the business cards he'd left at the front of the stage had vanished. Beer and wine flowed and people laughed and told their own Doris stories. Jen appointed herself Josh's unofficial assistant. The donations jar had to be emptied over and over again.

"Ladieth and gentlemen," said Elvis, "we've reached that part of the evening where we're coming to a close. I have to thank you all for being here tonight."

A chorus of boos washed up to him from the dance floor and he staggered playfully backwards.

"I know, I know," he said, waving a hand, "but as thomeone I can't remember once thaid, if I don't leave, how can I come back? Theriously, though, thank you everyone. We came together tonight to honor thith wonderful woman…"

A spotlight lit up Doris, who panicked for a second and then bowed and clapped her hands. She mouthed thank you before the light cut back to the stage.

"… and it's thafe to thay that we did that. You should all do thith again thometime. Next time, though, do it when you need no other reathon than to just get together and have a good time. I have one more thong to thing and then I'm hitting the cathino but, before then, I'd like to make an announthment."

Colin tapped a pedal with his foot and his backing music dropped in volume until it chimed quietly in the background like elevator music. The room seemed to tense as he spread his arm and gestured to the side of the stage. "Ladieth and gentleman, thith man hath thomething important to thay."

The stage curtains fluttered and Adam stepped nervously onto the stage and ambled into the center. Colin backed away until Adam stood alone underneath the mirror ball.

A burst of feedback squealed through the speakers as he stepped up to the microphone and tapped it, then pulled it toward him.

"Hello, everyone," he started. One hand clutched the mic, the other wrung at his side. "Most of you don't know me, and I definitely can't sing so you needn't worry about that."

Tom glanced across to Vicki who sat bolt upright, eyes wide and mouth open. Shock and surprise shot across her face, along with a hint of pride and curiosity.

Adam continued. "Someone gave me a stern talking to tonight, a talk about how fragile life is and how important communication can be."

He nodded and smiled at Doris. Doris blew him a kiss.

"It's easy to wake up every day and just breeze through it. To assume that you'll be able to do the same thing tomorrow and the day after that. You play little attention to what's around you because, well, it's always around you. Why worry, right? It's always there." He paused and scratched his chin. "It's taken tonight to make me realize that, one day, that next day won't come. It'll be too late to do all the things you wanted to do or say the things you wanted to say. You'll curse yourself for not stepping up sooner, when you had the time."

He turned to face Vicki and held her gaze. "There's a girl," he said as his voice cracked, "that I've known for years. She's amazing. Do you know that she still packs me a lunch for work? I'm in my thirties and yet, each day, I have a packed lunch waiting for me in the morning. And this shirt I'm wearing. When I get home tonight, I'll throw it in this wicker basket we've got, and it'll magically reappear in my wardrobe a few days later, clean and ironed. If I have a bad day at work, she's got this weird sense that can tell as soon as I walk through the door, and she'll give me a hug and rub my shoulders in a way that only she can. And I hear songs on the radio that take me to a place and time when we did something together. When I go shopping, I see things I think she'll like. And I know what she likes because I know her. She's the other half of me that makes me this person I am. If she wasn't there, I wouldn't be a complete person."

Tom gripped Emma's hand and moved back toward their table. Vicki still sat there, dabbing at her eyes with a napkin.

Adam walked across the front of the stage until he stood in the corner by Josh's studio, as close as he could get to the table. Then he walked down the stairs, stood under the trellis, and held out his hand. Vicki got out of her chair and walked up to him.

"For years I've just been drifting with you. I thought you were happy with the way we were, but a little bird," he said, and tilted his head toward Doris, "has set me straight."

He reached into his pocket and pulled out a shiny circle of metal. "Please bear with me, because I wasn't expecting to do this tonight, so for the time being and to make this biggest of gestures, I've had to improvise."

Adam searched the room for someone, then shrugged his shoulders. "I'd like to thank Rob for helping me out with such a quality piece at short notice, but he and Abby seem to have vanished."

He dropped to his knee as Vicki covered her mouth and gasped. "Victoria Brookes, will you take this piston ring from a Chevy 2004 SSR and make me the happiest man in the room by agreeing to become my wife?"

Vicki held out her shaking hand as tears streamed down her face and cried "Yes!"

Adam beamed and slipped the ring over her finger. She closed her fist around it to stop it from falling off.

"Yes, of course Adam Wilkes. And about frigging time."

Chapter Sixteen

Tom checked in with Emma as soon as he woke the next morning.

All the party guests seemed to get home in one piece, courtesy of the fleet of taxis provided by Rob's mechanic friends. Shane dropped Henry at Doris's place, made sure they were okay, and then locked the door behind him as he left. No one mentioned tic-tacs.

Adam and Vicki left in a whirlwind of romance. Vicki promised to keep the Chevy piston ring in a safe place forever, just as long as he bought her a proper ring.

Tom watched Emma climb into a cab and then drove himself home. They kissed and arranged to meet the following night.

Rob and Abby never reappeared. Tom texted him a brief 'are you okay' message from home and got a smiley face in return.

Colin dismantled his stage set-up and held an impromptu autograph session, where he joked and signed numerous napkins 'With thankth…Elivith'.

The work day moved along smoothly and, as the evening approached, familiar butterflies played games and danced inside Tom's stomach.

This would be their fourth date and he was entering uncharted waters. Their earlier dates had been spontaneous, so he had no fear of her not turning up. This time she might realize what she was getting herself into, or be fraught with stronger nerves that his, and bail on him.

As the day progressed his nerves wound tighter, until he forced himself into a cool shower before putting on a casual suit.

****

The forecast had called for rain but the evening was warm and heavy, with the chirp of cicadas fighting against the rumble of traffic. The tree-lined streets seemed to teem with them, rubbing their legs together as if the song the friction created would get them somewhere. They were like the call girls on West Garfield Park, but luckier. And warmer.

Tom stood in the restaurant entrance with his jacket draped across his arm. Something about the sound relaxed him but, holding his jacket this way, he could have been Russo or Scissors. Like he concealed a sawn-off shotgun beneath it before walking into a bank. He slung it over a shoulder and studied the parking lot. She was late. His watch read 7:35. They'd agreed on 7:30.

Hadn't they?

He dug out his phone and scrolled through days' worth of communication. The text message was almost at the bottom.

'7:30? Manganelli's?' he'd asked.

'Sure, I look forward to it.'

She was late. If she was coming at all.

Seeds of doubt blossomed and bloomed. This was their fourth date, but the first time that doubt had reared its ugly head.

Perhaps he'd been too forward, texted too often. Why had he put four kisses at the end of his last text? He checked the message thread again. Sure enough, he'd sent twice as many messages to her as she had to him, and she ended her texts with a solitary 'x'. It was obvious. He'd scared her off.

Right now, she'd be sitting on a sofa telling her friends about this stalker that had seemed okay at first. Now, he was a full-on lunatic who probably collected women's parts and kept them in a freezer in his basement.

Tom breathed into his hands and sniffed at the collected air. He knew his teeth were clean; his gums were tender from the scrubbing and the burn of the mouthwash. Another nervous glance at his watch. 7:42.

She'd stood him up. A quick text would have been nice.

Sorry, I have to cancel. A friend had an emergency. Sorry, would love to have met you again but my dog swallowed his own balls. Anything, just a sign to save him standing here like a failure while other couples paraded past him like runway models as they took their reserved tables. He was about to sit on the leather bench that lined the back wall when a car turned into the parking lot. Suddenly, all of his doubts disappeared. He checked his hair in the window and re-tucked his shirt.

The car slid between two other vehicles out of sight. The dancing butterflies in Tom's stomach took flight, and he rocked from one foot to the other, waiting for her head to appear above the top of the parked cars. A long minute passed before he saw movement, then a middle-aged couple appeared. First the passenger and then the driver emerged from between the cars, clasped their hands together and strolled toward the entrance.

Tom glanced at his watch yet again. 7:50. At twenty-minutes late, she wasn't coming. The smell of grilled steak drifted through the air followed by the laughter of happy couples. Tonight would now become 'comfort night'. Pizza and a few beers in front of the TV with Oswald.

He looped his finger into the collar of his jacket as a wash of light swept across the window. A sedan swung around the corner and nosed into a parking space beneath the sodium light that lit the entrance. Then, through the window, he saw her.

He watched as she pulled down the sun visor and checked her lipstick in the dim light. She did that thing girls do where they ruffle their hair and pat it down until it looks exactly the same. Then she pushed her upper lip higher and checked her teeth and did the same breath test into the palms of her hands he'd done moments earlier.

All of his doubts disappeared. Emma was cute and seemed to be really nice. Not the type of person to stand up a date without notice. Most important of all, she was here.

Tom heaved a sigh of relief and pushed open the heavy entrance door as she beeped the alarm on her car and locked the doors. As she turned and saw him she paused for a moment, then collected herself and strode toward him. She looked gorgeous, like a classy business woman.

"Hi! Sorry I'm late. The traffic on Clark Street's an absolute bitch and I couldn't get my damned Bluetooth to pair so I could call you." She paused and then laughed, a genuine sound that came from deep within her. It sang a nicer song than the cicadas. "I am so sorry. That wasn't exactly lady like was it?"

He placed his hand at the curve of her back as she passed him and stepped inside the restaurant. It was a discreet touch, but his senses screamed contact and he couldn't stop himself from smiling.

"It was honest. And don't worry, I haven't been here too long myself," he lied. "It seems busy out there tonight. Our tables ready, though, so you can relax and have a glass of something to unwind. Can I take your coat?"

Emma frowned, as if the practice had died in the Stone Age and she was surprised he was resurrecting it. She slid her arms out of the sleeves and offered it to him. "Thank you. You're quite the gentleman."

"Ah, wait until you get to know me," he said, and instantly regretted it and looked for a cloakroom to hide his embarrassment. There wasn't one. "Hang on, and I'll tell them we're here."

When he returned, a young girl led them through an organized maze to their table. Tom pulled out a seat for Emma to take and draped her coat over the back of it. She thanked him as she slid her legs under the table and took the seat. Her pale skirt rose to expose her knees and a hint of thigh. Tom's pulse beat in his ears as he hung his jacket over the opposite chair.

"This place is lovely," said Emma as she shuffled her seat closer. "Have you been here before?"

"No, a friend recommended it. Said the food was some of the best around here, and the atmosphere was even better."

She glanced around. A dozen or so tables were dotted around a small room in no particular order. Tall windows lined the wood-paneled wall on one side with gold colored curtains tied against their sides like angels' wings. An older man in a black tuxedo sat at a grand piano in one corner playing an old Gershwin tune. The soft jazz was loud enough to hear without affecting any conversation.

A mirrored bar ran down the other wall, the glass reflecting a dizzying selection of drinks. Behind it, a young man shook a cocktail mixer before deftly pouring the contents into a glass.

Tom nodded. "This really is nice. I'll thank him tomorrow."

A waiter materialized out of nowhere. "Good evening. My name is James and I'll be taking care of you tonight. Can I start you out with some drinks?"

Tom looked at Emma, who picked up the drinks menu and slid her finger down the list.

"All the names are written in a foreign language," she said. "Could I just get a glass of sweet white wine, please? Fizzy."

"Make it a bottle," said Tom. "I'll join you."

The waiter wandered off before Tom continued. "So, how was your day?"

"Busy, as always. That's a good thing, though, since we're trying to build up our business. How's your Viagra coming along?"

An older couple on the next table glanced across. The man gave Tom an understanding nod. Tom shook his head quickly as Emma laughed. "Sorry," she said and spoke a little louder. "How's your ad campaign coming along?"

"It's getting there. We've presented it to the Powers That Be. Now we're waiting for word to come down that we can move forward with it."

He handed her the food menu as their waiter placed a wine cooler on the table and poured two glasses.

"Thank you," said Emma. She lay her arms onto the table and leaned in. "So, Tom Lewis, this is our fourth date, not counting the fund raiser, and we still haven't asked the obvious question."

"Don't you think it's a little early for that?" said Tom. "Not that I'd complain."

"Not that question," she said with a disapproving glare. "The first couple of times we met, we were at funerals. I don't believe in coincidences and I could tell you didn't know either of those people, so can I ask you why were there? Not that I'm complaining either, I've had a great time since, and it's been a long time since I had a great time."

Tom took a deep breath and let it out slowly. "It's not exactly romantic dinner conversation material, but I suppose I should tell you if we're going to keep seeing each other."

He leaned in even closer and spoke softly. "A good friend of mine had me try to explain and I think he understood me, so I'll try the same thing here. Something in me has changed a little since I met you. Before that, the only way I can describe the way I was is to say that I was emotionally stunted. That sounds dramatic, I know, but I struggle to feel anything. I'm not sure you'll understand, but I'll try to explain."

"I understand more than you might realize," said Emma. "Please, go on."

"Okay. Well, I don't remember too much about my early childhood, but I do remember us being a close family. That all changed when I was eight. Years later, the police told me everything I'm about to tell you, but I still had to track down the details myself."

"Okay, now I'm intrigued."

"We were coming back from the cinema. The roads were wet and there was a mist in the air, and Dad lost control of the car. They said he wasn't speeding, it was down to road conditions, but he took a curve in the road and the car skidded off and ran down an incline. We smashed head on into a tree."

Emma put her hand to her mouth. "Oh my God, Tom. I'm so sorry."

"Dad wasn't wearing a seat belt. The impact sent him right through the windshield. They reckon he was dead before he hit the ground. Mom was crumpled in the passenger foot well. Somehow, she didn't break the screen. It broke her neck."

"How did you get out of there alive?"

Tom took a mouthful of wine. "Apparently, I was sitting in the middle of the rear seat, and I shot forward and flew right through the hole that Dad's body had made. They found me on the other side of the tree, bumped and bruised but otherwise okay. You want to know the weird thing?"

"Okay?"

"I've been out to the crash site. The tree is still there. If you drive half a mile in either direction, there's nothing but open land. That's the only tree in a one mile stretch of road. And Dad found it."

Emma reached across the table and took his hand. "I don't know what to say. Honestly, I have no words."

Tom shrugged. "There's nothing you can say that hasn't been said before. So anyway, I didn't know at the time but, when I look back, that day changed me. I won't lie, I've dated before, but I'm difficult to be with. Or maybe complicated. And I've been called all kinds of things, most of them prefixed with 'cold' or 'stone hearted'. I'm really not. It's inside me, I can feel it, but I can't let it out. That's why I go to funerals, hoping that the grief and bad feelings there will spur something inside me and help me get everything out."

"You might not believe me," said Emma as she squeezed his hand, "but I do understand."

He continued. "Just give me a chance okay? You're the first girl I've met in a long time that I can stand to be around and smile."

"Are you folks ready to order?" said the waiter as he materialized at the side of the table. Tom jumped as Emma picked up a menu.

"Sorry," she said. "Could we have a few more minutes?"

"Of course. I'll be right back."

The waiter wandered off as Emma leaned forward again. "I'm not going anywhere. Let's order food and I'll tell you my story."

Twenty minutes later, two well-presented plates appeared. They ate and made small talk, in between quiet moments of relaxing and listening to the pianist. Tom discussed the ad campaign and Emma dished the dirt on clients that Tom would never meet. The waiter took away their empty plates and left them with the dessert menu.

Emma peered over the top of hers. "Your friend wasn't wrong about the food. That was delicious. Did you leave room for dessert?"

Tom smiled and picked up the card. "I always leave room for dessert. It's my reward for eating all my greens." He glanced down the card and smiled wider. "Hey, they have salted caramel ganache."

"Well it made your day," she smiled. "Does it bring back a memory or something? And what exactly is ganache?"

"It does." He laid the card on the table. "I always wondered what it was, too. Ganache. It sounds so French. If it's French, it must be classy and rich tasting, right?"

Emma tilted her head to one side and rested it against her hand. "So what classy establishment prompted this interest? Were you in Paris? Or Marseilles? I've always wanted to go there to watch their soccer team."

"Nothing so extravagant. A while back I flew from America to England and got it on one of those plastic trays that barely fits in front of you. I ate spaghetti and meatballs, followed by ganache. I'm sure it's much classier in a French restaurant than out of a plastic cup. There's not much romance or class sitting in a seat with minimal leg room and strangers either side of you."

She laughed and sipped her wine. "You muppet. I thought you had an exciting story to tell."

"No," he continued, "but at least I got off the plane able to say I knew what ganache was."

"Well, come on," she said, "what is it? I'm intrigued now. It sounds like an extravagant cheesecake or something."

"To be honest with you, it tastes like a Rollo."

"What, the round chocolate things?"

"Yeah, like a Rollo but in a plastic cup."

"So why do they call it ganache? And why wouldn't you just buy a pack of Rollos?"

Tom picked up the menu and scanned the listing. "So they can charge ten bucks for it, why else?"

"Oh," she said with a raise of her eyebrows. "That makes sense. Well, in that case, I'll try the ganache, please."

The dessert arrived on a plate five times too big for it. It sat lost, like a small island in a huge ocean, with a drizzle of melted chocolate thrown across it for effect.

"So," said Tom. "You said that you'd mention why I keep seeing you at funerals and tell me your story. Is yours anywhere near as bad as mine?"

Emma paused with a fork full of dessert sitting an inch away from her open mouth and then laid the fork back on her plate.

"Okay. This goes back about two years," she started. "First off, my ex was a control freak. You have no idea how liberating it was for me to put on this skirt and blouse tonight. It was actually my choice."

"You look beautiful," said Tom. "I'm sorry, I should have said something earlier. Obviously, I'm out of practice."

She smiled. "Thank you, but you're okay. It used to be that my clothes would be laid out on the bed ready for me when I stepped out of the shower. I'm sure he thought he was doing me a favor, and it was nice at first. That someone would be so interested in me, enough to go to that effort? Then it got to be oppressive. It was like I was his full-sized Barbie and, if I moved to select something else, he'd get all moody. It wasn't worth the trouble so, after a while, I just went along with it."

Tom shook his head and opened his mouth to speak as she continued.

"Oh, trust me, I got over that eventually. It took a while, and a lot of arguments, but no one will ever dictate to me again. I'm my own person. I don't need anyone to complete me or anything like that."

Tom sat back in his seat, an unconscious retreat. He could tell she saw it and kicked himself.

"Oh, no," she said, "don't think I'm telling you to back off, but you should know that I'm strong-willed and very independent."

He smiled again but stayed in his seat.

Emma took a deep breath as if she was about to unburden herself. "So anyway, months later, I had a full day of appointments at the salon. One after another, from nine in the morning until six in the evening. It was great because we were planning a vacation and the money would have been handy. But at around lunch time, it snowed."

Right on cue, the promised rain materialized outside and spattered and ran down the long windows. Emma glanced at it and turned back to him.

"That's freaky. Anyway, all of my afternoon clients called to cancel so, suddenly, I had the whole afternoon free. Stuart, my ex, was working until five so I thought I'd cook us a nice meal as a surprise. I called into the grocery, picked up a few things and headed home. When I got onto our road, I was sure I recognized my folks' car parked about half a block away. I thought nothing of it and went into the house and unpacked the shopping. That's when I heard it."

Tom leaned forward again, intrigued. An old Sinatra standard twinkled through the air courtesy of the pianist as the rain hammered against the wall of glass.

"Heard what?" he said.

Emma blinked quickly. "Grunting and moaning, coming from upstairs. I stood there for a while and listened. Then I heard talking and, of course, I recognized the voices. Both of them, they were laughing and joking. In my house. I crept up the stairs and threw open the bedroom door."

"And?" said Tom.

"It was Stuart. In our bed. With my mom."

She sat there, her face like stone, as Tom flushed and reached across the table. He took her hands and cupped them in his.

"Shit, Emma, that's awful. What the hell did you do?"

"Threw stuff," she said. Her face was impassive, and she stared right through him. "They both jumped out of bed. Naked. Stuart was still excited, but I doubt it was at seeing me. Mom just looked at me with her mouth open. All I could think was that Stuart had probably been in there."

Tom shook his head as words failed him.

"I screamed at them both to get out. By the time he got dressed and reached the front door I was already throwing his shit through the window into the snow."

"You did…"

"Yes, I opened the window first. It was still my house, and they weren't worth wrecking it for."

"So then what happened?"

"Nothing. Literally, nothing. I took a shower and slept on the sofa, and I haven't seen or spoken to either of them since. It ruined my Dad. And since then, I've felt nothing. Just like you. God knows, I'd love to cry. I'd love to scream and scratch things and make myself feel something, anything. That's why I go to wakes and funerals. All I want is to cry. But I can't. It's like dragging a stone around."

Tom squeezed her hands again. "Emma, I don't know what to say. At least in my instance the whole thing was an accident. There's no one to blame, I just don't know how to express it. But you…"

"Oh, don't feel sorry for me," she said. Her voice took on a harder edge. "It showed who they both were. Being betrayed by not one, but two people you should be able to trust is a killer. My Dad went to war, you know? He did and saw things that no one should, and he came back almost the same man. Mom didn't fire a single shot, but in one moment she destroyed him. But at least I'm still here. And I can promise you it'll never happen again."

"And this was two years ago."

"Yes."

"And you've never cried."

"No."

Tom sat there for a minute. "So, if you don't mind me asking, how many dates have you had since?"

When she looked up at him, her eyes shone like glass and looked as hard. "First dates? A few. Fourth dates? One. This one."

"Damn, I've never met your ex but I hate him already."

She tensed and frowned. "Hate is a very strong word, Tom. Why would you hate someone you haven't met?"

He leaned forward. The flicker of the candles danced in her eyes as he gazed at her. This was his first fourth date too, and he wanted a fifth. And a sixth. Suddenly, he wanted to share this woman's pain and ease it.

"Because he broke you. And he broke you so much that, now, you won't let anyone fix you. I see an amazing woman, Emma. You should let someone in. You deserve to be happy."

In an instant the atmosphere changed, as if all the air was sucked out of the room. Emma leaned far back into her chair and crumpled up her napkin. A cloud seemed to cross her face as her brow furrowed. The rain drove even heavier into the windows.

"So you think I'm broken?" She spoke low and steady.

Tom could barely make out her words above the sound of the weather. Her brows shaded the anger in her eyes. Before he could answer, she continued, her voice growing louder until she was almost shouting. "And if I was, what gives you the right to assume I need fixing? Maybe I don't want to be fixed. What? Do you have me on some kind of fucking couch or something?"

She reached for her purse and slammed a handful of money on the table. Tom held up his hands. "Look, I'm sorry. I never meant to…"

"Meant to what? Analyze me? Are you my hero, come down from some special place to fix me? Fuck you, Tom. I don't need you. Or anyone else. I can take perfectly good care of myself. And you can shove your stupid ganache where the sun doesn't shine."

The chair legs screeched against the floor as she forced it backwards away from the table. Other diners turned as she balled up her napkin and threw it. It unfolded in mid-flight and covered his face. By the time he removed it she'd grabbed her coat and was storming out. A bustle of whispers erupted around him as he summoned the waiter.

"Er, can I get the check please?"

Chapter Seventeen

It took two weeks for the girls to notice a difference as Emma buried herself in her work. The moment came as a flower delivery walked through the salon's door.

"Delivery for Emma Cairnes?" said the fresh-faced youth.

Emma's head snapped up from her work as she watched him walk up to the counter. "Would you excuse me for a second, Mrs. Jacobs?" she said with a grim smile. "I need to take care of this."

The delivery man stopped by the desk as she approached. "You can take them back," she said. "I don't want them."

He looked confused, as if this was the first time someone turned away a delivery. "Ah, I'm sorry, but I can't leave without a signature."

Emma huffed, picked up a pen and signed his delivery note. He nodded his thanks and hurried back through the door like a scolded child.

"Those are beautiful," said Mrs. Jacobs as Emma returned to her chair.

Emma reached inside the plastic wrapping, wrenched off the attached note and placed the bouquet on her client's knee.

"You like them? They're all yours. Thank you for your custom, Mrs. Jacobs." She dropped the note into a trash can full of hair and continued her work.

"Well... thank you," said Mrs. Jacobs, "but are you sure they're not for you? You didn't even read the note."

"Oh, they're for me. And I know who sent them. I can imagine what the note says, too, and I have no interest. Why do men send flowers to say they're sorry? Even on a good day, if someone sends flowers, don't you wonder what it is they're apologizing for that you're not aware of yet? No, you should take them home and get some enjoyment from them."

Vicki and Jen closed in, one on either side. "Okay," said Jen. "Is all not rosy in the green garden of Emma and Tom?"

Emma coughed out a dry and cynical laugh. "That garden is covered in weed killer," she said, "and blooms are dying by the second. It turns out he's just like all the others."

"Oh, oh. So how tall is this new wall you've built? And is it brick or some kind of reinforced concrete? What did he do, offer to make you really happy?"

"Jen? I don't appreciate your sarcasm," said Emma, "but for the record, this wall is unassailable. I'm done with men. Why do they always think they can…"

Her voice tapered off into an uncomfortable silence.

"But you seemed so happy at the fund raiser," said Vicki. "What happened?"

"I'd rather not talk about it."

"It was the usual, wasn't it?" said Jen. "The usual thing happened and now you've resigned yourself to be a lonely old spinster again."

"Really?" said Emma. "And old?"

"Yes, and you'll get a dozen cats and stay home and knit and become a crazy cat lady. Is that what you want? You want to be crazy cat lady? Do you own a rocking chair? Because you'll need one of those to complete the effect."

"You're really not helping," said Emma. "Why can't people just take you for who you are? If they could, I'm sure they'd Photoshop out all the bits they didn't like. Why do they think you have to become a project or something? It's as if it's the manly thing to do; step up and mold you into who they want you to be."

"So he didn't like who you are?" asked Jen.

"Well, no," Emma said with a pause, "it wasn't like that."

"So he didn't like what you did?"

"No, we always had a great time. I didn't do much more than be me."

"Did he not like what you were wearing? Did you or he say something unforgivable? Oh no," said Jen as she paused for effect. "Did he discover your love of Dr. Hook?"

"Hey," said Emma, "lots of people like Dr. Hook. And no, it was none of that. He struck a nerve, okay? We got talking about the past and some things came out and I didn't like the reaction I got."

Vicki walked around the back of the chairs and draped an arm around Emma's shoulder. "Did it ever occur to you he might be taking more than an average interest in you because he likes you? I mean, really likes you? And he wasn't sure how to react because he's never met anyone like you before, so you might have misread him? The poor guy must feel like he's walking through a minefield. In flip flops. In the dark. Drunk."

Emma shook her head and shrugged off Vicki's arm. "No. I know what I heard. He's a lovely guy, he really is. But there's always this thing that happens, this hardening."

Jen's eyebrows shot up.

"Not that kind of hardening, you pervert. Me. My hardening. Emotionally. You know me well enough by now. I daren't take that chance because I'll be really happy and let someone in. All of my defenses will be down... and it'll happen again and I'll be devastated."

Mrs. Jacobs turned her head with intrigue written across her face. "What will happen? And sorry, it's none of my business, but I'm here now so I'm somewhat invested."

"Betrayal, Mrs. Jacobs. The big letdown. It comes in many forms; betrayal of trust, a sly insult that starts the demeaning process, the attempt to change you into something they want, the cheating. Anything. They're all the same."

Mrs. Jacobs turned her chair to face Emma. "Let me tell you something. Not all men are born equal." She shuffled back in the seat until she seemed to have grown a few inches. "When you're young, it's easy to paint them all the same way. I'm almost sixty and I'm on my third marriage, so I speak from experience. I got put through the wringer a few times and had my share of upsets. But you should listen to your gut. Your heart is soft, regardless of what anyone might say or what you might think. It's just the way it is. The heart wants to be happy at all costs and can be an idiot at times and ignore all the signs. But the gut? The gut learns and you'll build up experience in there. Listen to your gut. The day your heart and gut are anywhere near the same place, you might as well go for it. If you don't, you'll wake up one day and open a birthday card from no one special that says Happy 60th on it, and you'll wonder where the years went. And believe me; you think they go by fast now? You have no idea."

"Well shit, Mrs. Jacobs," said Emma. "Should I thank you for your advice or run out into the street and throw myself under the first bus I see?"

****

"It's like navigating a maze," said Tom.

"Okay. Of course it is. I can see that." Rob crumpled his empty beer can and tossed it into the recycling basket. "What is? What the hell are you talking about?"

"Getting to know Emma. It's like trying to navigate a maze."

"Look, you've had your first falling out. Have you got any idea how many times Abby slammed my car door after an argument? And it was a '71 Ford Pinto. It's amazing the piece of crap didn't shatter under the impact. Give her a week. She'll be in touch and you'll be fine."

"It's been two weeks, Rob."

"Oh," said Rob. "Shit. Sorry."

"I really put my foot in it. And I didn't mean to, I mean... I was trying to be caring, because that's how I felt. I wanted to be there for her."

"Be where?"

"I can't say. It's kind of personal."

"Okay. Well, that helps. So, the maze thing? What's that about?"

"You know my history with women, and you needn't smirk. It's like being in a maze and I think I've got it all worked out. I've turned corner after corner and gone down avenues I haven't dared go down before. And then, suddenly, I turn a corner and it's a dead end. A solid wall. And that's it and I come to an abrupt stop. There's no way forward and I've forgotten how to get back. So I'm stuck in limbo."

"That group should be meeting again tonight, if you want to..."

Tom smacked his hands against his thighs. "Rob, I'm being serious. I really like her and I don't know what to do. I've sent her a few texts, but she's ignored every one of them. I've even sent flowers but I've heard nothing."

"Have you tried calling her?" said Rob. "Remember that? The long lost art of conversation? People used to talk to each other. With real words. Weird and scary, isn't it?"

Tom gave him a look that could turn water to ice. "And say what? Hi Emma, it's Tom. Sorry I'm such a dick, I can't help myself?"

"Chances are, she's already worked that out. And I thought you said you cared? How does that make you a dick? She's nice, Tom, and gorgeous, too. She seems to be good for you, so if you don't work this out then, yes, you're a dick. But still, I'm just saying. Texting is lethal. There's no tone of voice. Almost everything you write can be taken at least two ways. Dial her number and call her. Speak and say real words and tell her what you meant. If you care and you're genuine, it'll come through in your voice. And then, it's up to her. But if you don't try, you'll never know. She's got to be worth a phone call?"

"Of course she is," said Tom. He picked up his phone for the hundredth time that day, illuminated the screen, and checked for missed calls or messages. The screen displayed his usual icons. He tossed it back onto the table.

"That doesn't look much like making a call," said Rob.

"Enough about me. You still haven't explained what happened at the fund raiser. Where did you and Abby disappear to? Colin started playing and I remember seeing you both on the dance floor laughing, and then you vanished. Did you get bored?"

Rob smiled a beaming grin that stretched from ear to ear. "Far from it. Where did we go?" he asked himself. He thrummed his fingers against his knee and tilted his head in mock concentration. "Well, we went to the ladies' room because their stalls are bigger. We went outside behind the kitchen. Later we went into some trees outside..."

"Rob?"

"Yes, Tom?"

"Do I want to know what you were doing?"

"No, you don't, although if you're not sure by now I have a book you can borrow that explains everything. Especially given your current situation."

"Hilarious," said Tom. "So, any news?"

"Other than I'm tired? No, not yet. But I have to tell you, we were both so relaxed on that night that, if nothing else, it helped us rediscover ourselves. I'm not sure how to explain it. It's like we've been trying for so long to do it to have a baby, we'd forgotten how to do it just for ourselves. Does that make sense?"

Tom nodded. "Yes, I think so. I'm sure it'll work out for you. It would be nice to have something positive come from that night given the reasons it happened in the first place. And you did it in the ladies' room?"

Rob smiled again.

"Animal." Tom stood, picked up his phone and walked toward the kitchen. "Okay," he said. "I'm doing it. I'm making that call."

****

Emma turned into her street and allowed the car to coast to a stop beside the curb. The advice from Mrs. Jacobs still rang in her head. 'If you don't go for it, you'll wake up one day and open a birthday card from no one special that says Happy 60th on it, and you'll wonder where the years went'.

She still had a few years to go until the big six-oh, but she couldn't help but wonder what the future held. The only person in her life that had seemed to find true happiness was Doris. Now, Doris was riddled with cancer. Was that karma playing its last hand? Making her pay for the good times? Making her give something back for the times she'd lain awake at night smiling while Bill faced the wall, knowing full well that, tomorrow, he'd be facing her?

From her father down to her friends, she doubted anyone was living with true happiness. So why should she be any different? Did it even exist? What was true happiness anyway? A sun-soaked island, with endless beaches and romantic sunsets? With a man that would cater to your every need? Who found that?

But what if, maybe, it was something as simple as opening a card from someone special. Or leaving work and going home to someone. Someone who had the oven warm, with nice smells filling the house. Who took you to the bedroom and massaged away the challenges of the day while hot water splashed into a tub full of bubbles. Who placed a glass of cold wine on the tub and washed your back, and then toweled you down and allowed you to just be.

To just be.

It was a dream, surely. Tom seemed to be the kind of person that could offer that. He hadn't said the words, but his demeanor and attitude suggested he would be like that. Still, if he didn't understand her, what was the point?

She grabbed her purse and her phone, climbed out of the car and locked the doors. As she walked to her door, the phone buzzed and vibrated again. She glanced at the screen.

Tom. He was calling this time, not texting.

Temper and stubbornness had stopped her from replying to his earlier messages. She doubted she could respond in a manner that wouldn't seem aggressive anyway even though, deep down, she was certain he was no threat. He was trying to push into the center of her, the part of her that no one would ever hurt again. She couldn't allow it. It was too vulnerable. The pain and humiliation still stabbed at her from the last time and she'd never feel that way again.

The phone's screen danced to a jolly tune and pretty colors flashed across it.

Swipe left to answer the call, to the pleasant green phone that screamed 'Go', or swipe right to the angry-looking red phone that said 'No way in Hell'.

She swiped right.

Chapter Eighteen

Three weeks after Tom's rejected phone call, Emma overheard the one she'd been dreading. Vicki put the call on speakerphone and they all listened. Henry's voice was heavy, as if he was speaking through a thick fog.

"She's gone," he said. "They had her sedated, and I held her hand while she faded away. She's in a better place now."

Emma held Vicki as she sobbed and thought back to their chat in the salon with Mrs. Jacobs. Just like that, a bright light had snuffed out. Here one day, gone the next. Seventy-nine years of experiences, of knowledge and life. Seventy-nine years. Gone.

She glanced at Vicki's chair, the chair that Doris had sat in two weeks ago, laughing and joking but looking drawn and tired. The feelings built, the pressure that wanted to break free. She held it tight inside her and hugged Vicki even closer.

The proceeds from the fund raiser made a sizeable dent in the cost of Doris's funeral. Emma posted the check to the home, and the girls made sure that arrangements were as close to what Doris wished as they could get them.

On the day, Jen drove to the funeral home. The sky looked like gray cotton, heavy with rain, and looked as if it wanted to unleash a torrent. It matched Emma's mood, the pain in her pushing at every pore to escape and leave her body. Looking through the pictures they'd used for the notice board, along with a night of sad songs and wine, had failed to breach the wall that held it back. A few times, she'd picked up her phone to text Tom, but always placed it back on the table. That door had closed.

The radio worked hard to break the silence.

Finally, Vicki spoke. "Come on girls, she would have wanted us to celebrate her life. We have to cheer up. If we get there like this, we'll have people jumping through the windows. Some of those folks are so old they won't make it up to the sill. The place will be littered with broken bodies."

"You're right, Vic. Okay, think of good Doris memories," said Emma from the back seat. "I'll start. Remember that time she told us about that baptism at their church?"

Jen glanced over her shoulder. "I don't think I heard that one. Was I working that day?"

"I'm not sure, maybe. Anyway, she said they were at church, I think it was in the sixties, and this new family came in with a teenage boy. They wanted to get him baptized right away and asked if their preacher would do it. He said he would after the service. So they make it through the service and the preacher invites the family up to the altar. They all gather around the font while the preacher says a few words, and he leans the boy forward and splashes water on his head."

Sun tried to peek through the clouds and the sky glowed a dim yellow.

"Oh my God," said Vickie, "I remember it now."

"Carry on," said Jen, "I definitely missed this."

"Okay, so the preacher's splashing water and, just as he says 'I baptize you in the name of', the boy's mother reaches over and dunks her son's head into the font. Doris said they heard it hit the bottom. It made a proper 'thud'. She holds it there and screams 'out with you demons. Let them out, baby, you can't hold them. Be gone demons, out'."

Emma laughed. It felt so good to let something out.

"She held his head under until he passed out. They had to carry him to the car and watch over him until he recovered."

"Oh my God," said Jen, "the poor kid. Was he okay?"

"Yeah, he was fine. Had a big bump on his head, though. And I'm sure the demons left him."

"Okay, my turn," said Vicki. "Remember that time she and her husband took their first foreign holiday? She said they'd never been on a plane before and they were fifty something. They got to the check-in desk to find their case was over the weight limit, but they'd scrimped and saved to make the flight and had no extra money. So her husband took out every item of clothing that fit him and put them on. He took ages to get through security because all the belts he had on his trousers kept setting the alarm off. Once they boarded the plane, they had to turn all the air conditioners on him because he thought he'd pass out!"

"Ha ha, I bet he looked like the Michelin man," said Jen, "and walked like a Weeble. Remember them?" The car fell silent again. "I don't have a Doris story, but it sounds like she lived a good life, doesn't it? I will really miss her."

Vicki dabbed at the beginnings of a tear. "Me, too. I dyed her hair that crazy blue color for years. Oh God," she laughed, "what are we going to do with all of that blue dye? No one else uses it and we bought a load to get a discount."

"We could paint a wall in the salon with it," said Emma. "A Doris Memorial Wall."

The entrance to the funeral home appeared in the distance. She pointed through the window. "It's down here Vic, on the right."

Vicki steered the car into the parking lot and pulled up outside the entrance next to a catering truck. There were still twenty minutes to the official start time but there were already a dozen cars dotted about.

Emma led the way to the viewing room. She could get there with her eyes closed. The girls followed behind, walking with a quiet reverence. They turned past a large picture of Doris and headed for the kitchen. No one glanced to the left where the shell that had held the lady with the blue hair lay displayed in a half open casket. A few people milled around.

Emma's chest tightened as the familiar feelings rose in her again, and she made the kitchen door her focal point until she reached it. It swung open as a caterer exited from the other side. The edge of the door grazed a pile of empty aluminum trays he balanced on one arm, but he staggered backwards and juggled them with practiced precision.

"Shit, I'm so sorry," she said. "Oh God, please excuse my potty mouth. This isn't place for that kind of language."

"No shit, Sherlock," said the man with a smile, "or for using the Lord's name in vain."

He was around Emma's age, and the tight shirt and dress pants he wore accentuated a toned-looking body. She blushed as he used a leg to hold open the door for her. "Whoops," he said, "I'm sorry too, but at least we can call it quits in the bad language department."

Jen leaned forward and nudged her in the back. "Well, go on," she whispered. "What are you waiting for? He's gorgeous, and it's obvious he likes you."

"Well," she stuttered to the caterer, "I'm still sorry. And I'm sorry that I caused you to have to be sorry, too. Anyway. I'm sorry. Seriously. Sorry."

She blundered past him as her face burned and she almost ran to the far side of the room.

Vicki caught up with her. "Are you okay? That was like watching Abbot and Costello do their who's on first base sketch."

"I'm not ready," said Emma. "I'm just not ready. I thought about Tom all night but I still couldn't pluck up the courage to text him."

"Everything happens for a reason, Em. If he had any interest he'd have texted you, right? Or better still, he would have called. And surely he'd know how upset you'd be about Doris."

"I don't think he knows anything's happened. And I was so abrupt with him the last time we met. I'm sure I've scared him to death. And he called. I rejected it."

"He's a big boy. I'm sure he can handle himself and anyway, can you imagine dating a caterer? You'd never have to cook again. If he can iron and use a vacuum cleaner, he's a keeper. We should fix him up with Jen."

"Er, I'm right here," said Jen from behind them, "and I'm doing fine, thanks. And anyway, I wasn't the one having wobbly knees moment."

Emma picked up a huge plate of sandwiches and placed them on a side table. "Come on girls, let's get this food set up and get out there. I'm looking forward to meeting some of Doris's friends."

Fifteen minutes later, the kitchen held enough food to feed the five thousand. A babble of murmurs bled through the door from the viewing room.

"It's like when you go to the cinema," said Vicki, "and everyone is whispering before the movie starts. We might have a full room."

Emma tied back her long hair and wiped down her blouse as her stomach fluttered with nerves. This was unlike any of the funerals she'd visited before. She picked at her nails. "I'm actually nervous. And emotional. And I'm not sure I like it."

Vicki wrapped an arm around her shoulder. "Em, it's a funeral. You're not supposed to like it."

"Yes, but..." she started, and then stopped. The earlier visits here were no one's business, regardless of their suspicions. She wasn't here for the regular reason. Over the years, Doris had become more like the salon's mother, not another client. With her infectious smile and contagious laughter, she'd brightened up many a miserable day and her advice, however blunt, always came across with genuine affection. "But it's Doris," she continued. "I really did love her."

Vicki squeezed her shoulder and shepherded her toward the door. "We all did Em. Let's pay our respects."

They wound their way through a maze of living bodies. The average age of the room appeared to be around a hundred, with more wigs and false teeth than a fancy dress store. Henry had full control of his wheelchair and was weaving it in and out between furniture and people. He waved and forced a grim smile.

Doris must have mentioned the salon to everyone, and it took almost twenty minutes for the girls to reach the casket. The conversation was pleasant and the commiserations sincere. Doris may not have had any family, but she'd had a lot of very nice friends.

Streams of tears already flowed down Vicki's cheeks as the girls held each other and filed in front of the oak box.

"I can't do it," said Emma.

Vicki clung to her and held her tight. "It's okay, Em. We all feel the same."

"I can't look at her. She won't be smiling. She won't tell me about how she made her husband do the chores before she'd sleep with him. She won't ask me why there isn't a ring on my finger. And she won't be smiling, Vic, she'll be lying there all pale and still."

"Emma," said Vicki, "what's going on?" She wiped away an errant tear. "Don't you come to these places all the time? I don't need to know why, but we know, okay? Aren't you used to this by now?"

"This is different. And no, you don't need to know, although I think you already do. But this is real. I have this pain in me, Vic. It's eating away at me and I can't let it out. A piece of me disappears every day and I'm terrified that I might wake up and find there's none of me left."

"What the hell are you talking about?"

Emma shook her head. "It doesn't matter. I have to do this. Come on. Let's say goodbye to Doris."

Bright cream silk draped across the back of the casket and cast a light across Doris's face. Subtle red spotlights set into the ceiling above gave her a healthy blush.

"She looks so peaceful," said Emma as she reached out to touch the sleeve of Doris's dress. "I can't believe we won't talk to her again." A sensation formed behind her eyes, long lost but familiar. She could sense Vicki and Jen looking at her from either side and she turned away and glanced around the room.

It was full but, out of the entire crowd, a form materialized. Through the mass of moving bodies, on the opposite side of the room, she saw someone who looked familiar. It was weird, because it could have been Tom, but there was no reason for Tom to be here. He would be away, doing whatever Tom did when he wasn't with her. Drinking in the bar with his friends or helping his mate with something. He'd be doing anything other than being here. Unless...

It was definitely him. There he was.

Seeing him opened the floodgates and everything rushed at her like a tsunami; Jen's troubles in finding a man and the change in her since she met Josh. Abby's trouble in conceiving and the work and sacrifices both her and Rob had made. Doris's passing, and the hole that that would leave. Her Dad's complete and utter loneliness. And her own insecurities, her fears and worries she'd be alone forever. That she could never have an equal partner but remain independent. Everything married together like a dozen tributaries converging into a river. The river washed over her. The feelings built layer upon layer and pushed at her very being and heaved against her walls.

And then the dam burst.

At first, her view became blurry and her breath caught in her throat. She opened her mouth to release it and a gasp sounded, followed by a sob. It sounded like someone else made the noise. Her face flushed warm as waves of heat rolled across it, and she fought it with every fiber of her being. But, finally, after years of trying and living with a heartbreaking burden, she cried. Everything she'd held back flooded out. Her shoulders heaved and her breath came in gasps as tears streamed down her cheeks.

"Oh God, what's up with me? This is awful," she panicked. "I don't like it. Please make it stop."

A pain throbbed through her chest as she covered her face with her hands. Her friends closed in, wrapped their arms around her and, as the heavens opened and lashed at the windows, they held her tight.

****

Rain hammered against the car so hard that the wiper blades struggled to keep the screen clear. Tom flicked the lever to have them fly across double time and leaned forward to trace the lines in the road. His phone lay on the seat beside him, its screen dark. Emma hadn't responded to any messages since the argument in the restaurant. That was over a month ago, but he still kept the phone visible at all times.

Deep conversations shouldn't be held with anyone until after at least six months. That would be the new rule. He determined that it was like texting. Everything was so open to interpretation. One crossed wire and the whole thing could blow up, just as it did.

Tom could still remember the waft of air as the crumpled napkin hit him in the face, and the sight of Emma storming away as he removed it. The embarrassment of a room full of gazing eyes didn't come close to masking the loss that swept over him as the glass doors closed and she faded away into the night on the other side of them.

Thunder crashed overhead and snapped him back to the present. Tom jumped and gripped the wheel tighter, his knuckles white. His mood was dropping faster than the rain. Grief welled up in his eyes but wouldn't complete its escape and just hovered there, draped over his thoughts like a heavy blanket.

A sign flashed by on the roadside, blurred through the rivers of water washing over the car. Tom still knew what it said.

Last Stop Funeral Home.

Hadn't that been where he first met Emma? The entrance was a few hundred yards further along on the right. As he grew close, he glanced across to it. There wasn't a single space in the parking lot, with some vehicles pulled up onto the grass verges that lined it. He stared at the road and drove stubbornly past, then swung around into a side street and stopped.

He held onto the wheel and took slow, measured breaths. Now would be the perfect time to let these feelings out. Every one of those cars had a driver and maybe even a passenger, too. That was a lot of people grieving. Either every viewing room was in use, or someone very popular had passed away.

He turned the car in the narrow road and pulled out and drove back to the Funeral Home parking lot. The only place to park was at the far end away from the entrance. By the time Tom reached the home, his clothes clung to his body like a second skin. Cold water dripped from his nose and ran from his hair down his neck.

As the door opened that familiar smell hit him. It was almost comforting, like coming home. A crowd milled around the first room. The corridor beyond lay empty.

All of these people were here to see one person.

The ever-present easel stood against the door with pictures of the deceased. The main picture was of an old lady who looked like someone's favorite grandmother. Tom's breath caught in his throat as his stomach lurched.

Doris Wellnick, said the print. Preceded by a loving husband. There were no family members mentioned, but a list of clubs and accomplishments filled the rest of the page. She was a popular girl. Of course, he knew all of this.

Below the main picture was a mosaic of smaller snaps. In her youth, Doris had been beautiful, with shoulder length cascades of dark curls framing a face of porcelain skin. The same man, presumably her husband, appeared in each picture. From start to finish they showed a timeline of them growing old together. The final shot was of her sitting in Emma's salon, craning her head and flashing a beaming smile of perfect dentures to the photographer. Tom smiled. The avalanche of dark curls had aged and changed into a tight knit of pale blue hair, but a spark of fiery spirit still burned in her eyes. She looked like one of those 'life and soul of the party' people. He remembered her dancing to Elvis tunes.

As he rounded the corner, he paused in the doorway to take in the sight. The owner of every car parked outside was packed into this one room. There were no cliques or groups of hangers on. The room throbbed with emotion that washed over him as if he'd walked under a door heater. The sensation made his skin crawl, and the wet hairs on his neck sprung alive. People hugged and consoled one another, or laughed and shared good memories.

At one side of the casket stood a group of younger girls, huddled together arm in arm, their shoulders shaking and fingers clasping one another. It was hard to tell if the shaking was from crying or laughter until one of the group peeled away and wiped her eyes. Tom recognized her at once. It was Vicki.

He squinted his eyes and studied the rest of the group. It took a moment for him to pick out Emma. She'd pulled up her long hair. She wore a light colored blouse with a black knee-length skirt and black heels that made her bare legs seem pale against the dark colors. As she turned to face him, he reeled in shock. Her face was ruddy, with gray lines of make up running like veins from the corners of her eyes. She didn't seem to care. Even from this distance, he could see she was crying.

Emma was crying.

The same feeling he'd had in the restaurant overwhelmed him; the need to comfort her, to make her happy. She was such a good person, she didn't deserve this pain. He wanted to ease her burden, but was wary of the last time he'd mentioned that same thing. This was not the place for a repeat performance. As the girls consoled one another, he ached to walk over to the group and just hold her. To show her she wasn't alone, and that there was someone that cared. He held back. If she'd been interested at all, she'd have returned his call, or even just answered a text.

This was not a regular funeral to her, if such a thing existed. This was personal, involving someone she'd cared about. Tom felt like an intruder and decided to leave and sneak out before she noticed him. As he turned on his heel, a voice cut through the background murmurs.

"Tom?"

Shit. She'd seen him. He glanced up and tried to appear surprised as Emma made her way through the crowd. He watched her again, weaving and turning to move through the mass of people. She stopped a foot in front of him. Her perfume washed over him and made him giddy as she reached out and brushed his arm.

"Hi. What are you doing here? God, you're soaked. Did you know this was Doris's funeral?"

He could tell she was forcing the words out, trying not to break down again. Then, her eyes widened as realization set in.

"Oh, no you didn't. You were just doing your thing. I'm sorry, I should leave you alone. I'll just go back to the…"

"No, I'm sorry. I had no idea. I was driving by and… it doesn't matter. Are you okay?" he said and leaned in closer to her. He returned the touch. Subtle, but he hoped it would serve as a peace offering. "I'm the one that should be apologizing. If I'd know it was someone…"

Her eyes fluttered and sent another tear careening down her face. "Tom?"

He lifted his hand and wiped it away with a finger. "Yes?"

"Please shut up." Her voice just rose above the sound of the room. "Don't say anything, okay?"

Tom closed his mouth, and they gazed at each other. Then, she wrapped her fingers around his wrist and dragged him from the room. As Tom opened his mouth to protest, the look on her face silenced him. She pulled him through the entrance. The ever reliable fountain trickled away in the corridor as they turned left and moved away from the noise of the crowded room. He stumbled to keep up as Emma led him past an empty viewing room and down toward the end of the corridor. It ended with a huge padded sofa that separated two doors. One said 'Office', the other said 'Cleaning'.

Emma turned to face him. "I can't cope with this," she said. Tiny rivers of tears rolled down either side of her face and met at her chin. They tumbled to the ground and smashed like glass on the carpet. "I knew this was inside me, this pain, but I want it gone. It's too much. If I smoked, I'd put a cigarette against my skin. I want to feel something else, anything, just not this."

She pushed open the door that said 'Cleaning' and walked into the small room, pulling Tom behind her. They stood in darkness as the door latched shut with a click. He fumbled against the wall and searched for the light switch.

"Leave it," she whispered. Hands landed on his shoulders and pushed him back to the wall. Her perfume washed over him again and then her lips pressed against his. Her tongue probed and lunged between his teeth. The sensation took his breath away, and he pushed back, cupped her head and kissed her deeply. Her hands ran up and down the side of his body before they found his belt. His stomach tensed as she pulled it tight, and then the pressure released. A moment later, he stood against the wall with his underwear around his ankles.

Her breath came in ragged and desperate bursts as she rained kisses up and down his neck. Tom responded and reached down to lift her skirt as she wrapped a leg around him. His back muscles tensed as she locked her hands behind his neck and hoisted herself up to his waist. Hot breath breezed across his face and she wrapped her other leg behind him and forced him away from the wall.

"Now. I want you now, Tom."

She reached between them and then gripped him between her legs as Tom cupped her buttocks and gave himself to her. Cans crashed and shelves rattled as they staggered around in the darkness, but they held each other, joined as one. Emma bucked and pushed until her breathing was broken by small sobs and gasps. Tom held her tight as her warm body shuddered. She bit into his shoulder to stifle a cry and the pain lit up every nerve as he fought his own urge to shout.

And then she unfolded her legs and placed her feet on the floor. He heard her ruffle her skirt. A soft kiss landed on his lips and then he shielded his eyes as a shaft of light shot through the opening door. Then it closed, and he was alone.

Tom laughed as shock and surprise overwhelmed him. He pulled up his rain soaked pants and tightened his belt. Then he slid down the wall and sat on the floor. He threw his arms around his legs and pulled his knees up to his chest.

And then he cried.

Chapter Nineteen

Hot water mingled with tears as Emma scrubbed at her body in the shower. The feelings that coursed through her left her even more confused than before. Were these tears for Doris, or a result of the shame that racked her?

The pain of her loss was eating her alive. The girls had supported one another through the time at the Funeral Home but, now alone, she relived the moment again.

She'd used Tom; taken what she needed and then discarded him like a used toy. Her mind and body had craved something to take the pain away, and he was right there. Wasn't it said that we take out our worst moments on the people closest to us?

As she'd walked away from the closet, Tom's laughter had bled through the closed door behind her. Emma applied more soap to the sponge and thought about its tone. It hadn't sounded light and jolly, like he was laughing at a joke, but hard, as if he'd been shocked and didn't know how to react.

She'd left this man, who'd opened himself to her, alone in the dark after she'd practically raped him. Of course, he hadn't said no. After they'd entered the room, he was a more than willing partner. But still, she'd used him and left him. And he deserved better than that.

But then, he'd got too close to her. And now he was chipping away at her wall.

She couldn't allow that.

The skin on the inside of her thighs glowed red and tender and would be clinically clean by now. Painful stings jabbed at the skin as warm water ran over it, so she turned the handle until the temperature grew hot enough to scald. Her body shivered from the pain and her lungs burned from the suffocating steam. Through gritted teeth she took the punishment until she could stand it no longer, then turned the handle the other way. The stream lessened in intensity until a small drip seeped from the shower head. Her eyes did the same thing as she stifled her cries yet again and steeled herself against her shame.

She stepped out and toweled down and let her bathrobe soaked up any remaining moisture as she tied it around her waist. The sofa wheezed a protest as she collapsed onto it and turned on the TV. Would Tom be home now, or would he still be wandering the funeral home looking for her?

Tears fell again.

Now the dam was cracked she seemed unable to stop, and she punched at her sore legs in frustration. He'd been the best thing to happen to her in years. Someone honest, trustworthy, patient and fun. She wouldn't find a better partner. Now he'd seen her cry, and she'd given herself to him. So why couldn't she let him in?

Dad was still alone. His sadness on her last visit was bleaker than ever. He'd said he could never forgive or even begin to forget what had happened. The bitterness weighed him down and his shoulders slumped as if he wore a lead cloak, as if he'd already resigned himself to eternal sadness. Emma didn't want to be like that. By all statistics, she still had more than half her life to live. Mrs. Jacobs's words rattled around her head again. In a nutshell, life's too short. It's up to you to live it while you can. No one can do it for you.

A vibration broke her thoughts, and she glanced at the coffee table as her phone's screen lit up. Her heart pounded, blood rushed in her ears, and her palms sweated as she leaned forward and scooped it up. How would she respond to Tom's questions? The act at the funeral home was so impulsive and so out of character, there was no other explanation than to be completely honest. She'd needed relief, and he was there. Simple as that.

Would she be able to apologize, to say 'Sorry, Tom. It was nothing personal'?

Except is was personal. It was special.

She swiped the screen and read the message. 'Google Play. Update available.'

A cry of despair and frustration left her throat. She leaned her head back against the sofa to let it out. The phone buzzed again, and she almost dropped it. Maybe this time.

It was a text from Jen.

'About to leave. Where did you go? Are you ok? Worried about you xx'

She dabbed her eyes against the back of her hand. 'Yes, I'm ok. All got a bit too much xx'

Jen's response was instant, as if it had been on her screen, waiting.

'Tom was here, too. Wasn't sure if you saw him xx'

'Yes,' she replied. 'I saw him xx'

This time the response took a little longer.

'Here if you need to talk, girl. Love you xx'

Suddenly, a wave of utter loneliness overwhelmed her. The room seemed to spin and her vision darkened. She shook her head to clear it.

'Thanks, but I'll be ok,' she texted. 'Talk to you in the morning. Love you too xx'

She placed her phone on the coffee table, stood and walked to the bedroom. The bed was cold to the touch but provided a refreshing contrast after the boiling shower.

Emma curled up, rested her head on her hands and tried to sleep. The cold sheets made her shiver and, after the burning shower, she enjoyed the sensation, relaxed into the cold and drifted.

****

Tom stared at the picture as if the people in it had somehow changed. It had faded a little, the image of a young boy nestled between his parents. Looking at it through sore eyes made the people all the more tangible. It was more than a picture to him now. These people were real, his parents. Something in him had broken free, and he felt able to grieve for that moment and the moments he'd lost. They'd never seen him graduate school. They'd never met his first girlfriend or congratulated him on his first job. These people, his Mom and Dad, had been taken from him. For the longest time, he couldn't deal with that loss and the hole it left.

Now, his chest heaved and his head ached at the constant pressure that pushed inside it. Emma had breached the wall and earned his trust in no time at all. Perhaps it was the way they met, sharing such unusual common ground. The disorientation of so much emotion could have freed up their own emotions enough for them to bond. Perhaps it masked something they might otherwise have seen. Or, in simple terms, they were just good together and were meant to be. Whatever had happened between them, the effect he'd been searching for had finally been realized. At least he had that.

As he collapsed onto the sofa, her scent washed over him. His collar still wore her perfume and he lifted it to his nose. It was her smell, the musky fragrance she always wore. Her other scent was on him, too, mixed in with the weather and his own nervous sweat.

What had she done? He shuddered at the pained look in her eyes. They normally bristled and sparkled with energy and enthusiasm. At the funeral home they were flat and lifeless, her large brown irises surrounded by a bloodshot red that now haunted him.

She'd used him. But the short moment before she climbed down from him, when she clutched him tightly and shook against him? That moment made it all worthwhile. Without asking, she'd taken from him.

But he'd wanted to give, anyway.

Then she'd left him. Alone and frustrated. Missing something. The feeling had moved inside him, the wanting and the needing to give everything. She'd taken her pleasure from him, but his was still there to share. It left him aching, and the aching moved deeper until it forced out the thing, the burden which had been in him since childhood.

And he'd cried.

Finally. After years of crushing pain, he'd cried.

His skin flushed and released more sweat which drifted up to him and overpowered Emma's scent. He needed to shower, but doing that would wash her off him and he wanted this moment to last forever.

The TV remote blinked as he chose a channel. Oswald leaped onto the sofa beside him. The cat nestled a head against his side, then flinched and raced away.

Tom grimaced, apologized to the cat and then got up to shower.

****

Three weeks passed. He woke, went to work, came home, showered and ate, and went to bed. Rinse and repeat. A monotonous cycle.

His phone was a constant companion, the screen visible at all times. Even in the bathroom it sat next to the sink staring back at him, silent and taunting. Many times he nervously checked to make sure that a hacker hadn't operated the camera without his knowledge.

Early one morning, Steve called from work. Tom had snatched it up so hard that it flew from his hands and over his shoulder and had narrowly missed a bowl of cereal. Viagra had accepted the pitch at the highest level and graphic designers were creating ads to match their theme to run as the next campaign. Tom took the slaps on the back and the hearty congratulations but, deep down, he just wanted his phone to light up and for Emma's name to appear.

He maintained his weekly ritual of meeting the boys at the Irish bar. Yet another cover band was playing, this time a group of studded and leather clad guys named Spin Lizzy.

Josh shouted an answer to his question over the well-known bass line of The Boys Are Back in Town. "No," he said. "Jen says that Emma hasn't mentioned you. Having said that, she said Emma doesn't mention much of anything. Apparently, she's like a well-functioning zombie at work. She does the job as well as she ever did, but she's got no expression. When she told me, it made me shudder, to be honest. She said the light had gone out of her eyes, like she just turns up, works, and then goes home."

"Know it well," said Tom. "I've texted a couple of times and even called once. It got cut off quickly. Not like when it rings and they don't hear the call and it goes on and on, but like when they can see your number and they don't want to talk and just kill the call."

He was at a loss to explain, being too respectful to mention the meeting in the cleaning closet. As far as Josh and Rob were aware, they'd met once after the fund raiser and then argued about something vague. They must have seen the look on his face and didn't push the conversation any further.

"What else can I do?" he continued.

Rob leaned forward. "Why don't you go to the salon? Do that thing John Cusack did in Say Anything. Record a really meaningful song and stand outside with a ghetto blaster and play it at full blast until she comes out."

"I wouldn't know what song to play. Or even what mood she's in," said Tom, "other than not very talkative. And she might be really annoyed. I don't even know if she has a carry concealed license. She might come out incensed and pop a cap in my ass."

Both guys gave him a tight smile and a head shake of disapproval.

"Okay, maybe it won't be that bad. But I have no idea where I stand. What do I do for the best? I mean, I've never met anyone like her, but this silence? It's deafening, but it says nothing. It doesn't really matter what I say, it's going to be wrong."

"Tom?" said Josh. "I have the perfect solution. Say nothing."

"Wise words from a muppet," said Tom as the crowd cheered and clapped the band. "Welcome back, Josh of old."

Tom drained his beer as the next song started. He recognized the guitar intro to one of his favorite Thin Lizzy songs and the band began their version of Still in Love With You. How apt.

And then his phone vibrated across the bar. He glanced at the screen to see who was bothering him now. Centered in the picture of Oswald's pale fur, a name flashed.

Emma.

Chapter Twenty

Jerry Springer was on TV trying to incite a riot. Some woman's baby-daddy shouted and cursed at her, waving a tattooed arm in the air. Another guy sat on the other side of her and countered with his own verbal assault. Only a lip reading expert would understand any one sentence because of the constant beeping to censor the curse words. Jerry was egging them on with a ten-foot tall security guard standing by, ready to step in five minutes too late to stop the inevitable fight. The crowd bayed for blood as if they were seated in a Roman Colosseum.

Emma shook her head. When did fathers become baby-daddies? Was there a difference? Once someone fathered a child they become a father, right? Isn't that why the word existed?

The word pricked her conscience, and she picked up her phone. It had been a few weeks since she'd spoken to her father. Texting was one thing, but it wasn't the same as hearing his voice.

"Hello?" he answered.

"Hi, Daddy, it's Emma. How are you?"

Dad had never got a cell phone and relied on a good, old-fashioned land line. She wasn't aware of anyone else who had one. Even Doris had owned a cell phone.

"I'm doing okay," he said in a voice that conveyed everything but okay. Not quite monotone, but not far off. It ran along, the way a heart monitor flat lines as a heart stops and paramedics try to shock life back into it. The occasional spike, but otherwise flat.

"Are you sure? You sound a bit down. Do I need to come up there again? It's no problem, honestly."

"No, you have you own life there, now. How's that young man of yours? Tom, right?"

Emma's heart beat in her ears and her stomach tumbled at the mention of his name. "Ancient history, Daddy. It didn't work out."

Dad couldn't have sounded more depressed. "Oh, Emma, I do worry about you. Do you want to talk about it? You're such a lovely girl, but for the love of all things holy, would you please give someone a chance?"

"It's okay, Dad. Really. We haven't spoken in weeks. It's all over now, and I'm fine with that."

All she could do was take a breath and wait for the inevitable advice. He couldn't help it.

"There's concern in your voice when you speak to me," he continued. "I'm not stupid, Em. Just because I live alone doesn't mean I don't know what's going on. I'm an old fart with life experience. I've lived my life and I've loved and lost. But at least I've loved. I pray you will too. And even an old fart knows what 'fine' means."

"Daddy, you're not an old fart. You've got years in you yet. Don't forget, sixty is the new fifty."

He snorted and laughed down the line. Emma smiled. He didn't do that anywhere near enough these days.

"Be that as it may," he said, "you're not half way through your life yet, and you seem to have already given up. I didn't raise you to be a quitter. You're much stronger than that. And don't you dare confuse strength with the crap you do when a good man comes along."

His voice had grown stronger. He sounded like a lecturer speaking on a subject he felt passionate about. Emma could imagine him pointing fingers to emphasize a point. As she opened her mouth to protest, he continued in an even firmer tone.

"That's not strength. That's fear. Fear of change. Fear of the unknown. Fear of taking a leap to let someone in and give them a chance. You've heard the saying, it's better to have loved and lost than never to have loved at all?"

"Of course. From Lord Tennyson's poem."

"Correct. And well done, I knew you paid attention at school. Still, I think that's a pile of bullshit…"

It was Emma's turn to snort, and she raised a hand to her mouth in shock. "Dad!"

"Well, he married his childhood sweetheart so what the hell would he know about lost love? Still, it hints at taking chances. You deserve to be happy. I saw the way your eyes sparkled when you spoke about Tom. And he helped you with that cancer thing even though he'd only just met you. People like that are rare, Emma, people that want you to be happy, with no agenda or wish for repayment. They're rare. When they turn up, hold onto them. Or at least give them a chance. They don't come along often. And as for sixty being the new fifty, I remember being your age like it was yesterday. It seems every year knocks a week off the calendar. Stop wasting your life. It's not a rehearsal, it's a one-off. This is it. Take a chance."

Just like Mrs. Jacobs had said.

Emma sat in silence for a moment as the few memories of Tom she had played through her mind like a movie trailer. The time he'd stopped her sitting on a splinter, and the way he'd held her leg while she climbed onto his shoulder to find an exit from the maze. The way he'd smiled when she thrashed him at bowling. The impromptu picnic he'd turned up with. And their date at The Sizzling Wok.

Her eyes misted over at the timid way he'd introduced himself to Doris and, damn him, Dad was right about how he'd helped with the fund raiser. Truth be told, he'd done most of it while she was out of town. And the way she'd exploded when he'd mentioned something that pushed her button so hard she had no choice.

But she did have a choice. Tom wasn't aware of her feelings up to that point. How could he be, they'd only just mentioned it?

"Em? Are you still there?"

She jumped at the voice. "Sorry. Sorry, Dad. Yes, I was miles away."

"Em?"

"Yes?"

"Why don't you call him? What's the worst that could happen?"

She sighed. The expression on his face in the restaurant as she'd stormed out had been heart wrenching. Just before the napkin had covered him, he'd looked like a little boy who'd been reprimanded with no idea why. Perhaps it wasn't too late. Dad was right. What was the worst that could happen? He'd ignore the call like she'd ignored his. And sure, she'd be upset, then deal with it for a while and try to move on. Or, he might answer. Things would be awkward at first, but they had to start somewhere.

"Okay. As soon as I hang up, I'll call him."

Somehow, she could hear his smile from hundreds of miles away. "Good girl. Now go. Get off the phone and make the call. Trust your Dad, I'm sure it'll be okay."

"Okay, Dad. I'll call again soon, okay?"

"I look forward to it. And Emma?"

"Yes?"

"I love you, darling. Be happy."

Emma disconnected the call and sat on the sofa. What the hell was she supposed to say to him when she called? Hi Tom, long time no speak. Anyway, I'm a lost cause, trying to find someone who might be able to handle me? Fancy the challenge?

She did have one thing that Dad never had in his day. It was the coward's way out, but she was scared and she took it. Hear my confession and deal with it... I'm a coward and I'm scared.

Emma swiped the phone screen, selected Tom's name from her contacts, and texted three words.

****

Tom pulled into the parking lot and swung the car around to a stop at one side of the entrance. The twin beams of his headlights swept across the side of the building and through the glass doors. A slender female shape was silhouetted against the wall. She was already here, waiting for him.

As normal, his stomach lurched as he pulled on the parking brake and he took a moment to compose himself. She was standing in the same spot he had the last time they'd been here. Tom hoped this wouldn't be a repeat performance. Everything was reversed. He'd set the date before. He'd been here to meet her. He'd picked the table, and he'd started the conversation that left him sitting alone as she stormed out.

It seemed as if, this time, she'd taken control. No, wrong word. Not control. Never mention control again. The initiative. This time she'd taken the initiative.

He wondered if he'd be walking on the same eggshells during the meeting to follow.

Her text had simply said 'can we talk?'

After such a lapse in time, he had no idea what she might want to talk about, but the gap in his life had grown larger by the day. Oswald seemed to sense it, but it seemed that only she could fill it.

So he'd replied, 'Of course'.

Over a few more texts, they'd agreed to meet at Manganelli's, to return to the scene of the crime where their big bust up had occurred.

The cold Chicago wind blasted him and ruffled his hair as soon as he opened the car door. Tom stopped and checked it in the rear-view mirror, then laughed to himself. If he checked his teeth, he'd be copying her there, too. He climbed out and walked to the door. The shadow inside drifted forward and opened it.

Emma looked amazing. Gone was the classy business look and instead was a stunning woman in a small black dress and heels. Her hair dropped around her shoulders like a horse's tail and her nervous smile lit up the foyer as she greeted him.

"Hello again," she said. She fluttered her eyelashes as her voice wavered.

Butterflies swarmed yet again in his stomach, and Tom didn't know whether to hug her, kiss her on the cheek, or just reply. Their last meeting was a complete contradiction. The pain and sadness of loss, the discovery of feelings for both of them, then a passion Tom had not encountered before. And then nothing. A parting of ways and a shutdown of communication.

Until now.

He decided to tread lightly. Eggshells.

"Hello, Emma, it's nice to see you again. You look incredible, by the way."

She blushed and turned her head. "Thank you. And thank you for coming. I didn't think you would after we, you know, after the last…" She shook her head. "Whatever. Thank you for coming."

"Thank you for texting," he said. He leaned toward her with renewed bravery to kiss her. Another customer came through the door and brushed between them and the moment was gone.

Emma seemed to relax and gave him a knowing smile. "People can be so rude. Come on, our table's ready and I took the liberty of ordering our drinks. Follow me."

He followed her to the table, by the windows this time, and pulled out her chair.

"I'm surprised he isn't staring at me," said Tom as a waiter appeared with two glasses of wine. "Maybe we're not the first couple to argue in here."

Emma bit her lower lip and glanced down at the table. "Perhaps not, and I'm sorry about that although, you must admit, you can't say you didn't have it coming. I hope you learned your lesson, Tom Lewis."

Tom's eyes widened in mock worry, and then he relaxed a little and smiled. "Yeah, I did. I try to make a habit of learning after the first mistake."

"Well, you clearly didn't realize the full extent of my situation. You do now, so consider yourself warned." She smiled, too, an awkward and shy-looking gesture, just to take the edge off the warning.

"So what changed your mind?" asked Tom. "Why did you ask to meet me? After the funeral I thought that was it, like a one-off, and you wanted nothing else to do with me?"

She blushed. "God, I'm sorry about that too. That was so selfish of me. It was what I needed at the time but I promise I'm not normally like that. I can't say it was one thing."

She reached across the table and rested a finger against his wrist. It was the smallest of touches, but it was a reach across no-man's-land.

"I missed talking to you. Somehow, you seem to understand me and I'm not sure that anyone else does, so I suppose that makes you special. And my Dad gave me a really serious talking to. He even said a bad word, and he never does that."

Tom turned his arm and reached for her hand but she leaned back and picked up her drink. He frowned at the retreat but left his hand in place as a peace offering. Tiny steps. "Well, then I need to thank your Dad. You're special too, Emma. I've never met anyone like you. And I've never had a fourth date before either, a fifth if you count the funeral."

Emma let out a short laugh and put her glass back on the table. "Would you call that a date? A nice moment in an otherwise shitty day is probably the best description for it. In one day I went from being distraught, to feeling a moment of tenderness, to sheer panic. I never feel anything."

Tom wondered what she was feeling now. "So what happens next? You're still not giving much away, not that I'd ask for anything, but you asked me to come here. You've woken something in me, too. That must mean something. And I regret what I said the last time we were here, it didn't come out right. I know you weren't looking for sympathy or, what was it you said, a fucking couch?"

They smiled together as Tom continued. "But I can't change who I am. And I do want to make a difference in your life because you've already done that for me. And not because you need it either, but because I want to. I really want to. Something good happened here, to two people that have never had whatever good is. All I want is a chance to show you what we might be able to do. And sure, there are no guarantees, but if we don't try…"

"We'll never know?" Emma finished. "One person can't truly fix another. There'll always be something in me that's broken, as you'd say, or maybe there are even parts of me missing. My past has made me who I am, for better or worse. But I suppose that person could show them something new that might at least paper over the cracks. They could create something unique between the two of them and, I don't know, in doing that allow them time and space to be themselves? To carry the burden willingly? What's the saying, a load shared is a load lighter? I've always had a reason to grieve, but perhaps that's like putting a band-aid over a knife wound. It won't cure it, but it might slow down the bleeding."

She took a deep breath and exhaled slowly. "I do believe that no two people are the same together as any other two people. In every couple there'll always be something different because everyone's unique. And if you can find the person who has the parts you're missing, wouldn't that sort of make you complete? Know what I mean? Your patience to my lack of it, or the way you consider things, to the way I rush headlong into things and mess them up? You make me stop and think when, before, I'd have charged ahead and regretted it."

She placed her hand back on the table and gazed into his eyes. "Tom? You might have my missing parts."

Tom sat in silence for a moment and then inched his hand closer across the table. Emma leaned forward and took it.

"It would be perfect if I did," he said. "And if that's the case, what do we do now?"

"Well, have you seen the movie The Sixth Sense?"

Tom nodded. "The Bruce Willis thing. Where they see dead people."

"Yes. How about, like I said before, instead of us seeing dead people we see each other? Only this time we do it properly. With a lot of patience. No walls. No expectations or, as my Dad might say, no bullshit."

"I'd like that. A lot."

"Okay, well what we do now is you get me another drink and we have a nice night. After that, we tackle tomorrow. And if we make it through tomorrow, we tackle the next day." Emma paused. "But like I said, you'll need to be patient with me, right? This won't take six dates. Probably not even ten. I'm going to open a door and let you into the home of me, and I'm trusting that you won't ransack the place. One day, if it's right, I might give you your own key."

Tom nodded and squeezed her hand.

"And if you ever try that 'fix me' shit again," she continued, "I'll kick your ass to the curb so fast it'll leave skid marks. Understood?"

"Understood," he nodded.

"And I don't like to make rules," she said.

Tom sighed. "Good. Thank God for that."

"But there are rules."

"Oh."

"I want complete honesty. No skirting around things. Don't be afraid to say what's on your mind. And don't treat me any differently to anyone else. I don't want you telling me my clothes look nice just for the sake of it, like some kind of affirmation. Feel free to make suggestions, you won't offend me. Now, if you lay my outfits out on the bed for me, you may become the first man I know to be strangled to death with a bra strap."

Tom leaned over the table and placed a gentle kiss on her forehead. "If I said that I just want to make you happy, would that sound cheesy?"

Emma sat stone faced and appeared to be deep in thought. His heart raced. He'd already said the wrong thing. Then she looked into his eyes. "Yes Tom. Cheesy as fuck."

They erupted into laughter. "I can't believe you said that," said Tom.

"Toes, Tom Lewis. Got to keep you on your toes. Enough of this serious talk. Get me another fizzy wine and let's order some food. All I've eaten today is a piece of toast and that was first thing this morning."

Tom raised his arm and signaled the waiter

Chapter Twenty-One

Two years later.

A small postcard inside an elaborate glass case stated that 'Hubert Jones, 86, would be laid to rest at this place on Sunday September 19th at 2.30pm'.

Tom studied the statement. What exactly did that mean, laid to rest? They'd bring Hubert's body into the cemetery next door and put him in the ground. How did that translate to laying him to rest? Surely, at the precise moment he took his last breath and ended up horizontal, he was at rest. He was dead. Lay him any way you like but, at that moment, he's laid to rest. He will never rest any more than that.

"That's tomorrow. And I thought you'd worked through this shit."

Tom jumped and turned. "What?"

"The funeral stuff. I thought you didn't do that anymore."

Tom placed a hand on Rob's arm and adjusted his friends' tie so it fit snugly into his collar.

"I don't. I was just looking at the notices. Tell you what, this is the first time I've seen you in a suit. You're normally sporting the grease monkey look. Turns out you clean up well. In a non-gay way, of course."

"Of course. I wore one for Morgan's christening. You should know, you were both there. And I'm over the gay thing. I'm sure you're straight. This is proof enough."

"I remember the christening well," said Tom with a smile. Then he winked, "As for the gay thing, you remember Elton John? He married a woman. Look how that turned out."

He looked around the room. Dark suits filled the place. It looked like a room full of FBI agents waiting for the go order on a kill mission. Except this wasn't a kill mission.

In one corner, Adam fought with a pair of cufflinks. Every time he got them in place they slid out of his grasp and lay against the dark fabric, mocking him. Tom stepped forward.

"Let me get that for you," he said. He pulled the shirts' cuff tight and threaded the links through the button hole.

Adam grimaced and clapped Tom on the shoulder. "You'd think a decade of waiting would give a man enough time to get over the nerves, but Jen's been so excited about today. I don't want to mess it up."

Tom laughed and threw an arm around him. "You won't. Look around, my brother in matrimony. There are three of us Musketeers here, all bound by what, Doris and Elvis?"

Tom, Adam and Rob wore identical outfits and were crammed into a small room at the side of the chapel. The walls were washed beige and the only things in there were a table, a bench and a tall mirror in the corner.

"Where's Josh?"

"In the chapel, adjusting his tripod," said Rob.

Three pairs of eyes locked and then creased in laughter.

"Pervert," said Rob. "That'll get him in trouble. And I speak from experience."

"You can't have any complaints," said Tom. "After all the practice you've had, it was bound to happen eventually."

Rob leaned forward until his forehead rested against Tom's. "Yes, and I've never been happier. And now it's your turn. I can't thank you enough. For that time in the bathroom? Chances are, you saved my marriage because I was about to lose it."

"That's what friends are for," said Tom. "I love you, man. Thanks for doing this."

"Do you two need a moment?" asked Adam, "Cos I can go for a quick walk and leave you to it."

"You're going nowhere," said Tom. "It took over a decade to get you here, right? Talk about keeping a girl waiting. Who's to say you won't walk outside and run off down the street in a panic like a little girl?"

They laughed again as Josh burst into the room. "Okay guys, we're all set. I've got three cameras rigged, one in each corner at the front of the chapel and one over the congregation. Sorry it's a bit last minute, I couldn't get access to the church any sooner, but I promise it will be amazing."

Tom had another flash of FBI imagery and shook his head. "Are you ready?"

Josh spread his arms wide like a jazz singer and grinned. He wore the same suit and the same shirt, and his tie was immaculate.

"Shit, you big girls blouse. I guess you are," said Tom.

Rob hoisted himself up onto the table, stood upright and clapped his hands. The noise silenced the room.

"Oh hear yea and all that crap," he announced. "We're gathered here together…"

"You can't say that," interrupted Josh. "Those are the main man's words."

"Oh. Crap," said Rob. "Okay, oh room full of men who resemble a bunch of penguins. I would like to take a moment to ease the brevity of the situation and thank you all for being here."

"Aren't you supposed to do this afterwards?" asked Josh. "You know, the best man's speech?"

"I'm sure I am," said Rob. "I've never been best man to three men at the same time, though, so you'll forgive me if I admit I'm shitting myself right now."

"Don't do that," laughed Tom. "The rental place only had the suits we're wearing. We can't get replacements if we mess these up."

"Soft and tender's not my strong point so let me speak, okay?" said Rob. The room fell silent. "Each of you has played a part in my life, in getting me to this point. Without you, Abby and I wouldn't have little Morgan. And I'd probably be divorced and strung out on drugs or something by now."

The other men shook their heads as he continued.

"Adam? We've only got to know you recently, thanks to Elvis. But you're a good man. Vicki's a great girl and you'll make a great couple. And you need to because she's a better wrestler than you are. She'd give you a proper kicking."

Adam smiled, bowed his head and pointed at Rob with a 'you've got me' expression.

"And you," said Rob pointing at Josh. "I've never seen such a transformation. You and Jen are perfect together. I always knew you were a good guy, but she's brought that all out of you. You were a male whore before she straightened you out... in the nicest possible sense, of course."

"Of course," echoed Josh.

"Seriously, though, it's good to see you happy, man. You deserve it. It makes me proud to stand with you."

Josh leaned forward and slapped Rob's thigh. "Likewise."

"As for you," said Rob as he jumped down from the table and squared up to Tom. "As for you, you're the most complicated person I've ever met. But, you always give everything you have to anyone who asks. And you always see the good in people, even when everyone else has painted them black. You never ask for anything in return and you're always there."

Tom blushed and took a step back. Rob followed him and stepped forward again.

"And you're done backing off," he continued, "in every sense. I've watched you let this amazing woman into your life, knowing what I know, and you've taken that leap of faith. And now look where you are."

"Bankrupt?" squeaked Tom.

"Maybe," said Rob. "But when you've got what you've got, do you really need money?"

Tom leaned forward and hugged Rob. "Thanks, man. And thank you for being there for all of us. It means everything." He pulled back his sleeve and glanced at his watch. "It's almost time, guys. Adam. Josh. Are you ready?"

The four men gathered in a huddle, hugged and back slapped and then opened the small door into the chapel. The whisper of many hushed voices grew a little louder.

"Okay," said Tom. "Let's do this."

****

Emma shuffled across the seat to see her reflection in the mirror as the long car bounced over a pothole in the road. "My hair's all over the place!"

"Emma, your hair's the same as it was when we left the salon," said Jen.

The back of the limo resembled a lace factory. Three girls, each wearing a wedding dress, lounged in the rear of the stretched car.

Frilly white material sat in an untidy but carefully arranged mound between the seats. Abby, Rob's wife, sat up front with the driver while the brides and their clothing filled the rear compartment.

"My make-up is too thick, then. I could be one of those Japanese geezer women."

"Emma?" said Vicki, "The geezer women are mainly in Thailand, but over there they call them lady boys. Now please be quiet, you're starting to sound like Doris. And I think you meant to say geisha women. Totally different thing."

"Yes," said Emma. "What you said. And my stomach is sticking out, too. I'll be waddling down the aisle, not walking."

"You're seven weeks pregnant, not nine months gone. Will you please stop moaning?"

"I'm sorry, but I want everything to be perfect. Really, my hair's everywhere. I look as if someone's dragged me through a hedge backwards."

"I'll drag you through a limo backwards if you don't shut up," said Vicki. "I'm sure it's your hormones, but we're all in this together so get a grip."

She leaned forward and dropped a small panel in the back of the car to reveal a row of small crystal glasses and a bottle.

"I have just the cure," she said, and poured three drinks. The champagne froth climbed the sides of each glass and settled into a whirlwind of bubbles.

Jen held out her hands to take two glasses and passed one of them forward to Abby. Vicki took the other as Emma turned her head to follow each glass and then frowned, empty handed. "Feeling a little left out here, Vic!"

"Oh, yes. Sorry." Vicki reached forward into the compartment again. "Here you go," she said and handed Emma a bottle of water. "Better get used to that, Em."

Abby laughed from the front seat. "Been there, done that. Morgan's two in a couple of weeks. Someone told me it's called the terrible twos, so I need all the practice I can get." She raised her glass in the air. "I'm sure I'll have a bottle on hand daily. Don't worry, Emma, you'll get used to it."

Emma screwed the lid off the bottle and raised it into the air, too. "I have to do a toast, and I think it's only right that we toast the one woman who's missing that really should be here. Who'd have thought that meeting a lovely lady with blue hair would result in all three of us getting married?"

"No shit, Sherlock," said Vicki. "I, for one, never saw that coming. For nine frigging years. And you know what? I reckon Doris is with us. Can't you feel her? She's right here, and she had a hand in this entire thing."

Emma smiled as her eyes misted. It happened at the drop of a hat now. "To Doris. May she be loving wherever she is, especially since Bill is facing her now. And he didn't have to do any chores."

Laughter rang through the car followed by a chorus of 'Doris' and 'Lucky Bill'. Glass clinked against glass as the limo slowed to a stop outside the church.

Abby got out and opened the other doors. "Well? What are you waiting for? Come on girls. Destiny awaits."

"You're so dramatic," said Jen, "but thanks for pulling all of this together. Even with Morgan wrapped around you all day."

Abby took Jen's hand and helped her from the car. "When I see those three wedding rings appear, it will all be worth it."

Emma stood by the road and looked up at the church. It was a beautiful gray stone building with arched windows. Brilliant sunlight bounced off the stained glass and painted the grass outside in a mix of deep color. A small bird with blue feathers perched in an apple blossom tree looking down at them.

"Girls? Look. I think Doris is with us."

She pointed into the tree as the bird tweeted a greeting. Then she heard a click and the church door opened.

Emma broke away from the group, lifted the train of her dress and ran up the crazy-paved path to the entrance as her Dad appeared in the doorway.

"Dad! I'm so glad to see you."

Like the others, he wore a dark suit. Framed in the church entrance he looked ten years younger than he had when she'd first mentioned Tom. His regular posture was back, and he stood tall and proud as she grew close to him. When he smiled the expression radiated throughout his entire face and caused handsome crow's feet to form by his watering eyes. He reached out and held her hands as another hand appeared over his shoulder. A pretty woman stepped forward to stand beside him.

"And Susan. I'm so glad you could make it," said Emma as the woman wrapped her arms around her. "You two make a lovely couple. I'm so happy for you."

"Calm down, Em," said Dad. "Let's stick to three weddings today, okay? Leave us old folks to make our own way."

The comment earned him a slap across the back of the head. "Old folks? You speak for yourself, old man," said Susan.

She stepped aside as Jen and Vicki rushed up the steps to meet their fathers. After some jostling and a lot of adjustment, the three women stood in line, dads at their sides.

Emma glanced over her shoulder. "Ladies and gentlemen? Are we ready?"

Each couple nodded and smiled and they walked into the church, then paused as ooh's and ah's bounced around inside the stone building. Then the traditional music sang from the organ and the procession walked down the aisle.

Emma picked out Tom, sandwiched between Josh and Adam. He was smiling and crying. At the sight of him, her own tears ran once more. Dad squeezed her hand.

"Are you okay, Em?"

"I've never been better, Dad. I hadn't cried in years before I met him. I had no idea it was so much grief."

Dad smiled. "You're preaching to the choir. Come on, there's a wedding waiting for you."

THE END

Thank you so much for reading my story. The greatest thing you can do to help an author is to leave an honest review. It helps to get our names out there and encourages others to pick up our books.

I would be truly grateful if you'd take five minutes to post a few words on Amazon and/or Goodreads to let them know what you thought of my book, good or bad!

I'd also love to hear from you. Email any comments to mickwilliamsauthor@gmail.com, and come and say hi to Mick Williams Author on Facebook. I promise to say hello back.

Keep reading for sneak peeks of my other two novels…the first few chapters from A Guy Walks Into A Bar and Whatever It Takes, both available now from Hydra Publications.

ABOUT THE AUTHOR

Mick Williams wrote his first short story (which linked a local celebrity to a spate of killings) in High School. His teacher noted 'he has quite an imagination'…she never mentioned whether it was good or bad. Since then he has written a romantic comedy and three adventure/thrillers.

After a decade in Kentucky, USA, he has recently relocated back to his hometown of Stoke-on-Trent, England, and shares a house with his wife and two demanding and needy cats, Crash and Thud.
In between working and writing, he is an avid reader and enjoys watching football. Both kinds.

Other novels A Guy Walks Into a Bar and
Whatever It Takes are available from Amazon.
Exodus – An Old Farts Club story is coming soon!

A Guy Walks Into A Bar

Mick Williams

Prologue

I should listen to my gut more often.

Roses are red. Other than the dangerous thorns, roses are nice, right? A symbol of love men across the ages have given to lovers as a sign of affection. Blood is red too. It feeds the body, transporting valuable oxygen to keep us alive and invigorated. We'd die without it, something I'd soon find out first hand.

The vision, dressed in red, was at the other end of the bar. Her slender legs, tipped with a pair of glossy red stilettos, were perched on the chrome footrest of the barstool. I think they stretched all the way from here to Canada. Maybe even to Heaven.

The first time she caught my eye, she did that hair thing girls do when they want something. She twirled her brown locks around her fingers as she maintained eye contact long enough for me to see that they matched her hair.

I always knew most predators had retractable claws. Hers were extended and painted a shade of red that looked as if she'd just ripped the bartender's throat out. In fact, he was missing, and my glass was empty. I hoped she hadn't killed him.

The devil is red too. And stop signs.

So why didn't I stop? Why didn't I just leave my empty glass and go back to my room?

Yeah, I should listen to my gut more often.

1

I help people. It's my calling. They have money, and I help them to get rid of it by selling them drugs. The large pharmaceutical company I work for rakes in billions of dollars every year by selling overpriced medicines to doctors. I don't get billions for my trouble, but they pay me well enough, which is why I'm in this bar, in this kind of hotel. It's a nice enough bar that I can sit here with no worries about the clientele, but not so nice that I can't afford to buy a drink or two.

There are four of us facing the large mirror mounted behind the bar, each separated by the barrier of an empty stool. Sitting between me and what I hope will become the focus of my attention for the foreseeable future are two people. One is a middle-aged woman who's just painted her claws, maybe to compete with the dream sitting next to her, and is fanning them as if she's waiting for an invisible Polaroid to develop. The other is a bulky man, dressed like me, but his clothes are twice the size of mine. I tend to keep fit, eat well, exercise. I do everything in moderation. This guy doesn't, evidenced by the extra stomach hanging over his belt. He's also looking for the bartender, but unlike my solitary wine glass, he has three empty beer glasses and a couple of shot glasses lined up to attention, awaiting new instructions like soldiers.

Because they banned smoking in hotel bars, without the overriding stench of tobacco, other smells have become prevalent. They didn't ban nail polish. I was about to tell nail lady they produce the stuff without the cloying aroma when the bartender reappeared. He was a young man, but he was sweating for some reason and looked as if he was trying to catch his breath after a heavy run.

"Sorry everyone," he said to his captive audience, "had to switch out a keg."

Bulky did the nod thing, and the bartender removed his dead soldiers and replaced them with a new recruit. Its frothy cap slid down the side of the glass onto the shiny bar top. A shot of Makers Mark followed it. Nail lady raised her painted hands in defeat when the bartender caught her eye. She spun her stool around, slid off it with the elegance of a rhino, and left the bar. It was just the three of us now. My stomach lurched as my dream leaned forward enough to catch my eye again and then leaned back. Her necklace swung out in front of her. It was the only jewelry she wore. No rings. Subtle, but I'm a man of the world. I know what to look for.

I pointed to my glass, and it vanished for a moment and reappeared full of merlot. One small sip for courage and I grabbed it by the narrow stem and walked casually to the other end of the bar. Bulky man watched me in the mirror. He was sizing up my chances of success and his smirk showed he had little faith in me.

As a single man, I stay alert to opportunity, but picking up women in bars is not something I do on a regular basis. For one, it's tacky and can lead to all kinds of problems. The main reason is that it's a rare night when a woman as stunning as this one flashes the signs. One messy divorce scarred me enough to raise my standards. If I take a chance on someone, it had better be worth it. Therefore, the only thing I curl up with most of the time at night is a good book.

"Hi," I said, "I'm Paul." I offered my hand, and she wrapped those claws around it. Her handshake stroked against my skin.

"Hello, Paul. I'm Monica."

Monica? She looked like a Giselle or one of those names that promised all kinds of things, some of them legal. But she had a voice that would turn lions into kittens, and I couldn't look away from those eyes. They smoldered.

"Pleased to meet you, Monica," was the best sentence I came up with. "What brings you here?"

Damn it! What brings you here? Is this the first time I've ever spoken to a woman? Monica didn't flinch, though, just did the hair-twirling thing again and smiled. Something dormant stirred below.

"Just passing through," she said. "What about you? What do you do?"

"I sell drugs," I said. I always say it like that. It makes me sound like a dealer, which promotes excellent conversation. "And you?"

"Ah," she replied, "I kill people."

She kept a perfectly straight face and, for a moment, I forgot the entire English language. I think my mouth dropped open and there may have been drool. She smiled again, and her eyes smoldered even more. "Just kidding. I travel a lot."

Bulky laughed to himself behind me. Bastard. It seems that smirk was justified after all. Her glass had a lone olive nestled at its base, skewered with a pink plastic sword. It looked lonely. "Can I rescue that olive with a drink?" I asked. I can be smooth sometimes.

"Sure," she said. She lifted the glass as if it was a trophy awarded for finishing her drink, and slid the olive between her pouting lips. "Dry martini, with a fresh olive."

"Shaken not stirred?" I said with a raised Roger Moore eyebrow, trying to remain calm.

"I'm sorry?"

"Never mind," I said, deflated. I can fall flat on my face too.

Bulky was still chuckling to himself. I signaled the bartender to get her a new glass. He did and slid it across the bar toward us. I reached out to intercept it in a cool but casual fashion. The stem of the glass slapped the side of my hand, spilling some of the contents over my arm. I felt like a fumbling teenager who'd just discovered second base. Before things got any worse, I excused myself and headed to the restroom to regroup and clean up. My shoes made a good focal point as I shuffled past Bulky to the bathrooms. I prayed he didn't see my face in the mirror.

The men's restroom was cleaner than my kitchen; with white tiled walls that were so shiny you could comb your hair in them while you took a leak. The urinals had mountains of those weird-smelling cubes that drunks sometimes mistook for pineapple chunks. I ignored them with no call of nature to answer, placed one hand against the cold tiled wall and took deep breaths. My heart was slamming like a jackhammer and the clammy beginnings of a cold sweat were forming. I'm not saying it's been a while since I was with a woman of this stature but, well, it's been a while. Still, I couldn't stay in here all night. If this window closed, I'd never forgive myself. Hell, mankind would never forgive me!

I splashed lukewarm water on my face and wiped it off with a hand towel, slam dunked the towel in the trash can and made my way back to the bar. She was still there. Bulky had left, so now it was just the two of us and a bartender barely out of college.

"You're still here," I said with a smile as I slid onto the stool next to hers.

"Of course I am," she purred. "Where else is a girl going to go on a cool night in Kentucky?"

I started to give her the myriad of options and then reigned it in. "So, no concrete plans for the evening?"

"Only you," she replied.

I swear, she didn't bat an eyelid, just looked me right in the eyes. I don't think I cried aloud, but there was a strange mewling sound followed by that stirring down below.

"Me? You have my undivided attention, but what exactly do you mean?" I asked and rested my arm against the bar to prevent me from falling off the stool.

"Well. We're both here, both alone, and I assume both single. Do you have somewhere else you need to be tonight?"

"Me? No," I said, a little too quickly. Damn, I need to practice that. "I have all night."

"Then you only have one decision to make," she said. She leaned toward me, pulled the latest olive off the plastic sword with her teeth and took it between those red lips.

I think the next sentence came out in English, but I'd have to check the hotel's security cameras to be sure. "And what might that be?"

"Is this going to happen in your room or mine?"

After a second's hesitation, she passed me her glass to drain and we headed to the elevators. I pressed every polished button in that thing to make sure the ride to her room on the fifth floor took as long as possible to milk this moment. It was a miracle I managed it. My coordination was shot and I was grateful to get in there without getting the bulge in my pants jammed in the closing door. If the hotel manager monitored the discreet camera in the corner, he wouldn't be changing the channel any time soon. The mirrored walls gave me a great three-sided view as she slammed me up against them and put those lips to good use. They were inches away from my ear, but I heard no breathing from her, just my frantic panting. I felt like a three-hundred-pound man who just finished a one-hundred-yard dash. Then she did that thing where, without me realizing it, she pinned my hands to the wall above my head, and my entire body was exposed and vulnerable. Fine by me, I thought. Have at it.

I think a random body part of mine bumped into every wall and door in the hallway as we did an epileptic dance to her room. By the time we got inside, my tie had almost garroted me and she was already barefoot. I pushed her onto the bed to try to gain a semblance of control and sent her purse flying across the floor. Its contents spread out and sought the underside of every piece of furniture in range. We ignored it and, for the next few hours, I found heaven.

2

A white streetlight shone across one side of the Capitol Bank building on Hillbourne and Main, casting dark, shadowy fingers up the tall wall that ran parallel to it. Traffic was light at this time of night, and hidden on the fifth story parking lot across the road was the only occupied vehicle present.

Its two occupants watched as a lone figure climbed the wall and sat like a statue while a security guard made a routine sweep beneath it. Once the guard moved around the corner and out of sight, the figure dropped, landed cat-like beside the building and moved around the perimeter.

This was the fifth stakeout that Blaine Bell and Vince Molito had carried out together on American soil. Five out of five times they were successful and their reputation was growing as a competent and efficient team.

"You think that's her?" said Bell. He leaned over the steering wheel as if it would give him a better view.

Molito pointed at the bank. "Has to be. She's just like they said; stealthy, cool, efficient." He nodded, as if to confirm it to himself. "Has to be."

The dark silhouette checked the doors and windows, then leaped onto a dumpster and used the extra height to reach the top of the building. The jet-black clothing contrasted with the painted white of the roof and made her look like an ant crawling across a Formica tabletop. A large shoulder bag swung from side to side with every step.

"This I have to see," said Bell as he grabbed binoculars and slipped out of the car. He knelt below the lot's side wall and peered over the top. The figure reached into the bag, removed a tool and dismantled the steel mesh cover that protected a rectangular skylight. Once removed, another tool peeled back metal flashing from the edges and yet another removed the retaining bolts. The skylight slid to one side.

Molito joined the driver by the side wall. "Don't you think at least one of us should go in and watch her, see what she finds?"

"Yeah. You get down there, and I'll be ready with the car. Radios on."

They both flicked a switch behind their ears that opened channels on a top of the line wireless set.

As his partner began the descent to ground level, Bell raised the binoculars in time to watch the figure drop a small device through the hole in the opened roof. Seconds later, the streetlight and all other lights within a small radius blinked out, leaving the building in darkness. All shadows disappeared, and an eerie calm settled over the area. He strained his eyes enough to see the target rappel into the building. Torchlight danced across the window blinds before being quickly extinguished.

"What the hell?" he said into the mouthpiece.

"No idea," came a whispered reply. "That was so sudden I couldn't see a thing. Keep your eyes open."

Five minutes later, another light bounced in his peripheral vision as the security guard jogged back up the street to investigate. Nothing moved inside the building, but Molito had moved into position by the dumpster.

"Hey, you've got the guard coming your way," said Bell. "Get around the back but be careful. If he moves on the target, take him out."

"Got it. I hear movement on the roof. Get ready."

Bell strained his eyes again. The shadow moved along the parapet and back toward the dumpster. He crept back to the car, climbed in and turned the key in the ignition. The engine produced nothing but a click. He frowned. "What the fuck?"

He tried again, with the same result.

"Dammit," he said into the radio. "She must have dropped an EMP in there to disable the alarm. The radios are shrouded but the car's dead." A voice shouted from across the street. He looked again but saw nothing. "Molito! What's going on over there?"

"The guard appeared just as the target dropped onto the dumpster. As he reached the corner, she jumped him and chloroformed him. He didn't even have the chance to reach for his piece. Shit, she's seen me."

"I'm on my way," said Bell and ran down the stairs to the road.

He reached the bank and found his partner laid out next to the guard like two sardines in a can. He shook his head, pulled a knife from his jacket, and slid the blade into the side of the guard's neck before hoisting his partner over a shoulder.

****

When I woke the next morning, she was gone. No note on the pillow, no smell of coffee brewing, just my open half empty bottle of water standing by the lamp on the nightstand. Her bottle balanced on the drawers by the door, the plastic lid on the floor beside it. She must have left in a hurry.

I rolled onto my back, stretched my arms, and laughed. I'd never had a night like that in my life, and I still had that glow of pride you get after a job well done. In fact, after that performance, I figured I should promote the Captain to General.

My mouth felt as if it held more gravel than the bottom of a bird cage and I'm sure I had a purple tongue from the wine. The bottled water was lukewarm, but it was wet. I rinsed my mouth with a small sip and placed the bottle back on the nightstand but didn't slide it far enough. It dived off the edge, tumbled to the floor and cart-wheeled across the carpet. Water sprayed up the drawer fronts before the empty container landed upright on my untidy pile of clothes.

My bones creaked just as loud as the mattress as I slid out of bed and leaned forward to grab my pants. Something caught my eye under the nightstand, so I knelt by the bedside and reached underneath into the shadow. I pulled out a business card. The corners had curled with wear and there were lines of random numbers written on the back in black ink. I put it on the nightstand while I pulled on my crinkled clothes, then sat on the edge of the bed and looked at it. She must have missed it when she picked up the contents of her purse this morning, assuming she'd stayed until the morning. The front side had a line of professional looking font that said Monica Bridges. So her real name was Monica. That was disappointing. She worked for a company called SonicAmerica, but there was no job description, no branch address, just a cool logo and a cell phone number. I slid the card into my pocket. We could still try for a repeat performance in my room.

I was in the bathroom, zipping up after taking care of business, when I heard a knock at the door. My first thought was that I'd found the perfect woman and she'd just slipped out to get us breakfast. By the time I realized she'd have the key, the door burst open and a crowd of shouting, gun toting Feds filed into the room.

They fanned out like a synchronized dancing team and covered the room. Someone said 'clear' without too much conviction, maybe because they do it on TV. The lead agent peeled back one side of his standard issue black suit and flashed his badge at me.

"Sir, are you alone?"

Now, this wasn't the Penthouse. It was two rooms; one decent sized bedroom with a bed, a few pieces of furniture and a mini fridge, and the bathroom. The shower curtain made a staccato machine gun noise as he slid it to one side and stared at the empty tub.

"Ah, let me check." I paused for effect and stared with him. "Yes, it would appear so. What the hell is going on here? What are you doing in my room?"

"Unless you're Jane Bennett, which I doubt, then this is not your room. That's the name on the credit card that paid for it."

Touché, karma Gods, revenge is yours. Hang on, Jane Bennett? I followed him into the main room. His goons were doing a cursory search of the place while the hotel manager stood by the door. He waved his card key around as if he was trying to join the team.

The lead agent had one of those voices that commanded attention. He should work in radio. "So," he continued, "what are *you* doing in this room?"

"Okay," I said, "before we go any further, who exactly do you work for? Let's see some ID."

He flashed the badge again. I have to admit; it was pretty cool. Then he flipped open a wallet.

"Special Agent Lennon, F.B.I."

"Lennon?" I said. "As in 'John'?"

"Yeah, yeah, I've never heard that before, smartass. Your turn. ID."

My fingers brushed against the business card as I reached into my pocket to grab my wallet. I left the card in place for now and handed over my license. Before I gave too much information, I wanted to see what this was about.

"So, Mr. Howard," he continued, "what's your relationship with Ms. Bennett?" He passed my license to a colleague who wrote my details down in his little notebook.

Who the hell was Jane Bennett? So, was Monica Bridges really Jane Bennett? Was that even her business card? She didn't look like a Jane either. I'm still going with Giselle or Chantelle. Her name had to end in –elle!

"Well, relationship might be too strong a word," I started. I didn't need to finish. Lennon looked at me like I was one of his kids and I'd just spilled milk all over his new car seats. "And how long have you known Ms. Bennett?"

"You mean in the biblical sense, or…"

I got that look again.

"Okay. I met her at the bar last night. I'd never even seen her before then. What's this about, Agent Lennon?"

"And you were with her all night?"

"Yes. No. You know what, I'm not sure."

Lennon tilted his head like an attentive dog and smirked. "You have a lot to drink last night, Mr. Howard? Which was it?"

The weird thing is, I had no idea. My stomach felt fine, but my head was still all over the place. It seemed as if someone had crept into the room last night and drip fed me a bottle of bourbon.

"I know we fell asleep together, but when I woke up this morning, she'd already left."

"And you've no idea what time she left?"

"No. Not a clue. I must have crashed out. To be fair, it was a hell of a workout. And my head is a little fuzzy."

"Did she give you anything to eat or drink?"

"No. We came right here from the bar. I was drinking wine and she…hang on, I finished her drink. You reckon she spiked it?"

"Did you see it the whole time?"

I thought back to the sequence of events and couldn't be certain she'd drunk from her glass before she handed it over. I'd been in the restroom. Lennon was at least one step ahead of me.

"No wiseass answers this time?"

"I do that when I'm nervous. It's a defense mechanism. So, you think she drugged me?"

"You should know the answer to that, Mr. Howard, but I can tell you one thing. She definitely used you."

"No kidding," I smirked, "and I enjoyed every second."

"As an alibi. We need to talk to her about her connection with multiple murders. We've got a new one here in Louisville. Last night. When she was with you."

A tornado blew through my head and cleared it out in an instant, but the room spun with it too.

"Multiple?"

"Multiple. She didn't by any chance leave you with any contact information, did she? I doubt she'd be that stupid, but you can never be sure. You know how it is, in the heat of passion."

"Yeah, okay, you can quit the sarcasm. You've got my attention."

I thought about the card, but my curiosity was piqued. Since it belonged to Monica Bridges and not Jane Bennett, I had no idea where this would go. And I didn't see her as a murderer, so I figured I'd keep hold of it for now. "No, she left nothing. Other than giving directions there wasn't much conversation. We had more of a physical evening."

"No comments on where she was going, or where she'd been?"

"Nothing."

"And you made no plans to see her again?"

I wish. "No. Like I said, she left before I woke. I expected that kind of night, though."

"Did you take any pictures?"

The question surprised me. "I beg your pardon? I'm not sure that's any of your business, and anyway, I might not be that kind of guy."

Lennon shook his head. I think I disappointed him. "We have no idea what she looks like. She's hidden her face from every camera we've found. Even the one in the elevator. The card she used to pay for this room originated in Virginia. We've been following a paper trail to get here."

I'm sure my face blushed at the mention of the elevator, and then I tried to describe her. I'm positive I overused 'smoking', but I did my best. The phrase 'She was my dream woman' is not a description the Feds can put on America's Most Wanted.

"If you put Cindy Crawford, Princess Diana and Famke Janssen in a blender…well, it would be messy, but you'd end up with Jane

Bennett. She looked like a Bond girl and moved like a princess. And she had these smoking eyes."

Damn it. There it went again.

The room search turned up nothing, which didn't surprise me. I'd already picked up the only thing on the floor that didn't come in with me last night. Lennon gave me the "we'll be in touch" speech and they all filtered out of the room like a bunch of penguins heading for mating season. I think my description got them stirred up.

Whatever It
Takes

Mick Williams

1

Cory Keller had found the perfect place from which to kill.

The rental truck coasted to a stop in a small clearing beside the forest. Crisp morning air stung his nose as he stepped onto the roadside, threaded an arm through the strap of a scoped rifle and swung it behind him.

The truck's tailgate dropped to reveal a canvas kit bag. Keller sifted through its contents and checked them off against the list in his mind; protein bars and water, rope, a small tarp, binoculars, lighter fluid, and a blanket for warmth. The rifle and spare ammunition were checked earlier, but he still brushed his palm against the top of the razor-sharp knife wedged into a leather pouch on his belt.

He had everything needed for a prolonged stake out, except the one thing he couldn't pack.

Patience.

Keller looped the binocular strap over his head and stepped over a small wooden rail that divided the roadside from the entrance to a dense forest. A gravel bank sloped away to a well-trodden path that cut through the tree line and disappeared into darkness. He slid down the bank, swiped the smaller branches aside and began the walk to his destination, taking each turn by memory.

On this day for the past two years, Keller had made the same trip, checked in at the same local inn, and followed the same trail.

After a five-minute walk, he reached the place he'd visited the day before. The sun climbed steadily as he began his own climb up a makeshift ladder, twenty feet into a mature tree. Five minutes later, he was buckled safely into his deer stand.

The forest's canopy of greens and browns stretched out before him, becoming more vivid as the sun rose. The path he'd taken earlier snaked away to his left and back to the road. Behind him, an old wooden fence cut off the forest from old farmland surrounding a block of disused red metal barns and shelters. To the right, another path wound out of sight after a few feet, this one beaten firm with hoof prints. The stand offered a good, all-round view, and he knew his prey passed this way; he just needed to blend in and be silent.

Be patient.

As Keller reached for a protein bar, the bruised orange sun slumped toward the horizon. It had been a long day with few chances, and he began to doubt his preparation. Almost eight hours had passed since the first encounter. It was mid-morning when a target presented itself. He steadied the rifle, a Marlin 1894, and settled the scope's crosshairs where he knew the deer's heart and lungs to be. At this range, the sleek ten-point buck made a big and beautiful target. Beige dappling in its brown fur looked like bleach marks on dark silk, and its wet nose twitched as it searched the forest air for familiar scents.

He slowed his breathing and recalled his father's lessons. Once relaxed, he breathed out and squeezed the trigger, ready for the rifle's recoil to bite into his shoulder. Before the motion was complete, a startled bird flew across his field of vision.

His heart raced at the interruption and, distracted, he eased off the trigger. Inaccurate shots could cause the deer to suffer and leave a blood trail to spook any further animals. No real hunter wanted his prey to suffer. He exhaled and raised the scope again.

The deer had bolted.

Keller stretched his legs, regained his composure, repositioned his rifle, and settled back to wait for the next opportunity.

For the rest of the day, he relaxed and enjoyed the contrast between silence and the sounds of the forest. Part of the reason for the long flight to get here was that this forest, at least to him, was the perfect escape. No construction or heavy machinery, no gnarled traffic lanes or shouting drivers, just peace and natural beauty.

As the sun dipped beyond the far tree line, its rays cast intricate patterns over the blanket of trees. The multicolored leaves of the pines and walnut trees bounced a kaleidoscope of colors back to him. Arrows of orange and yellow light shot through any gaps and sparkled against the charcoal black streaks of trunk shadows.

Mother Nature, the greatest artist on the planet, put on a dazzling show. He enjoyed it as much as the hunt.

As dusk fell, Keller picked up his binoculars once more and swept the view for signs of life. His sweep presented no targets but, on the swing back to the horizon, movement in the distance snapped him to attention. It was nothing as fluid as a deer, but shadows danced back and forth in the shade of a huge walnut tree. The dim light painted the whole scene a muddy blur and hid whatever caused the movement. As the sun dipped lower, the shadows bent across the forest floor. He stared harder still, but saw nothing, and was about to give up when he heard them.

Voices. Two of them; one worried and shaky, the other strong, assertive and authoritative. Keller gazed through the lenses again as a man stumbled into the clearing. The guy staggered to a stop and turned to face whoever had pushed him. The distance and natural forest noise masked any words, but the man shrunk with fear and backed away from the tree. Muffled shouts echoed as he raised his hands in defense. Without warning, a puff of pink mist shot from the back of his head. His body hung upright for a frozen moment, then crumpled and fell like a dead weight.

Keller jumped. His stomach leaped, and he dropped the binoculars. Their metal casing clanged against the stand's front rail.

"Shit!" he cursed, "what the..."

In panic, his legs shot out and kicked the kit bag. It slid across the stand and tumbled out of sight. Keller held his breath, and then jumped again as it landed with a thud on the forest floor. He grabbed the binoculars and looked back toward the clearing.

The man behind the trunk stepped into the open and looked in his direction. From this distance his features were a blur, but there was something unusual about his appearance. Keller froze and considered his options. He was in a deer stand, twenty feet up a tree, in full camouflage clothing. And, surely to God, he couldn't have been that noisy.

He fought the panic and swallowed rising bile, trusted the camouflage, and waited. When he reported this to the authorities, he'd need proof. He reached for his cell phone, and then remembered there was no signal through the dense trees. He'd left it at the Inn.

Still, he could have taken pictures.

The man moved toward him. Keller considered standing with his rifle to confront him, to march him back to town like a Sheriff's Deputy. But, if the man fought back, he doubted he could shoot another human. The man ahead had no such issues.

Keller slid the rifle strap over his shoulders, unclipped the tether securing him to the stand, and clambered over the edge to the small ladder. His foot searched for the first rung and, with shaking hands, he began his descent. Ten feet below the stand, he heard a shout.

"Hey! Who's out there?"

So much for blending in, and being silent and patient. He took two more shaky steps, threw his rifle to the ground and leaped the last eight feet to the floor. He landed and dropped into a roll. The earth knocked the wind from him, but he snatched up the kit bag and rifle and ran, head down, toward the road.

Branches whipped his face, and vines grabbed his ankles as he blundered over pot holes and exposed roots. The binoculars bounced against his chest and chin as he thundered forward. He told himself not to trip like they did in the movies and did just that as his boot skidded off a leaf covered stone. He tumbled to the ground and almost lost the binoculars, then rolled back to his feet and ran.

There was no noise behind him. Trees would rustle or twigs would snap if someone followed. The roadside was a hundred and fifty yards away when the first gunshot whined past his head. The man was gaining ground.

Keller dug into his pocket and grabbed the key fob to open the trucks' doors. He surged forward and scrambled up the bank as his nails and knuckles raked over leaves and stones. His boots slipped with every step until he vaulted over the low rail onto the road. Hunched into the smallest shape he could make and breathing in quick gasps, he sprinted to the truck. A painful stitch stabbed at his sides as he pressed the fob to open the doors. The alarm beeped and lights flashed like a beacon of safety in the distance. He made them his goal, not daring to look back. Six feet from the truck, he launched his belongings into the bed and lunged for the handle. The door bounced against its hinges as it swung back. Keller got the ignition key in his fingers as the man stepped over the guard rail. He dove onto the driver's seat, fumbled the key into the ignition and turned it.

Nothing happened.

He glared at the gear stick, as if could help. The manual gearbox needed the clutch to be engaged for the engine to start. Climbing into the seat, he slammed the door shut, depressed the pedal and turned the key again. The engine responded with a roar and a belch of exhaust smoke. Rubber screeched and burned as the wheels spun to find traction. A gunshot cracked and a small side window shattered as the tires gripped the road and the shuddering truck shot forward. The momentum threw Keller back in his seat.

Framed in the rear-view mirror, the man knelt in the road with a pistol leveled for a second shot. Keller ducked below the steering wheel and willed the truck around a sharp turn ahead to put him out of sight. The engine screamed for a gear change as the driver's side mirror exploded in a shower of glass, and then the truck turned the corner and onto straight road.

He kept the accelerator mashed into the floorboard and checked the mirror until the safety of the town buildings appeared in the distance.

2

The sign at the entry to Watkins Forge, Texas, stated the town had a population comprising nine-hundred-and-seventy-two individuals. Faded paint showed its age, so that number might go a dozen or so either way but, regardless of number, this was a small town. It sat on the intersection of two highways. One ran from north to south, the other east to west. No simpler in terms of navigation, but still a blessing and a curse. Any directions to the town were so simple a blind man could drive there but in winter, if snow fell, the residents stayed put until the road was cleared.

Other small towns lay at the end of each compass point but the inhabitants rarely ventured into the next. They didn't need to; they had everything they needed. People grew up and died in the same house and never left town. Everyone knew everyone else and all the yards were tidy and filled with color. Watkins Forge had all the features of a Stepford Wives town, but without the white picket fences.

The sheriff's office sat between a hardware store and a small antique store on the central block of Main Street. To the side of the hardware store, side by side, stood a bar and a liquor store. To the side of the antique store was a small diner called Cathy's.

When Keller entered Watkins Forge, the sign blurred by the roadside since his speed didn't drop below ninety-five the entire drive. The truck skidded to a stop with a screech of rubber outside Cathy's. He slid from the seat and raced up the stone steps to the sheriff's office, then shouldered open the heavy door.

It opened onto a small counter which cordoned off a few desks and another two doors. The whole room looked like it came from an 80's movie, and an odor of old wood and ground-in dirt hung in the air. The modern screens and equipment on the desks contrasted against the rest of the room. It looked to Keller as if the place wanted to appear an 'old school' sheriff's department, but with the 'big town' facilities.

A sour face looked up from behind the counter. Its owner wore a name badge that stated her name was Amber Bates. An officer sat at one desk filling in paperwork behind her. Another glared from the corner. The other desks were empty. Amber stared at Keller as if he was here to raid the place. She pushed black framed glasses up the bridge of her nose and looked him over.

"Help you, Sir?"

Keller struggled to hold back words and took a deep breath. "Ma'am, I just saw a murder. I need to speak to the sheriff right now."

Amber jumped. "Oh shit!" She tapped a sheaf of papers against the desktop. "Please, pardon my French! Wait right here, Sir." She shot to her feet and called over her shoulder as she ran, "I'll go get him. And please, wait right there." She seemed to admonish herself at the repeated remark and made a swift retreat through the door to the left.

Amber disappeared for a while. Keller drummed his fingers on the counter, ready to call to the officer seated at the occupied desk, when the door opened and she reappeared with the sheriff.

The sheriff looked like a sixty-year-old man fresh from the gym. Alert, solid, and built like a lumberjack, the whole appearance capped off with close cut silver hair and a face of weathered leather. His uniform was pristine, with pleats sharp enough to cut paper. The overhead lights beamed like spotlights off his polished shoes. He had a ramrod straight ex-military manner and led the way, chest out, chin up, very much in charge. Amber seemed to take two steps to every one of his as he strode to the counter. He stopped before Keller and stared at him with experienced eyes that crackled with sparks of intelligence.

"Amber here tells me you saw a murder." It was more of a statement than a question. He held out a hand which Keller shook with a firm grip. "I'm Sheriff Holt. Follow me, son".

He walked away toward the door on the left. Keller moved around the counter, nodded to the closest officer, was ignored by the other, and followed the sheriff through the maze of desks and chairs.

Once through the door, he found the building went back further than it seemed. The corridor ahead had a few rooms on either side. Each had the standard police blinds behind the windows, all closed for privacy. Names on the door signs meant there were at least a couple more officers at this precinct. The door in the center of the corridor had 'Jesse Holt - Sheriff' stenciled onto its frosted glass panel.

Keller's hands still shook as he followed Holt. Other than the breakneck speed and frantic mirror checks, the drive here had been uneventful, but the moments before it still milled through his mind. Holt turned into the room past his office and had already pulled out a chair as Keller entered and closed the door.

He looked around the room. It could have come straight from TV; a small wall mounted camera high in the corner, basic egg carton soundproofing on the walls. A plain table with a small loop welded into its smooth surface for cuffs. And three plain chairs.

He took the solitary chair against the wall, by the loop, and faced the blinds. Moments later the door opened and the officer from the desk entered the room. He glanced at Holt, took the seat next to him, and placed a notepad on the desk. Its cover slapped against the table as he flipped it open and clicked the end of a pen.

Holt got straight to the point. "What's your name, son?"

"Keller, Sir. Cory Keller."

"So, Mr. Keller," said Holt, "You already know I'm the sheriff here." He pointed a thumb to his side. "This is my deputy, Rudy Gettinger. He'll take notes. If you'd be so kind, hand him your Driver's License so we can get your details."

Keller reached into his pocket to retrieve his wallet. His favorite picture of he and Harriet smiled through the shiny plastic window on the front. He pulled the valuable piece of plastic from behind it at the second attempt and handed it across the table.

Holt continued as the deputy copied out Keller's details. "Murder is rare in my town, so you'll pardon me if I seem a little abrupt. How about you start by telling us what happened?"

Keller shuffled in his seat, uncomfortable at the immediate question of doubt. "Sir, I was sitting in my deer stand in the forest, and I saw someone get shot. Right in front of me." The words came out like bullets.

Holt frowned and folded his hands on the table. "That's quite a dramatic statement to make. You're sure you saw a murder. I mean, you said you were in a deer stand. How far were you?"

Keller felt on edge and this two against one setup didn't help. Maybe murders were rare in this town. Still.

"Close enough. The back of his damn head blew out like a water melon so yes, I'm sure he was murdered."

Holt leaned forward. "Okay, son, no need for raised voices. Tell me exactly what happened. Where were you and what were you doing there?"

Keller took a breath. "I told you, I was hunting in the forest on the north road. I saw movement in the trees and thought my luck had changed. I've been out there all day. After a while I heard talking. Well, shouting. I couldn't make anything out at first, but then this guy stumbled into a clearing below me. I didn't see who pushed him, he hid behind a tree, but they argued about something. The guy in the clearing had his arms out like he was trying to calm someone down or he was pleading... and then the other guy shot him."

Keller leaned back and rubbed his face to calm himself. "I heard no gunshot, so I assume he used a silenced pistol, but the guy is dead. His head exploded. I panicked and ran. And I mean I ran, and just made it back to my truck before the other guy caught up with me and shot at me. He took out a window and a side mirror. The truck's parked outside the diner. You can check it. And it's a rental. They'll be pissed!"

"I can tell you've had a hell of a fright," said Holt. He eased back into his seat. "Can I get you a coffee?"

"No thanks, I feel sick. I'll just throw it back up," said Keller. He took another deep breath in through his mouth and breathed out slowly through his nose

"All right, but let me get the facts straight. You saw a guy get shot, but they were far enough away you couldn't hear what they said. So, from that distance, you're sure you saw what you saw? And then this other guy chased you and started shooting? Where exactly were you?"

"I told you, in the forest, in a deer stand. Oh, I had binoculars."

Holt sighed. "It's a big forest, son. Can you be more specific and narrow it down a little for me?"

The deputy smiled and continued to take notes.

Keller almost laughed as his nerves leaped and jumped. His stomach performed circus sized somersaults. He held out his hands. They still shook. "Sorry. Look, I know where, I'm just not sure how to describe it to you. I could take you there and show you? I drove there on auto pilot and paid little attention to my surroundings. It's a straight road most of the way. I park the truck in a clearing close to an opening by the forest. My stand backs onto old farmland. I wandered in there a while ago and found a great place to set up. Now I always hunt there."

Holt frowned again. "But you remember no landmarks? And how about on the drive back to town?"

"No, Sir," said Keller, "although to be honest, I'll admit I didn't stick to the speed limit to get back here."

"Well," said Holt with a wry smile, "under the circumstances we can let that one slide. Still, I want you to think back. When you drove away, did anything stand out to you? Road signs? Any exits? Buildings? Any marks on the road that would help us?"

Keller thought hard about the run through the forest, the climb to the roadside, and the mad scramble into the truck. Then he remembered the shooter kneel and level the pistol to shoot. "Yes. When I pulled away from the clearing, there's a sharp turn to the right. I hammered the truck to get there, so I'd be out of his line of sight."

"Okay. Well it's a pretty straight road. Give me a second," said Holt. Keller watched him mentally drive the road back to town.

The deputy beat him to it. "I've got it. I drive by there often. You were twenty minutes away from here. Just before you turn right at the ten-mile marker, there's a clearing at the roadside. It's not too far from the old McGuffie farm."

"All right," said Holt, "so now we know the location." He turned to his colleague. "Rudy, get a couple of cars out there to take a look."

"You got it, Chief," he said. He slid the pen and notepad over to the sheriff, stood and left the room.

"Now tell me about the guy in the forest. The shooter," said Holt. He grabbed the pen. "What did he look like?"

"To be honest, I panicked so much I didn't get a good look at him. If he wasn't in shadows, he was hidden behind a tree. I remember he seemed tall. He towered over the other guy. He had mousey colored hair and had my build. One thing for sure is he's in good shape. I ran all the way from my stand to the truck and had a good start on him. I'm in decent shape but he still almost caught me. He has to be fit. He must work out or maybe he's military." Keller paused for a moment. "There was something unusual about him, but I couldn't place it. He could've been anybody."

"That's not entirely helpful, Mr. Keller," sighed Holt. "You just described half the people in this town. And this town's quite small. Think again. What stood out about this guy? Would you recognize him, if you bumped into him again?"

Keller had considered this on the drive back to town. At such a distance, and in dim light, he doubted he could pick the guy out from a line up, let alone someone in shade. The only lead he had was the man's unusual appearance.

"Honestly, I doubt it, but I remember, and this is weird, something about the way he looked didn't seem right. I thought about it on the way here and it clicked. He wore white socks. Dark clothing, but white socks. In the forest light, they really stood out. It's like his slacks were too short for his legs and his socks glowed against the dark clothes. I couldn't work it out at first."

Holt smirked. "White socks? You want me to track a murderer based on white socks?"

Keller's frustration grew, and he slammed his palms on the desk. "Man, I was shitting myself. I wanted to put him way behind me, okay?"

Holt didn't flinch. "All right, I'm sorry. Like I said, we don't get many murders here. What about the dead guy? What can you tell me about him?"

Keller felt useless. "I'm sorry." He rubbed his face again. "Even less. I panicked and came right here, and it was so dark and happened so fast. I wish I could tell you more because I'm sure he saw me."

Holt raised his eyebrows. "And if he passed you in the street? Would he recognize you?"

For most of the time Keller had been running in the opposite direction. When the guy approached the deer stand, Keller had been too far away to see him without binoculars. He had to assume the same worked the other way. "I'm not sure. The only time he may have seen my face was when I got to the truck. Saying that, I ducked behind the door while I tried to get it started."

"Well, remember there's only one road here from the forest, so he knew where you were heading. Keep your eyes open. Meanwhile, we'll get a couple of cars out to the site. I have a few more questions for you, but I'll give you time to calm down, so stick around for a while. If you've been out there all day, then I'm sure you're hungry too, so grab some dinner. Wash it down with a beer or three if your stomach settles. Were you here for the day, Mr. Keller, or are you staying with us for a while?"

"Staying. I'm at The Comeback Inn, the small place at the end of the next block."

"Okay," said Holt, "I know it. Get something to eat, drink a few beers and get a good night's sleep. I'm sure we'll talk again soon. Oh, and for the love of God, please get out your camouflage gear. You scared the shit out of my receptionist."

Made in the USA
Columbia, SC
23 April 2018